Brannigan
Rides Again

by

B.K. Bryans

Brannigan Rides Again

by

B.K. Bryans

First Edition

ISBN 978-1-300-34800-9

This is a work of fiction. The cities mentioned exist. The areas around Tucson, Arizona and northern Mexico are similar to those depicted in the story. However, the names, characters, incidents, and other places are the product of the author's imagination. Any resemblance to actual persons, living or dead, business establishments, events, or locales is entirely coincidental.

Published by Lulu.com

Other books by B.K. Bryans

The Dog Robbers

Flight to Redemption

Those '67 Blues

Sand

Trouble in Tucson

Flying Low

Management Math

Most of them are available on Amazon.com at:

https://www.amazon.com/author/b.k.bryans

You are also invited to visit the author's personal website at:

www.brianbryans.com

The cover painting was done by Frederic Remington in 1906. (It fits the scene on Page 211 of this story.)

Dedication

To the working cowhands of the twentieth century.

Author's Notes:

Brannigan Rides Again is a sequel to my novel *Sand*, which features a hero as comfortable on a horse as he is in a gunfight, a man with persistence and guts: Dan Brannigan. Hence, the sequel is ... *Brannigan Rides Again*.

Titles such as this one have a history. *Destry Rides Again* was written by Max Brand in 1930, made into a movie starring Marlene Dietrich and Jimmy Stewart in 1939, and then made into a musical in 1959. One of the lesser actors in that movie was Brian Donlevy. My mother was a fan of that actor and named me Brian. The very first book I ever read was *Montana Rides Again* written in 1934 by Evan Evans (or Max Brand, depending upon which cover you got).

Finally, the setting for this novel is southern Arizona in 1957. For cost comparison, a $10 item there today cost only $1 back then.

B.K. Bryans

Chapter 1

November 1957 – Tucson

"You may step down, Mr. Brannigan. Thank you."

I glanced at the jurors on my way over to the little gate in the bar separating actors from observers. *Chickens on a roost. Not a horseman in the bunch. God help you, Jubal Pearce.*

The prosecutor started his summation, the words falling mostly unheard behind me, as I went out the courtroom's tall front doors.

Down the street, I gave the clerk at Hugo's Diner a dime for a cup of strong coffee, then took up residence at a small pedestal table pushed against the back wall. Staring into the cup, I tried to put the pieces together again, to understand Jubal's story.

"The winter of '55 was a bad one up on the Mogollon," he'd said. "It snowed all the way into April. And that's when it began."

April 1955 – Arizona's Mogollon Rim

Reining in his horse, Jubal Pearce pointed off to the left. "There she is, Pa. Down in the valley. Just comin' out of the tree line."

"I see her, boy." Aaron Pearce pulled his horse up alongside Jubal and leaned forward. The sun's late-afternoon glare was bouncing off scattered patches of snow and ice that still dotted the high-mountain valley floor, and Aaron had to squint against it.

Jubal's buckskin cocked his ears toward the mare in the valley, then he stretched out his neck and nickered. A quarter mile away, the chestnut mare in question tossed her flaxen mane and whinnied back.

"Look close," Aaron said. "Her bellies dropped; she's about ready to foal."

"Ginger's never wandered away before, Pa. Why'd she leave like that?"

Aaron's face screwed up into wrinkles. "I figure mares are kinda like women, son, they get restless just before giving birth. In Ginger's case, maybe walkin' helps ease the foal into better position."

In the valley below, Ginger suddenly squealed and broke into a hard run across a treeless stretch, her distended belly swaying. Crackling noises swept up the ridge as the mare's hoofs crashed through the frozen crust covering a broad strip of wind-swept snow.

A puzzled look on his face, Jubal asked, "Why's she running, Pa?"

"Can't be from us," Aaron said. He turned and scanned the swath of snow-encrusted pine trees behind the mare. "Oh shit, Jubal. *Wolves.*"

"I see 'em, Pa. Oh God, they're after Ginger." Jubal spun his buckskin to face the downhill drop-off, then touched spurs to the horse's tan flanks.

Lunging forward onto the steep slope, the horse immediately squatted on his haunches as he slid over bare rock and loose soil made slick by melting ice. Head down, forelegs pushing one way then the other, the horse slalomed downward, racing a following avalanche of ice-covered dirt and rock.

Yelling and whooping to scare the wolves, Jubal urged his horse down the slope toward Ginger, now struggling through ever-deeper snow.

Their dark and silent shadows flitting easily across icy crusts, the wolf pack closed in on the fleeing mare. The lead wolf, his body low, legs stretching for distance, drew ahead of the rest.

Still on the ridge, Aaron Pearce pulled a .30-30 Winchester rifle from the scabbard lashed to his saddle. He aimed at the pack leader now almost upon Ginger. "Got to be three hundred yards," Aaron muttered. "Too damn far." Then, holding his breath, he squeezed off a round.

The targeted wolf didn't break stride. Nor did others in the pack.

Jubal heard the shot, knew it missed, and realized he'd be too late. He screamed into the wind, "Noooooo!"

A second shot echoed across the valley as the lead wolf struck the floundering mare with stunning force, knocking her onto her side. Silently, the wolf tore at Ginger's throat.

Screaming in pain, the mare kicked and tried in vain to shake the wolf off her neck.

Yanking out his own rifle as he rode, Jubal fired five rounds at the rest of the pack as fast as he could lever shells into the chamber.

One of the wolves fell, writhing in pain, it's blood spattering the pristine snow only a dozen yards from the downed mare. The rest of the pack gathered there, seemingly confused. Another bullet smacked into a nearby rock and ricocheted away with a loud *whirring* sound.

Leaping away from his bloody victim, the pack leader snarled once, then led the others in a race back across the snow, away from the oncoming rider.

Whining, the crippled wolf tried to follow but slumped back down, biting at the wound in its flank.

Urged on by Jubal's scream and a touch of spurs, the buckskin hit the valley floor on the run and plowed a path through thickening snow banks toward the wounded mare.

She lay on her side, eyes rolling, blood staining the snow around her neck. Although her hind legs thrashed, sweeping snow and ice away, she made no attempt to rise.

"Hang on, Ginger," Jubal called as he swung off his horse. "Hang on." He leaned his rifle against the mare's distended belly and knelt in the bloody snow next to her head.

Recognition bloomed in the mare's eyes, then dimmed.

And Jubal understood; Ginger wouldn't live to have her baby. He stroked the mare's velvety nose and whispered to her. "Easy girl. Go easy."

Ginger's body suddenly shuddered.

Jubal looked up in surprise as the head and forelegs of a foal, encased in bluish-white amnion, emerged from between Ginger's hind legs.

"Get that membrane off the foal's nose," Aaron shouted as his horse slid to a stop next to the buckskin. "It's got to breathe." He swung down off his horse and waded toward the birthing.

"Yes, sir." Jubal stood and stepped around the mare's body. Then, as if it were happening in slow motion, he saw the crippled wolf rise and, amber eyes ablaze, lunge at Aaron. Grabbing for his rifle, Jubal yelled, "Watch out, Pa!"

Aaron spun around. "What the hell?"

The wolf sank his fangs into Aaron's left leg a second before Jubal's bullet ripped thorough the animal's neck. The wolf dropped, quivered once, then lay still.

"Oh Christ," Aaron said as he fell backward into the snow.

Dropping his rifle, Jubal grabbed the wolf's hind legs and

dragged the animal's body aside. Kneeling next to Aaron's bloody leg, Jubal said, "You're hurt bad, Pa." He pressed a hand against the wound. "It's really bleeding."

"The son of a bitch must have cut a vein," Aaron said. "I'll need a tourniquet. But first you have to do Ginger's job, get that membrane off the foal's nose."

"Pa?"

"Hurry, dammit. You get the membrane while I pull off my belt."

Moving to the foal, Jubal raised its head a few inches and gently scrapped the soft amnion away from the animal's nostrils. "Should I pull the foal out?"

"Not yet. Is it breathing?"

"I think so."

"Good. Now come here and help me pull this belt tight around my leg."

Hustling back to his father's side, Jubal asked, "You okay, Pa?"

"It hurts some, Jubal. But this should stop most of the bleeding. Damn. That's as tight as I can get it. Put one foot on my leg and see if you can pull the belt tighter."

Jubal tried without success.

Aaron winced from the pain, his jaw rigid.

"Okay, boy. Take out your pocket knife and drill a new hole in the belt so I can keep it this tight."

When the task was finished, Jubal sat back, ignoring the wet snow that dampened his clothes. "What now, Pa?"

"Pull the foal out. Look, he's moving his little head. He wants to get on with life. Better give him a hand, but do it easy. He's real fragile right now."

Moving over to the foal's head, Jubal looked down into its soft eyes. "Come on out little fella." He grasped the two forelegs and tugged. The new horse slid out easily and lay on its side, wobbly head turning to watch Jubal. Its spindly legs jerked as it instinctively tried to stand.

"Good job, son. Now use your knife to cut the umbilical cord. Not too close to his belly."

Bending to the task, Jubal said, "It's not a he, Pa." The knife flashed. "It's a filly."

"Well, I hope she becomes as good a mare as Ginger was. You done yet?"

"All done, Pa. Look, she's trying to stand up."

"Leave her be. I need your help now. Bring my horse over here."

"Yes, sir." Jubal waded through the snow and led Aaron's roan over to his father. "Can you ride, Pa?"

"No. Gravity would push more blood out of my leg. Drape me over the saddle like I was some dead elk you were packin' out. Then tie my arms and legs to the front cinch rings. That'll keep me in place."

"You sure about that, Pa?"

"Yeah, boy. I'm sure. Now give me a hand." With Jubal's

help, Aaron managed to stand. He grabbed his saddle horn and the cantle, then paused there, sucking in cold air. "And don't be surprised if I pass out before we get home. Understand?"

"Ah … I think so."

"Okay, Jubal, you push while I pull."

A moment later Aaron was draped across his saddle, both legs hanging down on one side, head and arms on the other. Jubal found two rawhide piggin' strings in one of the saddle bags and used them to tie his father in place.

"Now," Aaron said, "for the hard part. You got to lift that filly onto your own saddle, then get up behind her. Once you're aboard, put her on your lap. And remember, she's a fragile little thing."

"I know, Pa."

Jubal struggled for several minutes, but finally wound up in the saddle with the filly draped across his lap, two little hind legs to the left, head and forelegs hanging off to the right.

"Christ, I imagine we look a sight," Aaron said. "Now grab the reins to my horse, Jubal, and take us home. But for God's sake, don't gallop." A large drop of blood trickled down Aaron's left leg and fell into the snow, joining several others already there.

Turned toward home, the two horses settled into a ground-eating trot, picking their way across rough ground now being rapidly obscured by more falling snow.

* * *

The sun eased out from behind a dark cloud, threw a few farewell rays at the Mogollon Rim, then slid behind the mountains as Jubal rode out of the tree line. Across the valley, the corrals and dark buildings of their ranch home beckoned in the gathering dusk.

A freshening wind stung Jubal's face, and he shivered. Taking off his jacket, he draped it over the filly to ward off the sudden chill. He could feel her tiny heart beating against his stomach, and he talked softly to the little head bobbing along on his knee. A moment later, for the hundredth time, he glanced over his shoulder at the horse trotting behind and the still form draped over its saddle.

His father had been quiet for the last mile, and Jubal wasn't sure the man was still alive. He wanted to hurry, to goad the horses into a gallop for home, but he understood; that would surely aggravate the bleeding.

Lights were on in the ranch house when Jubal rode up to the corral. A head appeared briefly in the kitchen window, then Jubal's mother rushed out the front door.

She stopped half way to the horses, one hand to her mouth. "Is he alive?"

"I don't know," Jubal said. He eased back onto the saddle's Cheyenne roll, leaving the foal still draped across the seat.

Martha Pearce ignored both Jubal and the filly. She ran to Aaron, knelt, and looked up at his face. "He's breathing. What happened?"

"Wolves got Ginger. One of 'em bit pa in the leg." Jubal jumped down off the buckskin, then lifted the filly off the saddle. "Ginger left us this little gal."

Clawing at the rawhide strips that bound her husband across the saddle, Martha snapped out orders. "Put her on that straw pile in the barn, then get out here and help me."

"Yes, ma'am."

Jubal disappeared into the large barn, returning just in time to grab Aaron's shoulders and ease him gently off his horse.

Unconscious, the man still groaned as his wounded leg, wet with blood, hit the ground.

Choking back tears, Jubal gently laid his father on the dirt.

"Loosen that belt," Martha said. "Get some blood circulating in the lower leg. Hurry."

"Won't he bleed more?"

"Can't be helped, son. But we'll do it just for a minute."

A moan escaped Aaron's lips when Jubal loosened the belt. Blood soon trickled onto the dirt, and Jubal whispered, "I don't know about this, Ma." He tugged at the belt.

"Wait," Martha said. "Not yet." A small puddle of blood formed on the hard ground. "Okay," she said, "that's enough. Pull the belt tight again."

Once the belt was buckled, Jubal stood. "Now what?"

"Get some saddle blankets out of the barn and make a bed in the back of the pickup truck." Martha turned and ran toward the house.

Jubal called after her, "Why not put him in the cab?"

"We need to keep his wound elevated. Put that saddle your Pa's been draped over in the truck bed too." The kitchen door slammed shut behind her.

Just as Jubal threw his father's saddle into the truck bed, Martha returned with an armful of wool quilts that she tossed into the back of the truck. "Now," she said, "let's get your Pa onto those saddle blankets." She ran to Aaron's prone body, picked up his feet, and nodded toward his head. "Hurry."

A minute later, Aaron lay on his back in the truck bed, his head just behind the cab, his bloody leg propped up on the saddle.

Piling the quilts on top of her husband, Martha tucked in the sides. "I hope this works," she muttered.

"Sure wish we had a car," Jubal said. "We could put him in the back seat."

"If we had a car we couldn't get across Boar Creek."

Stepping up on the rear bumper, Jubal said, "I'll ride with Pa."

Reaching out, Martha put a hand on Jubal's shoulder. "I'll get him to the hospital, son. You take care of that filly. Get some milk into her."

"But—"

"You can't help your pa right now, Jubal. And the filly needs milk."

"From a bucket?"

"Yes. Use two fingers as a teat. You've seen me do it. And she'll need to be fed every two hours. Now get to it." Martha trotted around the truck to the driver's door. Pausing there, she turned to Jubal. "And it wouldn't hurt if you said a prayer for your pa."

"Yes, ma'am. You think he'll make it?"

"He damn well better. I can't run this place by myself."

Jubal watched the pickup's red tail lights until they disappeared into the trees on the far side of the clearing, then he bowed his head and prayed for the life of his father.

Finished, Jubal trotted around the barn to a small corral where the family's two Holstein milk cows were sheltering under a *ramada*. Using a handful of hay, he lured one of them into the barn and put her in a milking stanchion.

The cow seemed to appreciate the bit of hay deposited under her nose, but she looked sideways at Jubal as if to ask, "What's up? Why now?"

After dragging a three-legged milking stool over to the cow's left flank, Jubal sat on it and rubbed his hands together until his fingers were warm. Then he reached under the cow's udder and began to gently squeeze two of her four active teats.

Five minutes later Jubal had several inches of fresh milk in a stainless steel bucket. He led the cow back out to the *ramada* and gave her an affectionate pat on the rump. "Good cow."

As expected, the filly was standing in her bed of straw when

Jubal carried the milk into the stall where he'd left her. Her four skinny legs were pointed in various directions, and she wobbled, but she was upright.

Dipping two fingers into the warm milk, Jubal stuck them into the filly's mouth, and she eagerly sucked on them. He repeated the process as he eased down onto the straw.

Soon tiring, the filly lay down beside Jubal and continued her first meal.

As long minutes passed, Jubal talked to her in soothing tones. It occurred to him that perhaps he was comforting himself as well as the filly.

Dawn was streaking the sky when Martha eased the pickup truck back into the ranch yard and pulled up by the barn. She turned off the ignition and leaned back against the head rest. Eyes closed, she waited for the sudden weakness in her legs to go away.

Jubal was asleep, head propped up against the wooden stall, when Martha finally walked into the barn. The filly lay on a bed of straw, her head on Jubal's lap. A bucket with traces of milk remaining sat next to them.

Martha knelt by her son. "Jubal."

His eyelids fluttered. "Huh?"

"Wake up."

"Eyes suddenly wide open, Jubal stared at his mother. "Is he okay?"

"He'll live."

"Thank God."

"But they had to take off the leg."

A sudden wave of warm spring air coming up from Mexico had melted the snow by the time Martha brought Aaron back from the hospital. She parked the truck near the house.

"Drive down to the barn," Aaron said. "I want to see the new filly."

Martha laughed. "Leave it to you, the horse lover."

"I loved horses before I fell for you, sweetie."

Tiny tears in her eyes, Martha drove over to the barn. She parked, got a pair of crutches out of the truck bed, and waited while Aaron slid out of the cab onto one leg.

Still struggling with what he called his *wooden walkers*, Aaron made his way into the barn. Step, swing. Step, swing.

Jubal had his back to them as he curried the filly, now standing firmly on four good legs.

"You're spoiling her," Aaron said.

Jubal spun around. His eyes focused on the legless stump and his jaw clenched. When his eyes finally made their way up to his father's face, he whispered, "I'm sorry, Pa. I didn't know about loosening the tourniquet."

"Not your fault, son. Even if you'd done it, the wound was infected too bad. That wolf must have been chewing on some old carcass cause he had more in his mouth than bad breath."

Aaron shuffled forward and stroked the filly. "She's a pretty shade of red," he said, his voice low. "Sort of like polished copper. If her mane and tail stay light like her mother's, she's gonna be a *sorrel*. You got a name for her yet?"

"Ma said her color is called *sienna*, so that's what I named her."

"Sienna?"

"Yes, sir."

"Well, son, take good care of her. She's your mare."

It was a hot day in early July when Aaron Pearce thumped into the kitchen, his prosthetic leg still an unfamiliar appendage. He pulled a chair away from the table and slumped onto it.

Martha set a cup of coffee in front of him and asked, "How'd it go?"

"You know, I'm getting pretty good at shifting gears on the fly. This wooden leg is a hell of a lot better than pushing the clutch in with a stick."

"I meant how did it go at the doctor's office?"

"Oh, fine. He gave me some salve to rub on the stump, makes the skin tougher so it won't get so sore. But you better sit down."

Hesitantly, Martha moved around the table and sat. She licked her lips. "What's wrong?"

Aaron pulled a small stack of mail from his jacket pocket and set it on the table. Using one finger, he slid the top envelope towards Martha. "It's for Jubal. From the government."

Martha gasped. "He's been drafted?"

"Looks that way."

"Oh dear God. What'll we do?"

"We'll do what we have to," Aaron said. "Wave goodbye and pray for the best. At least there's no war goin' on right now."

"But Korea could flare up again any minute, Aaron. You know that. And the communists are threatening in Europe."

"Oh, Ike can handle all that."

"And Jubal's supposed to start college in September. Can't we get him a deferment?"

"Well I guess if he'd already started in school that might be possible. But I don't think he'd want a deferment. He's nineteen, and his country's called. He'll want to go."

"What about us?"

"We'll just have to make the best of it. You know, he'll be eligible for the GI Bill when he gets out. That would pay for a lot of college."

"Oh, Aaron. That is so crass." Martha stood and drifted over to the kitchen sink. There she proceeded to wash a dish she'd already rinsed and dried. Her eyes wandered up to the window. "Here he comes now, and with that filly right at his elbow."

"Yeah," Aaron said. "Sienna's going to have a broken heart when Jubal leaves."

"That'll make two of us," Martha said. She watched Sienna

turn away when Jubal reached the porch. The filly wandered over to a patch of grass and nibbled at the new growth.

The screen door banged behind him as Jubal strode into the kitchen and plopped down on a chair across from his father. "What did the doc say?"

"He said I'm fine. Here." Aaron pushed the government envelope across the table.

Sucking in his breath, Jubal stared at it. "I've been drafted?"

"Open it."

Martha walked over and stood behind Jubal. She handed him a paring knife, then rested her hand on his shoulder.

Jubal slit the envelope, paused, then extracted a folded form letter. "It's an order to report for a physical examination."

"That's the first step," Aaron said. "Where and when?"

"The fifteenth, in Flagstaff. At the armory there."

"Maybe you won't pass," Martha said, a wistful expression on her face.

"Of course he'll pass," Aaron chortled. "We'll *all* go. Haven't been to Flagstaff in a coon's age. We can do some shopping. What time does it say to be there?"

"One o'clock."

"Good. We'll have lunch first." Aaron leaned on the table and pushed himself erect. "Come on, Jubal, I need to get some work out of you before you go off soldiering."

Chapter 2

November 1957 – Tucson

"That jury is goin' to be out a spell."

Startled, I stopped staring into the dark depths of my coffee cup and looked up. An old man was standing next to my table. Once my eyes refocused, I recognized him. Ruddy face. Short, white beard. Looked like a leprechaun. He'd been at the trial earlier, back row, right under the big clock. Taking notes.

The man smiled, putting wrinkles around pale blue eyes. "I said that jury is sure to be out a spell." He pulled out the only other chair at my table and settled in, uninvited. "Mind if I join you?"

"Looks like you just did," I said.

"Don't mean to be pushy," he said. "Wanted to talk to you."

"Why?"

"Because you know the truth of it."

"You mean the trial?"

"I mean the man being tried ... and his crime, if any."

"Sounds like you think he's innocent."

"No one's innocent," he said. "At least not anymore. Just thought it would be good to have the truth."

"You've been at the trial," I said. "You heard all the facts."

"Yes, I did." He paused and took a sip from a paper coffee cup. *Funny, I hadn't noticed the cup before.* Then he said, "You know, there's usually a difference between the facts and the truth."

"Well, I guess you better explain that to me."

"Facts are obvious. The truth is almost always hidden away somewhere."

"That's too deep for me. Give me an example."

He took another sip. "Fact is, you were a witness for the prosecution. Fact is, you testified against the man. But the truth is, you want that jury to find him innocent. You want Jubal Pearce to go free."

"What makes you think so?"

"An old man's instinct." He put his paper cup down on the table and stuck out his hand. "My name's Darcy, Darcy O'Rourke."

Not wanting to be rude to an old man, I shook it. "Look," I said, "I'm not in a mood to talk."

"You will be, Mr. Brannigan. Waiting gets to a man. Women handle it a lot better. They're used to long waits I guess. Mind if I call you Dan?"

"Look, Mr. O'Rourke—"

"Call me Darcy. All my friends do."

"I'm not your friend."

"You will be, Dan Brannigan; I'm a likable old coot. Besides, we both come from Irish stock. Almost kin. Tell you what I'm up to. I'm a writer by trade. Been one for forty-some years. Got an assignment from *Life* magazine to do a story on this trial. Like you said, I got the facts in the courthouse. Now I want the truth, and figure you know it better than anyone."

"So you can make a fast buck off someone's misfortune?"

"That was not a kind thing to say, Daniel. Actually, I think the truth would serve your friend in the Tucson jail a lot better than those courthouse facts. You think on that while I get us some more coffee. Want a sweet roll?"

"No."

He came back with two mugs of coffee and a plate of cookies balanced atop one of the mugs. "Thought you might like a cookie," he said. "I'm not much for sweet rolls myself." He set the mugs and the cookie plate down as if he were dealing cards, then eased back onto his chair. "They're chocolate chip." He nudged the plate closer to me.

More or less against my will, I took one.

Darcy grinned. "Knew you were a cookie man. You think about what I said?"

"About the truth being kinder to Jubal than the facts?"

"That's what I meant."

"Yeah, I'm thinking on it."

I ate the cookie, washed it down with a slug of black coffee, then tried to consider just what was the truth.

The arrival of a pretty young woman at our table interrupted my thoughts. Women usually have that effect on me. This one wore a white blouse that showed off her long black hair, a blue skirt made out of what looked like Levi material, and moccasins. The moccasins were a surprise.

She glanced at me, then knelt beside the old man's chair and whispered to him. "The jury sent a note to the judge. They want to know the definition of premeditated."

Darcy winced. "That's not real good."

"They also asked about dinner options."

"Well, at least they aren't in a rush to judgment."

The woman laughed. "A rush to judgment?"

"You're right," Darcy said, grinning. "Make a note of that. It's a good phrase. Now get back to the court room."

"Wait a minute," I said. "Darcy, aren't you going to introduce us?"

Rising, the woman said, "I know who you are. I am Pilar." She turned and walked lightly away. And *lightly* seemed the right word; maybe it was the moccasins.

"Okay," I said. "Now I know her name. Who is she?"

"Oh. I thought it was obvious. She's my assistant."

"I see."

"No you don't, but that's not important." Then, dragging out a notebook, he flipped through several pages before asking, "What do you know about Jubal's girlfriend, Becky Welch?"

"Not an awful lot. Her dad's a packer, runs hunting trips into the mountains for rich dudes. Got a good reputation. I hear Becky used to go along sometimes. A real Tom-boy type, probably because her mother died when she was seven."

"How'd Jubal meet her?"

"He drove into Show Low his second day home on leave after his Army training and ran into Becky at a saddle shop."

December 1955 – Show Low

Becky Welch leaned on the top rail of a large corral containing a dozen mules and one horse, a blue-roan gelding. The horse was thin and showed the tell-tale dark marks of healed scars. "He looks kind of pathetic, Dad. Where'd you get him?"

John Welch tipped his hat back and scratched the stubble on his jaw, something he did a lot. "Went to an auction up at Holbrook to see if they had any good mules. They didn't, but they had this horse. Felt sorry for the poor critter and got to figuring that you're likely tired of riding mules around here."

"You mean he's a gift ... for me?"

"That's right. You got a birthday coming up. And then there's Christmas."

"Thank you, I guess. How old is he?"

"A long two, according to his teeth. Take a look."

Shaking her head, Becky said, "I hear you're never supposed to look a gift horse in the mouth."

"Ha ha. But you do need to be concerned with his mouth; it looks like somebody used a spade bit when they started to ride him. He's got sores in there. Best you get a hackamore."

"You figure he's really old enough to ride?"

"Barely. But you're not very heavy. I'd say go ahead. Turning him into a healthy saddle horse will be a good experience for you."

Becky slid between the rails, evaded two mules that came over to see if she was passing out sugar cubes, then walked up to the horse.

The horse eyed her warily but stood still as she reached out and stroked his nose.

"He have a name, Dad?"

"Not yet. That's up to you."

She rubbed the horse's neck, then leaned away to avoid the small cloud of dust that arose. She laughed. "Think I'll call him Dusty."

"Fair enough," John Welch said. He turned away and made short, quick strides toward the low-slung log house that was their home and headquarters. The leather chaps he wore almost daily had warped over time into an exaggerated version of the man's bowed legs, making him appear to waddle slightly.

Becky smiled at the scene and called out, "Thanks, Dad. For Dusty."

"*De nada.*"

* * *

The Show Low Saddle Shop had a limited selection of hackamores, but Becky spent some time looking them over. Holding them up one by one and turning to see how they looked at various angles, she sized up, instead, the handsome young man dawdling over the shop's selection of bridle reins. She smiled to herself when he picked up a pair of braided leather ones from the sales counter and clearly winced at the price tag.

Then he looked up.

Becky turned away. *He looking at me?*

A clerk approached the man. "Those are genuine *vaquero-braided romel reins*," the clerk said. "Good for horse shows. Real gentle on the hands."

"I imagine," the man said, dropping the reins back onto the counter. "Where are your hackamores?"

"Yonder," the clerk said, pointing toward the back of the store, toward Becky.

She pretended to admire a piece of braided rawhide.

The clerk persisted. "You want to buy these reins?"

"Nah," the man said. "I don't ride in horse shows." He turned his back on the clerk and walked toward Becky.

Looking up at him, she asked, "You work here?"

"Not really," he said, smiling. "But maybe I can help you."

"Well," Becky said, "my dad's a packer, taking hunting parties into the mountains, and all we've ever used are mules. But now I got a young horse, and I'm trying to figure out the best way to train him for riding." She held up a braided rawhide loop with a knot at the bottom. "He's got a tender mouth, and I don't want to start him on those snaffle bits we use on the mules. How would this work?"

"You know what it is?"

"Course I know."

"Okay, what is it?"

"Part of a hackamore."

"Right on, lady. You win a prize. That's called a *bosal*. It goes around the horse's nose, held in place there by a headstall, that's like the top part of a bridle. For reins, you take a horsehair *mecate* and tie the two ends to that knot under the bosal. Then you have a hackamore. Nothing easier on a young horse cause there's nothing in his mouth."

Becky smiled. "You said I won a prize. What is it?"

"A cup of coffee with me."

"That's all?"

"You had a better offer today?"

"Guess not." She hung the bosal back on it's peg. "My name's Becky Welch."

"I'm Jubal Pearce. You gonna buy that bosal?"

"I'll come back after lunch."

"All you won was coffee."

"But I'm hungry. You're going to look pretty silly when I order coffee and a sandwich, and you tell the waitress all you'll pay for is the coffee. Can you afford a whole lunch?"

"Yeah. I can even afford two of 'em. Let's go."

26

* * *

Becky turned the Chevy pickup off the pavement and sent her truck fish-tailing up a narrow gravel road. She laughed when Jubal grabbed the padded handle above the passenger-side door. "Don't worry," she said, "Haven't rolled this thing yet."

"Seems like this could be the day," Jubal said.

Just then the right front tire caught a rut, and the truck jerked to one side. Jubal's grip on the handle tightened. "How far to your place?"

"Almost there," Becky said. "It's just past that stand of pine up ahead." She tossed her hair and slowed the truck to a sedate forty-five. A moment later they passed through a belt of tall trees and emerged into a large meadow.

"This is it," Becky said. "One house, one barn, and a big corral. Not much, but it's all we need."

The mules in the corral took some interest in the approaching truck and moved closer to get a better look, perhaps remembering previous loads of hay. The blue-roan horse, likely with no good memories, retreated to the far side.

"Good-lookin' mules," Jubal said. "Assuming you like mules."

Becky brought the truck to a stop close to the corral. "We use them cause mules are more sure footed than horses in rough terrain. You ever ridden one?"

"Nope. Never felt the urge. That scraggly blue roan your new horse?"

"Yup."

"Looks like a rescue animal."

"He is. Dad felt sorry for him."

"I just may like your dad."

"Well, here he comes."

John Welch came out of the barn and hurried over to the truck. Leaning against the driver's door, he peered into the cab through Becky's open window. "So I'm not the only one who brings home surprises. Who's this?"

Jubal extended his hand past Becky. "Jubal Pearce, sir."

Shaking his hand, John asked, "You related to the Aaron Pearce who has a ranch a ways west of here?"

"He's my pa."

"A good man. But I heard his son was in the Army."

"I am. Just home on leave between training and Germany."

"Germany, huh. Hope a war don't start over there. What did the Army train you to do? What's your specialty?"

"Sniper."

Scratching his chin, John said, "Kind of an unusual skill. You ask for it?"

"Yes, sir. There are times when a man needs to make difficult shots. I wanted to be up to it."

"Reckon so. Should make you a good hunter when you get out. You aren't making a career of the Army, are you?"

"No, sir. I'm coming back home. I plan to study agriculture on the GI Bill."

"Smart man. You'll stay for dinner?"

Becky interrupted. "He's taking me out tonight, Dad. I just wanted to show him our place ... and Dusty. Jubal knows a lot about horses."

"Ah. Well, nice to meet you, Jubal. Good luck in Germany." John put one hand on Becky's shoulder. "You be careful, girl. I've heard stories about soldiers." He turned and walked back to the barn, not quite so bow legged without the chaps on.

"It's about time you met my folks," Jubal said. He eased his dad's Ford pickup through the shallow waters of Boar Creek and gunned it up the south bank.

"We've only had three dates," Becky responded. "Sure you're not rushing this?"

"I leave tomorrow."

"Oh."

"Besides, I want to show you my filly. She's a beauty."

"Well, if you're taking me home to show me a horse, that's different. Nothing too serious about that."

Jubal glanced over at the passenger seat. "Were you figuring I was getting serious?"

"It occurred to me. You sure acted serious last night."

"Yeah. Sorry. Can't blame a guy for trying."

"Yes I can. I did. How's your cheek?"

"Still smarting. You hit pretty good for a girl."

They both were silent until they emerged from the pine

forest, and the Pearce ranch buildings loomed ahead.

"Look," Jubal shouted. "There she is." He leaned out the window and gave a long, low whistle.

Two hundred yards away, Sienna raised her head. Then, copper coat shining in the sun, Jubal's filly galloped across the pasture to greet the truck. She whirled when she reached the fence that paralleled the road, then raced the truck toward home, flaxen mane and tail flying.

"She is beautiful," Becky whispered. "I see what you mean."

"And growing like a weed. I figure she's got about ninety percent of her adult height and seventy percent of her final weight. She'll be about big enough to ride by the time I get out of the Army."

"I think she's too pretty to just work cattle, Jubal. Got any plans for her?"

Jubal laughed. "Maybe I'll go back to that saddle shop, get those genuine *vaquero-braided romel reins,* and ride her in horse shows."

"You should find a good stud and breed her," Becky said. "You think her offspring would keep that color?"

"Well, she's a chestnut. That's a horse with their mane and tail lighter than their coat, and no black hairs. Other breeds don't distinguish, but she's a quarterhorse, and the American Quarter Horse Association calls a chestnut with that copper-red shade a *sorrel*. Now I read that chestnuts are produced by a recessive gene, which means if you mate two chestnut horses, you get a chestnut every time. So I figure we could make sure Sienna's offspring are chestnuts all right, but I don't know if they'd be that exact same color."

"I'll try to find out," Becky said. "I'll write you when I do."

"You're going to write to me?"

"Of course, silly. You think I'll just forget all about you when you go?"

"I'll write back, you know. Here we are." Jubal pulled up next to the porch where his parents waited to meet the young woman Jubal talked about so much.

September 1957 – The Mogollon Rim

Twenty-one months later, a contract Pan American Airlines Boeing 377 carried Sergeant Jubal Pearce and ninety-eight other happy warriors from Ramstein Air Force Base in Germany to New York City.

There, in a brief flurry of paperwork, Jubal and the others were mustered out of the Army. Six hours later Jubal caught a United Airlines DC-3 flying to Chicago, Denver, Flagstaff, and San Francisco.

Becky Welch was waiting for him in Flagstaff. Two hours later, he was almost home.

"It's good to be back," Jubal said. "Thanks for picking me up at the airport." He pointed ahead. "You know, that mountain over there hasn't changed a bit in the last two years."

Becky wheeled her Chevy pickup around the next curve, and a stand of tall pines cut off their view of the mountain. "I think that's a safe bet," she said. "But how about you?"

"What do you mean?"

"Have *you* changed?"

"Oh, a lot I guess, but not my feelings about you." He leaned over and kissed her cheek.

The pickup's right wheels slid onto the road's narrow shoulder. "Stop that," Becky squealed, laughing. "You'll make us crash." She easily guided the truck back onto the hard dirt.

"I doubt that. Want to get married?"

"Don't know. No one's asked me yet."

"I'm surprised. A pretty girl like you?"

"That what the Army taught you? How to sweet talk a girl?"

"You mean it's working?"

"Maybe. I'll have to think about it. After all, four dates while you were home on leave and a dozen or so letters hardly makes a relationship."

"Yeah, but I've spent a lot of time thinking about you. Becky, will you marry me?"

She slowed the Chevy truck, eased it off onto the shoulder, and brought it to a stop. Leaning back against the headrest, Becky closed her eyes.

Jubal reached over and touched her cheek. "You considering it?"

"Yes."

"And?"

Opening her eyes, Becky gunned the pickup back onto the road and accelerated. "I'll have to wait and see. But thank you. Next time somebody gets nosy, I can truthfully say that I *have* been asked to marry."

"Okay," Jubal said. "Guess I'll have to court you a while like Pa did to Ma."

Laughing, Becky asked, "Did it work?"

"Well, here I am."

"And here's your ranch." The pickup rolled around the final curve, and there was the home spread, short grass and tall trees shining in the sun.

"I hear a truck," Martha said.

"Got to be Becky and Jubal," Aaron said. He pushed his way up from the kitchen chair and clomped toward the door.

Martha undid her apron and tossed it on the counter. "What are you going to tell him?"

"The truth. Had to be done."

"You know he won't understand."

"He'll have to. Now come on, woman, let's meet him on the porch."

"Well, at least break it to him gently."

"There ain't no way to do that I know of."

Jubal leapt from the truck and ran up the three steps to the porch. "God it's good to see you both again. Haven't gotten a letter in two months. How are you?"

Grabbing a parent under each arm, Jubal brought the three of them together in a big group hug.

Martha kissed Jubal's cheek before stammering, "Well ..."

Aaron winced and said, "Easy, son."

Letting go, Jubal stepped back. "What's the matter, Pa?"

"Oh, I got horned by a steer a few weeks ago. Not quite healed yet."

"You got gored?"

"Yeah. I was working with a few head in the corral. Tried to do something on one leg I should have done on horseback. My own damn fault."

Sitting down on the porch railing, Jubal asked, "How bad?"

"Bad enough," Aaron said. He stepped over to a chair and sat down. "Got my insides torn up a bit. Your ma got me to the hospital." He laughed. "They remembered me. At any rate, the docs patched me up real good. I'll be okay in a month or so."

Looking at his mother, Jubal asked, "He telling me the truth?"

"Never knew your pa to lie. He's still sore, but he'll mend."

"Good," Jubal said. "Come on, Becky, lets go say hello to Sienna." He stood and vaulted over the porch rail.

"She's not there," Martha said.

Jubal spun around and looked up at her. "What?"

Aaron eased up from the chair and leaned over the porch

railing. "I had to sell her."

"You're funnin' me," Jubal said. He stepped next to the porch, reached up and grabbed the railing. "You wouldn't sell Sienna. She's *my* horse."

Tears formed in Martha's eyes. "We had to, Jubal."

"Why?"

"Hospital bills," Aaron said. "It was the only way we could get the money to cover all the bills."

Slamming a fist on the railing, Jubal shouted, "You could have sold some cattle!"

"We did, son. All we have left is the breeding stock. If we'd sold that ..."

Jubal turned and stared across the valley. "I have money saved up. I'll buy her back. Who bought her?"

"Some movie producer. He came through here looking for pretty scenery for one of his films and saw Sienna romping in the pasture. Drove right up here and offered us nine hundred dollars."

"Nine hundred dollars?"

"That's what he offered. Got him up to a thousand. He really wanted that horse."

"Well, I have enough saved up. I'll buy Sienna back. Where did he take her?"

"He said they were shooting some television westerns at a movie set west of Tucson. She's gonna be the hero's horse."

"She's never been ridden, Pa. How in hell is that going to

work out?"

"The movie fella said they have a horse wrangler who's got a lot of experience breaking horses to saddle."

"Breaking? They're going to have some yahoo with spurs and a quirt break her to ride?"

"I don't think he meant it that way, Jubal."

Turning to Becky, Jubal asked, "Will you drive me to Tucson?"

Becky nodded.

"Then let's go," Jubal said. "I'll get my saddle and gear from the barn. Can I borrow the horse trailer, Pa?"

"Guess so, son. But I don't think the man will sell her."

"Oh he'll do it," Jubal said. "I'll make him sell her."

Chapter 3

November 1957 – Tucson

"Whoa," Darcy said, spilling a few drops of coffee on the table top. "Did Jubal actually say that? He'd *make* the movie producer sell the horse?"

"Can't swear to it," I said. "Wasn't there."

Darcy gave me a calculating look while he mopped up his spill with a thumb. "You know, those words could be construed as a threat. And it speaks to premeditation. But nothing like that came out at the trial. Why didn't you mention it?"

"For starters, nobody asked me. Furthermore, it's hearsay, something other people told me, not admissible in a court of law."

"Yes, I know. I'm wondering just how much you kept to yourself."

"Everything I could."

"Huh. Maybe you should tell me about *your* relationship with Jubal Pearce."

"Why?"

"I'm trying to write the truth about Jubal. And that apparently involves you."

I took another sip of coffee. "Where do you want me to start?"

"Why, right where you came into the story, of course. How did you get involved?"

"The usual way. I met a pretty woman."

"Oh did you now. When?"

"Two months ago. Right about the time Jubal Pearce came home."

September 1957 – Cañada Del Oro Valley

Old Blue saw us coming. The steer tossed his massive head, raced into tall brush, and disappeared.

My mare needed no encouragement, she lunged forward. A thick line of mesquite trees loomed ahead, and we hit it at a dead run. The mare didn't hesitate, she lowered her head and aimed for a sweet spot that showed slightly fewer thorny branches. I crossed my arms in front of my face, grabbed my hat, and yelled "Hooah!"

Branches cracked, several of them raked the backs of my exposed hands, and we burst through the grove—right into space.

I had one brief glimpse of boulders and sand strung along the dry wash bottom some twenty feet below, and then we were rolling into a forward summersault. I saw blue sky and then the saddle horn—*coming down at me*. Grabbing the pommel, I pushed sideways.

Slam!

The horse and I smashed into the sand, side by side, both of us flat on our backs. By some miracle we'd missed the boulders.

Turning my head, I looked at the mare.

She looked back at me with large eyes. All four of her legs stuck up in the air, and she didn't move for several seconds.

Neither did I. Then I heard applause.

We scrambled to our six feet. Twenty yards up the dry wash, what looked like an Army-surplus jeep was hunkered down in deep sand. A woman I'd be proud to describe as drop-dead gorgeous sat on the hood, clapping. She wore hiking boots, khaki shorts, and a pale-blue shirt. Some sort of floppy fishing hat sat on top of a lot of golden curls.

"That," she called out, "was just about the most amazing thing I've ever seen. Mind doing it again?"

"Yeah," I called back. "I mind."

The mare shook herself and started to move away from this strange apparition, so I grabbed the trailing reins and led the animal over to the jeep. The woman had deep blue eyes.

"What," I asked, "are you doing out here?"

She gave me an appraising look, like maybe I wasn't too bright. Then she slammed one dainty fist down onto the jeep's olive-drab hood and said, "I'm stuck."

After moving around to get a better look, I had to agree.

"Yeah, you sure are. Need some help?"

"Oh, no," she said. There came that look again. "I'll dig myself out just as soon as I conjure up a shovel. Or maybe I'll just hoist the damn jeep onto my shoulders and carry it out. Who needs help?"

"That's what I thought." I led my horse a few feet away, tossed the far rein around and over her neck, then swung up into the saddle. "Have fun."

Smiling goodbye, I rode the mare past the jeep and moved off in the direction Old Blue had been headed. I figured I'd get about thirty feet before she called me back. I was wrong; it was twice that.

"Okay, cowboy," she shouted. "You win. Please. I do need help."

Turning the mare around, I walked her back to the jeep. "Get in and start it up."

A tug on the leather thong that lashed my thirty-foot lariat to the pommel released it. I shook out a loop and dropped it over the jeep's front bumper.

With a quiet purr, the jeep's engine came to life. Its driver looked at me expectantly.

"Okay," I said. "When I pull, you drive this thing towards me. Got that?"

"Got it."

I rode away from the jeep, dallied my end of the rope around the saddle horn, and took up the slack. Urging the mare down the wash, I yelled, "Now!"

When the rope went taut, the horse's haunches squatted and she leaned into the task. I shifted my weight off to one side as the lariat twanged back and forth across the saddle.

The engine roared, sand flew, and the olive-green beast slowly rose out of its trap. Ten feet down the wash, the jeep found firm footing, and I reined in the mare. I rode back to the jeep, coiling my rope.

"Thank you," the woman said, turning off the jeep's engine. "I'm sorry about the smartass comments. What's your name?"

"Brannigan. Dan Brannigan. And you are ..."

"Sugar Holliday." Guess it was my turn to give an incredulous look, because she went right on. "I know. I know. It's a strange name. My daddy is a strange guy. I have a sister named Honey. Daddy likes sweet things."

"Ah. And besides being stuck in the sand, what are you doing out here in the middle of nothing much."

She smiled ... sweetly. "I'm looking for scenery."

"Scenery?"

"Yeah. For a new television series. A western. You know, background stuff. When the hero rides off into the sunset, we need some pretty mountains and cacti in front of the sunset. That kind of scenery."

"I see. And you're out here alone?"

"Of course. Why not?"

"Well, you never know what or who you'll meet out here.

There are some pretty rugged customers drifting around."

"Like you?"

"Worse. Some of them don't have a sense of humor."

"I'll keep that in mind. And what are *you* doing out here in the middle of nothing?"

"I'm looking for—"

An explosion of brush about a hundred yards beyond the wash yanked my attention away from Sugar. A large steer with a four-foot span of horns charged out of the scrub into a clear area. He gave a little buck and headed south on the run. Old Blue looked like he was going home. In a hurry.

Then I heard the *crack* of a rifle, and a spout of desert dirt sprang up near the racing steer. A horse and rider came out of the hole in the brush Old Blue had left behind. The horse's dark brown body was stretched out in a hard run. The rider stood in his stirrups, tall in the saddle, with a Winchester at his shoulder. Another shot rang out, and Old Blue swerved left.

"Him," I shouted. "I'm looking for that steer."

There was no need to spur the mare, she knew. We came up out of the dry wash like a Fourth-of-July rocket, then raced to head off the rifleman. The rope was already in my hands, so I built a loop as we closed on the rider ahead.

Old Blue was still running strong, but the shooter was gaining, and he raised his gun for another shot.

I threw my loop, dallied my end of the rope around the horn, and turned the mare. The man's rifle discharged into the air as I dragged him from the saddle and dumped him onto the ground. His hat flew off and disappeared in the small cloud of dust that marked the landing.

The man rolled over, swore, and swung the rifle in my direction. I didn't give him a chance to lever another round into the chamber, I spurred the mare, and she leapt away. The man's gun spun off into the desert as he bounced from sand to cactus and back to sand again.

Thirty yards of this and I reined in the mare. The man at the end my rope was clearly at the end of *his* rope. He lay across an anthill, and didn't seem to care.

He looked like any other local cowhand, and there were a few real ones still around Tucson in 1957, but I didn't recognize him.

"You son of a bitch," he croaked.

One tweak on the reins and my mare backed up six feet, dragging the man off the anthill.

"Enough," he said. "Enough. Let me up."

Keeping the rope taut, I said, "First, tell me why you were shooting at Old Blue."

"That steer?"

"Yes. The steer."

"This is Pump House land. That damn steer don't belong here."

"You ride for Pump House?"

"Yeah."

"So, you figure to kill anything that wanders onto the property?"

"If I feel like it. What's it to you?"

"I know the nice lady who owns that old steer. She'd cry if anything happened to him, and it upsets me to see her cry. That good enough for you?"

He chewed on that for a couple of seconds. "Yeah. Can I get up now?"

"Sure." I slacked the rope.

The man scrambled to his feet. "You gonna catch my horse for me?"

"Nope." Coiling my rope again, I loped the mare over to the dropped rifle. Leaning down out of the saddle, I scooped it up. It was a Winchester 94, one of the storied .30-30s first built by John Browning in 1894. A good gun for brush country. I rode back and stopped my mare twenty feet from the cowboy.

"Nice rifle," I said. "I'll drop it off at the sheriff's office tomorrow. You can claim it there."

"Shit."

"If I remember right, the Pump House home spread is about four miles due north." I glanced up at the sun, about twenty degrees above the west horizon. "You should just about have time to hoof it there before dark."

He looked kind of dazed. "You're shittin' me."

"Don't think so. I figure about an hour and a half to sunset."

"You mean you're gonna make me walk back?"

"Well, you might be able to catch your horse, but he headed north a good bit ago."

The cowboy looked around for salvation and spotted the jeep a couple hundred yards away. "Well, howdy do. Guess I'm saved."

Jacking a round into the rifle's chamber, I propped the gun on my right hip. That drew the cowboy's attention away from the jeep.

"No," I said. "You're walking north. That jeep is going south, same direction that the steer and I are going. *¿Comprende?*"

All he said was, "What's your name?"

"Why do you care?"

"Cause I want to know who to look for when the odds are better."

"Brannigan's the name. I'm easy to find."

He gave me the finger and started looking for his hat.

I rode over to the jeep, which had worked its way out of the wash and now sat on a rough desert road.

Sugar Holliday turned off the engine as I rode up. "Jesus," she said, "you do lead an active life."

"*Caca pasa.* That means—"

"You don't have to tell me what it means; I live in Los Angeles. You interested in a job?"

"Doing what?"

"Working with me."

"Finding pretty scenery?"

"Yeah. I've been thinking about what you said ... about me being out here alone. Maybe I do need competent assistance, and you look pretty damn competent. Interested?"

"Maybe. Which company you with?"

"Paradise Pictures. Wait a minute, you a stunt man?"

"No way. I'm unemployed right now. But I've been known to help film companies out with local problems when I'm hungry. One of the Hollywood big boys once referred to me as a *fixer*."

"Well, then you know the drill. You hungry enough to work?"

"I'll think on it. You staying at the Santa Rita?"

"Yes. How did you know?"

"That's where all you Hollywood types stay when you're in town. It has a lot of the local flavor Californians seem to like. I'll meet you in the coffee shop there tomorrow morning."

"What time?"

"Whenever you're ready. I spend a lot of time there when I'm not working." Using the rifle, I pointed west. "Now, follow this trail. You'll come to a gravel road in about a mile. Take it south and you'll get to Tucson. You know south?"

"Yeah. I'll keep the setting sun on my right, just like I knew what I was doing. And thanks ... for everything."

"See ya." I turned the mare and rode southeast.

The cowboy was a couple of hundred yards away, trudging

north like a good fellow, but I watched the jeep navigate the rutted road until it disappeared around a clump of trees. Then I picked up Old Blue's trail and put the mare into a fast trot.

Fifteen minutes later I came up on Old Blue. There was no sign of blood, but his right horn was now about two inches shorter than it had been, a bullet had clipped off the tip. The old steer tossed his head and rolled his eyes in greeting, but kept up his steady slog for home: the small ranch owned by Rosalinda Correa, *Rosie* to her many friends.

Old Blue and I crossed the bit of downed fence that had given the steer his short-lived freedom, and I stopped to prop up the wires. Still in a hurry, Old Blue moved on.

I caught up with the steer in time to ride into Rosie's ranch yard right behind the four-legged felon. I kept the cowboy's carbine propped up on my hip, just like John Wayne always did.

Rosie held the corral gate open and watched Old Blue move past, head down.

The steer aimed right for the water trough and buried his nose in the tepid water.

Slamming the gate shut, Rosie looked up at me and asked, "Where in hell was he?"

"North of here on Pump House land. The fence was down up by twin forks, but I fixed it on the way back."

"Any trouble?"

"One of the Pump House riders tried to shoot the old boy, but all he did was knock off a couple inches of horn."

Turning, Rosie stared at the steer for a moment, then looked up at me. "Old Blue's lucky. That the cowboy's gun?"

"Yeah. Thought I'd let the man cool off. I'll leave it with the sheriff tomorrow."

"You took it away from him?"

"He dropped it, and I picked it up." I held it out so Rosie could see it better. "It's a classic Winchester 94."

"Careful, it looks cocked. Is it?"

"Yeah. Let's see how it handles." I aimed at a fence post fifty yards away and let fly.

CRACK. The post shook, splinters flew, and the sound whipped across the ranch yard.

The mare danced around a bit, but Old Blue ignored the sound, apparently now used to the sound of gunshots.

"Nice shot," Rosie said. Then she stepped closer and gave me the once over. "Your shirt looks like you took a spill. You reopen any of those wounds? You okay?"

"I'm greater than grits, Rosie. Speaking of which, am I invited in for dinner?"

She laughed. "You always are. And that mare looks like she could use some feed too. About half a coffee can's worth of oats should do it."

Rosie tossed her pet steer some hay, then walked up to the house. Her two giant German Shepherds, Mutt and Jeff, appeared from behind the barn and cavorted by her side, eager for dinner.

After I unsaddled the mare, I rubbed her down with a dry saddle blanket and put her ration of grain in the tin bucket nailed to the side of a corral post. She shouldered her way past me and stuck her nose deep into the pail.

The two animals chomped away as I closed the corral gate and headed for my little apartment above the detached garage. I needed a shower.

Rosie's big, black telephone on the kitchen wall rang halfway through dinner. She answered, listened a lot, and said things like "oh no" and "damn." Then she hung up and walked back to the table ... real slow. She sat down, picked up a fork and played with her mashed potatoes. "That was the sheriff's office," she said. "Seems you roughed up one of the Pump House cowboys today. That the guy who tried to shoot Old Blue?"

"Yup. Guess he made it back home. He had to walk."

"Why?"

"I roped him off his horse, and the critter ran home. Did the cowboy call the sheriff's office about getting his gun back?"

Rosie smiled one of her Cheshire-cat smiles. "Not exactly. He called the sheriff's office to inquire about filing assault and theft charges against you. Said he'd come in tomorrow morning. Want some more pot roast?"

November 1957 – Tucson

Pilar materialized at the blurry edge of my field of vision. She glided up to the table, ignored me, and turned to Darcy. "The judge just ordered the jury to knock off for the night. He's sequestering them over at the Santa Rita Hotel."

Darcy looked surprised. "Sequestering? Why?"

"A waitress overheard a couple of unidentified men in a bar talking about killing someone, maybe at the courthouse. She called the cops, but the men were gone by the time the law got there. The prosecutor thinks it may be a threat to the jury. I guess the judge agrees, he's afraid something might happen if the jurors are out and about."

Darcy looked at me. "You know anything about such a threat?"

"Well," I said, "it's possible some friends of the Pearce family are trying to influence the trial's outcome."

"With violence?"

"Hey, the Mogollon Rim country is home to Apaches and Mormons. Both are pretty darn familiar with violence; it's a good piece of their history."

"Is Jubal Pearce a Mormon?"

"Probably. Pearce is a common Mormon name."

"You know the Pearce family well?"

"No."

"Well, you seem pretty familiar with them."

"Used to be a cop. I ask a lot of questions. It's a habit."

"A lawman, huh. That explains a few things. Tell me, why

are you an ex cop?"

"It's a long story."

"Uh huh. I bet it is." Darcy grinned at me, then turned back to his alleged assistant. "Pilar, why don't you circulate around the courthouse and see what you can find out. Maybe the plot is thickening."

"Will do." Pilar flashed me the very briefest of glances before wafting away on moccasin feet.

I watched her until she disappeared out the door. When I looked back at Darcy, he seemed to be smirking.

"She doesn't like me much," I said.

"You testified for the prosecution." He looked at my empty cup. "Want another?"

"Not this late in the day."

"Me neither. Why don't we go over to Carlotta's Cantina, have a couple of drinks and dinner. I'll buy."

"You bribing me?"

"Damn right." He stood up to reinforce his suggestion.

Not being adverse to freeloading, especially when I'm between jobs, I stood also. "Why Carlotta's?"

"They like me there."

Enjoying the late afternoon air, we walked the two blocks north to Carlotta's Cantina. That place has been one of my favorite haunts for years, and likely will be so long as Carlotta is around. It's mainly a watering hole for the locals, especially the legal crowd; the Mexican food served there is a bit too spicy for the tourists. I could understand why Darcy liked Carlotta's place. As I was to learn, the place liked Darcy because he was a big spender. My kind of host.

We beat the legal crush that usually rolled in about five fifteen and got a quiet booth in the back. Settling in, I asked, "How will Pilar find you?"

He laughed. "She'll know where I am."

A waitress appeared bearing the obligatory basket of chips and a bowl of mouth-burning salsa. "*Buenos tardes*, señor Brannigan. *¿Qué tal?*"

"*Bien*, Chita. This is señor Darcy O'Rourke."

"Oh," she said, tweaking Darcy's beard, "we all know señor O'Rourke."

Señor O'Rourke grinned. "Call me Darcy. What you drinking, Dan?"

"Johnny Walker Red on the rocks."

"Make it two," Darcy said.

As Chita strolled away, hips swaying, Darcy dipped a chip, then made a face when the salsa hit his tongue. "A hot one," he said, looking in vain for something to drink.

"I assume you're talking about the salsa."

"Of course. Tell me about Rosie's ranch."

"Not much to tell. It's a few miles north of here in the Cañada del Oro Valley. Just a few hundred acres, mostly mesquite. She raises horses, not cattle, but keeps Old Blue around as a reminder that it used to be a cattle ranch back when her husband Ben was alive. He was one of the Marine officers who landed on Okinawa in April of 1945 and never made it off the island. Rosie sold off some land and went into the quarter horse business, an operation small enough that one woman could handle it by herself."

"You live there?"

"I lease a little apartment Ben built above the garage for his hired hand. I'm a bit slow with the rent sometimes, but Rosie doesn't fret about it."

Darcy got busy writing in his notebook, so I dipped a chip into the salsa and tried some myself. Darcy had used the right word: *hot*.

Chapter 4

November 1957 – Tucson

Pilar showed up the same time as our drinks, and Chita stood aside when she saw that the lady was headed for our booth.

Ever an optimist, I slid over to make room for Pilar, but so did Darcy, and she eased onto the plastic bench next to him.

"Figured you'd be here," Pilar said. "I talked to one of the deputies. He seems to think there's a legitimate threat to some juror."

Butting in, I asked, "Which one?"

"He wouldn't say."

"What I meant was, which deputy?"

"Oh. Earl Castillo. You know him?"

"Yeah."

Chita finally stepped up with our drinks. She leaned in front of Pilar and set Darcy's scotch down on the Formica. Turning her head toward me, Chita winked and said, "*Lo conozco también.*"

"I bet you do," I answered.

She laughed, handed the other scotch to me, and swished away.

Looking quizzical, Darcy asked, "What did she say?"

Pilar snapped, "She knows the deputy too."

So, the lady speaks Spanish and is already jealous. Castillo is not wasting any time. But then, he never does.

Darcy turned to look at Pilar. "You joining us for dinner?"

"No," Pilar said, sliding out of the booth. "I have a date with the famous deputy." Turning to me, she asked, "Any advice?"

"Yeah. When Castillo starts to sing, it's time to leave."

"Really." Pilar wrinkled her nose at me and left.

"Well," Darcy said, holding up his glass, "Here's to fast women and pretty horses."

"Amen."

We both drank, then Darcy went back to business. "Did that cowboy get you arrested?"

"Not quite."

"What happened?"

September 1957 – Tucson

Early that next morning, I hustled over to the Santa Rita Hotel's coffee shop. I was on my third cup of java when Sugar came in. She wasn't alone, and this disturbed me for some reason, as if she'd brought along a spare man on a date.

The man at her side wore one of those tan safari suits you

see in movies about Africa. He was tall, slender, and what I'd call distinguished looking, with white hair and a white goatee. Maybe he was the sweet-liking Mr. Holliday. Maybe not.

Sugar saw me, pointed, and led the man over.

"Hi," she said. "Justin Cromwell, meet Dan Hannigan."

"It's Brannigan," I said, standing up and extending my hand. Cromwell's handshake was firm, his palm was dry, and he had good eye contact. It was just the sort of meeting you'd expect from someone distinguished. Naturally, I took an instant dislike to the man. "Pleased to meet you, Mr. Cromwell."

"Call me Justin."

"Okay, Justin. Have a seat."

They both sat. I noticed that Sugar pulled out her own chair.

After moving the leftovers from my toast-and-marmalade breakfast out of the way, I waved at the waitress.

Sheila, the waitress, managed to take their breakfast orders without ever taking her eyes off good old Justin Cromwell, man of distinction.

I asked the side of Sheila's head for more coffee and got the briefest of nods for an answer.

Justin dismissed our waitress, then turned to me. "Well, Mr., ah, Brannigan, Sugar tells me you fix things for movie companies here in Tucson."

"Sometimes."

"Well, she feels the need for some, ah, assistance out in the bush, and suggested I hire you. Interested?"

Sugar reached across the table and briefly touched my hand. "I told Mr. Cromwell about our meeting yesterday, and the way you handled that bully."

"Might be," I said. "Sorry, I don't recognize your name, Mr. Cromwell. Just what is it you do?"

"Please call me Justin. I'm a director ... usually of documentaries. You probably don't go to many historical motion pictures."

"I saw *Gone With the Wind*."

"That hardly qualifies."

"Hmm, guess not. You shooting a documentary around here?"

"No. Actually, we're creating a new television western series called *Vaquero*. It'll be filmed at the Old Tucson lot and various sites around southern Arizona. Sugar's job is to find photogenic scenery for those remote shoots."

Sugar leaned toward me while kissing up to her boss. "Mr. Cromwell was selected to direct because Paradise Pictures wants the series to be as factual as possible. His documentary background will be invaluable."

"Ah."

Their breakfast arrived: juice, coffee, and sweet rolls. Obviously, none of us was going to put on much weight here.

Sheila did a creditable job of parceling out the goodies while fixated on Cromwell. And I did get more coffee.

After Sheila left, Justin took a dainty bite of sweet roll,

downed half his orange juice, and got to the point. "How much will it take to bring you on board, Brannigan?"

"I get paid by the day and the job. What's the job?"

"Can you guide Miss Holliday to appropriate areas for her search?"

"Sure. And if she needs to find something I can't lead her to, I'll get help. What else?"

"Keep her out of trouble."

"That," I said, smiling at the lady, "shouldn't be too difficult. Fifty a day plus expenses."

Justin chewed on the rest of his sweet roll and my proposal. "Done," he finally said. "We'll try this for a week. I'll pay you then."

Laughing, I said, "Two hundred now and the rest then, Justin."

Good old Justin Cromwell reached into an inside pocket of his safari suit and pulled out a checkbook. "Very well. But my employees call me Mr. Cromwell."

"Okay by me, Mr. Cromwell, but I'll need cash."

Sugar volunteered to go with me to drop off the cowboy's rifle at the sheriff's office. Her reaction when she saw my car was typical: "What in hell is that?"

"That," I said "is a brand new Ford Edsel. One of the first in town."

"Ohmigod. It's weird looking."

"The folks at the Ford dealership tell me it's destined to be a classic."

"Classic what?"

"Get in. It's a long walk."

Deputy Charley Lopez was behind the service counter when Sugar and I strolled into the sheriff's office. The Pump House cowboy was on this side of the counter, his back to us, filling out some form. I could guess what that was.

Chubby and relentlessly cheerful, Charley looked past the man and grinned at me. "You're just in time, Brannigan; this man says you stole his gun."

The cowboy spun around.

"Here it is." I stepped past the man and set the rifle on the counter. "Like I told this fellow yesterday; he could claim it here today."

Charley eyed the cowboy. "That true?"

"Don't remember it that way. No, sir. This *pendejo* just took it."

Trying to look serious, Charley asked, "Why'd you do that, Dan?"

"He tried to kill Old Blue with it."

"That steer Rosie keeps as a pet?"

"Yeah."

Mustering up some inner strength, Charley actually glared. "Why'd you want to do a dumb thing like that?"

"It was on Pump House land. I just chased the critter away."

"You knocked two inches off a horn with one of your shots," I said. "That's pretty close for just chasing."

"I saw it all," Sugar said.

We three men turned and stared at her.

She went right on. "This cowboy was trying to kill that poor animal. Mr. Brannigan took the man's gun to prevent a grievous crime, and I heard him say he'd bring it here today."

The cowboy glared at Sugar. "That's bullshit, and—"

Charley cut him off. "Mister, I recommend you take your rifle and leave before I have to arrest *you* for something. Cruelty to animals and filing a false report both come to mind."

The cowboy snarled something under his breath, grabbed his rifle, and walked backward towards the door as if he were some gunfighter leaving a saloon after a shooting.

I was suddenly glad the gun's shells were still in the trunk of my car.

Charley watched the cowboy until he disappeared. I figured the deputy didn't know the rifle's magazine was empty. Finally, Charley turned to Sugar. "Was what you said the truth?"

"Most of it. I didn't hear what was said. I was too far away."

"It's not nice to lie to law enforcement officers, young lady. Makes guys like me and Brannigan here itchy, don't it Dan?"

"*Es verdad.*"

Sugar gave me a weird look. "Law enforcement? You?"

"Tried it once ... it didn't like me."

"Don't you believe it," Charley said. "Brannigan here was a damn good cop, right up to the day he punched out the chief."

"You hit your boss?"

"Well—"

"Dropped him like a pole-axed mule," Charley said.

"Why?" Sugar asked.

"The chief pissed me off," I said.

"He had it coming," Charley said, "The chief bad-mouthed Dan's dad."

Sugar shook her head. "Brannigan, you are something else. Have you ever thought of becoming a private eye, like in the movies?"

"He won't have to," Charley said. "The sheriff hired him. He's going to be a deputy shortly. When is it, Dan?"

"November, if the doc gives me an up chit."

Looking concerned, Sugar asked, "You been sick?"

"Shot twice. That was after I was a cop. It's a long story. Come on, let's get to work so I can bill your great white hunter for today. Where do you want to start?"

"At the Arizona Historical Society. Know where it is?"

"Amazingly, I do." I waved at Charley, then took Sugar by the elbow and steered her towards the door. At the threshold I turned and called out, "Hey Charlie, what's that guy's name?"

"The one who was going to have you arrested?"

"Yeah."

Charley picked up the uncompleted form, scanned it, and

said, "Billy Joe Dupree. Must be a southern boy."

It took us two hours at the Historical Society's Tucson headquarters to find what Sugar was after: a map that showed the old Butterfield Stage Line route between Tucson and Lordsburg, New Mexico. She traced it onto a current map of Arizona, then looked up with a smile of satisfaction. "Let's go eat, I'm hungry."

I turned the Edsel into Johnny's Drive-In on Speedway. The food there was designed for teenage tastes, but pretty young women on roller skates brought your orders right to the car. I liked that.

Sugar took one look at the operation and said, "You don't date much, do you?"

"You're not a date."

"But you need to practice. Let's go to a real restaurant."

"Jeez." I waved away roller-skate girl and drove back out onto Speedway. I picked out a little Mexican restaurant a half-mile farther east and earned a benign smile from Sugar.

The lady ordered two tacos with rice and a Budweiser.

"I'll have the same," I told the waitress, "but with a Dos Equis."

Out came the map, and Sugar studied it while we waited. I could have been at another table. When our beer arrived, Sugar took a long swig from the sweaty Budweiser bottle, then went back to the map.

More than a little aggravated, I asked, "Why are you so interested in the old Butterfield Trail?"

"Mr. Cromwell read about an Apache Indian raid on one of the Butterfield stagecoaches, and he wants to recreate it. It happened in a marshy area somewhere east of here, so we need to find it."

"You're looking for a marsh?"

"Yeah."

"*Cienega Creek.* A *cienega* is a marshy area."

"Where?"

"Look on your map, just this side of the Cochise County line about thirty miles east of here. It's where US-80 parallels the Butterfield Route you penciled in."

"I see it," she said, bouncing up and down in her chair. "There's a little dashed line on the map labeled *Cienega Creek.*"

"That's the place. The raid probably happened somewhere along that stretch. I can't think of another marshy place anywhere else on that route you copied."

"You know," she said, "I've driven down *La Cienega Boulevard* in LA hundreds of times and never knew what the Spanish meant. How incredibly stupid of me."

"How very normal."

"Mr. Brannigan, I think you've earned your pay today."

I raised my beer bottle. "Want to go there after lunch?"

"You bet." She clinked her bottle gently against mine. "We'll take the jeep."

"Good, cause I'm sure as hell not taking the Edsel out there."

Lunch arrived and stopped our mini celebration. Sugar splashed a copious amount of salsa onto her rice and dug in. I admire a girl who eats hearty and stays thin. My mother was like that.

We spent an exciting few hours that afternoon traversing some of the Butterfield Trail in Sugar's jeep. It was exciting only because she drove.

And we actually found a marshy place suitable for filming. Sugar was ecstatic and showed it by bouncing up and down on the driver's seat.

Late in the day, we separated at the Santa Rita and headed for our respective showers. I gave her directions to The Inferno, a nice little supper club that just happened to be owned by my sainted father, and promised to meet her there at seven.

Rosie was pitching manure into a two-wheeled trailer when I drove into the ranch yard. She made a bit of side money selling the fertilizer to a woman who raised flowers on Tucson's east side. Rosie stuck the fork into the mound of glop in the trailer and walked over to the car, the two dogs in tow.

"Well," she said, "I guess you talked your way out of jail."

"Charley Lopez was on duty when I turned in the cowboy's rifle, and he let me off the hook."

64

"Just like that?"

"The woman I told you about—the one in the jeep—went there with me and corroborated my story. Charley chewed out the cowboy and sent him packing. End of story."

"Maybe not. I called Clete Johnson, the man who owns Pump House, and bitched about my prize steer getting the tip of his horn shot off."

"Did he ask if you were now raising short-horn cattle?"

Rosie snorted. "He wasn't that amused. Said he'd fire the cowboy when he got back from town."

"Good for him."

"Maybe. But I'm going to sleep light tonight. Clete says that cowboy has a mean temper, and getting fired over my steer may not set well."

"I'm having dinner at dad's place tonight, but I'll be back about ten. Don't shoot me."

"I'll keep it in mind." Rosie turned and went back to her manure pile.

The Inferno was crowded, and Dad was busy behind the bar when I walked in a few minutes before seven. He nodded at me, added a wink, and went back to mixing something frothy.

I grabbed a stool at the end of the bar and focused my attention on the pretty woman carting drinks toward a rear booth.

This was interrupted by a soft touch on my shoulder and a

voice that asked, "Making new friends?"

Turning as I stood up, I gave Sugar a quick smile. The white blouse, tan skirt, and leather sandals suited her; she looked like a native. "Just checking out Dad's new waitress," I said. "It's one of my many duties here."

"Oh, this is your father's place. How convenient for you." Sugar looked around. "Yes, very nice indeed."

Never one to pass up an introduction to a beautiful woman, dad came hustling over. "Son, I'm proud of you. You've inherited your old man's taste in beauty."

"Ignore him," I said. "He's old enough to be my father. Come to think of it, he is. Sugar Holliday, this is my dad."

Sugar held out her hand, and for one brief moment I thought dad was going to embarrass me by kissing it.

Instead he merely shook it gently and said, "It's a pleasure to meet you, Sugar. Did I hear that right? It's Sugar?"

Laughing, Sugar nodded. "Yes. I have a sister named Honey."

"Her dad likes sweet things," I added.

One of the waitresses standing a few feet away with a drink order tapped on the bar.

"Well," dad said, "enjoy yourselves. Duty calls." He winked at me and turned away.

"He's a nice man," Sugar said. "Your mother must be happy to have him."

"She died some time ago, I said. "Cancer."

"I'm sorry." She glanced down the bar. "Does your father get lonely?"

"Not anymore. Dad and Rosie, my landlady, have a thing going on."

"A thing?"

"You'd probably call it a relationship." I took Sugar's elbow in one hand. "Let's get a booth and some dinner. I recommend the prime rib with stir-fried veggies."

"You're kidding. Stir-fried veggies? With steak?"

We slid into an empty booth. "Yeah. Dad's cook is an old Chinaman, and he likes to play with his wok. Any order that lets him do that gets special attention."

"He likes to play with his wok, does he? What about you?"

"I don't wok here. You want to go with the stir fries?"

"That woks for me."

It was no-moon dark when Sugar and I walked out of The Inferno and into the parking lot. I'd parked in the back to leave the prime spaces open for Dad's patrons, and Sugar had parked her jeep next to the Edsel, so both vehicles were in deep shadow. I didn't see the man leaning against my car until we were close, and I didn't notice the Bowie knife in his right hand until we were even closer.

Sugar stopped, but I moved in until I was sure. *Yup, it's the cowboy.*

He shrugged his lean body away from my car and went into

a slight crouch, the knife held low. "You were right, Brannigan, you *are* easy to find. And the odds are a heap better now."

"It's Dupree," Sugar said, her voice as cold as the steel on that knife.

I raised my eyebrows. "Dupree? Your name's Dupree?"

The man hesitated. "Yeah. So what?"

"From Louisiana?"

Now he looked confused. "Yeah. New Orleans."

"I'll be damned," I said, putting a big grin on my face. "My mother was a Dupree from Louisiana. Little place forty miles north of New Orleans." I moved closer. "We must be cousins." I stuck out my right hand and stepped right up to him. "Put 'er there, cousin."

He got one of those *deer-in-the-headlight* looks on his face and shifted the knife to his left hand.

That's when I hit him: five rigid fingers of my left hand into his solar plexus followed by a right hook to the chin. Dupree staggered back against the Edsel; the knife clattered onto the ground.

Sugar screamed, "Watch out!"

Something hit the side of my head, and I went down. The world turned fuzzy gray as I rolled over onto my back.

Dupree recovered first. He knelt next to me and put the knife to my throat.

Events like that tend to focus one's mind. As my vision cleared, I saw a man standing a few feet away, someone I hadn't seen before. He held in one hand what I took to be a sock, probably filled with sand. A makeshift *sap*.

When Dupree pressed the knifepoint into my skin, the urge to pee competed with the pain in my neck.

Then I saw Sugar. She leaned down and pulled up her skirt. Her right hand ran up a long, graceful leg until it stopped at a small leather holster strapped to the inside of one thigh. Sugar's hand emerged from under her skirt with a little Remington two-barreled derringer that barked once: a *snap* like a slammed screen door.

His knife still poised at my throat, Dupree froze.

The stranger with the sap turned and ran.

Sugar moved slowly towards us. She cocked her little gun again. "Get up, you louse. I've got one shot left."

Moving the knife away from my neck, Dupree stood.

"Now get lost," Sugar ordered.

Dupree glanced down, and for just a second I thought he might risk a cut at me, but then he turned away and strode off in the direction his accomplice had taken.

Lying there, I tried to regain my composure; the sight of all that leg must have befuddled me.

"We're even," Sugar said.

"What?"

"Even. You rescued me when I was stuck in the wash, and now I rescued you."

"Huh. I didn't know anyone was keeping score. Where'd

you get that flea biter?"

"Daddy gave it to me on my eighteenth birthday. Isn't it cute?"

"It's adorable. What did you hit with it?"

"Gosh, I don't know. She looked past me. "Oh, oh."

"Oh, oh?"

I sat up and looked behind me. There was a small, round hole in the Edsel's left door. It was letting that new car smell escape into the evening air.

November 1957 - Tucson

Darcy began to scribble, so I let my eyes wander around. And there, charging toward our booth like a three-masted schooner under full sail, came Carlotta herself. People darted out of her way.

She wore her customary outfit: a long-sleeved white silk shirt with lacy front, tight black pants, and a silver concho belt that must have weighed a good five pounds. It took a mighty buckle to support all that silver, and she had one: a four-inch square of brushed silver with a dollar-sized piece of blue Kingman turquoise mounted in the center.

The heels of Carlotta's black leather boots made little popping sounds as they struck the Mexican-tile floor. It occurred to me that she could easily pass for an ageing flamenco dancer.

"Ah, there you are," Carlotta said, aiming at our booth. "We are honored to once again have the famous Darcy O'Rourke in our humble cabaret." She slid onto the plastic seat that had so recently held Pilar's dainty derriere. *"Bienvenida*, señor O'Rourke. I was hoping you'd come in tonight."

Not surprisingly, Darcy stowed his notebook and beamed his own welcome. "You flatter me, *señora*."

Carlotta picked up Darcy's half-full glass and sniffed the rim. "Not our best scotch," she said. "I'll get you better."

Raising one arm above her head, Carlotta snapped two fingers, and Chita appeared. "Take these and bring two replacements," Carlotta ordered. "Blue label this time."

"Si, señora." Chita almost bowed, then hurried to comply.

Acknowledging me for the first time, Carlotta blessed me with a toothy grin, then returned her attention to Darcy. "I went to the Tucson library today," she said. "I wanted to see if they had that book you mentioned. The one about the Confederate Navy during the Civil War."

"Oh really," Darcy said. "And did they?"

"Seguro. I checked it out. A fascinating read."

"I'm glad you liked it."

"And I learned all about you on the ... what do you call it?"

"The flyleaf."

"Yes, that is it. You are indeed a famous man. All those books. And the many magazine articles. Where did you get all that talent?"

"I went to a good school."

"And worked hard, I imagine. As I did." Carlotta twisted her way out of the booth as Chita arrived with two new glasses of more expensive scotch. "With my compliments," Carlotta said. "*Apetito bueno.*"

We both watched her stride away. Once again, staff and customers moved out of her way, then reassembled in her wake.

"Smart woman," Darcy said. "She checked me out."

"Yeah. Here's to smart women."

Darcy and I clinked glasses again and drank, sipping this time."

"That," Darcy said, giving his glass a loving look, "is damn good scotch."

"Amen."

"Okay," Darcy said, setting his scotch down and picking up his pencil. "Sugar is an interesting woman, but when did you lay eyes on Jubal Pearce?"

"The very next day. And that's when the trouble began."

Chapter 5

September 1957 – Tucson

I got to the Santa Rita's coffee shop early that day and enjoyed a light breakfast while I watched a young Hispanic women on duty at the cashier counter.

Sugar came in about nine o'clock ... alone this time. She was wearing a dress, a yellow, sun-bright job with frou-frou trim. Frankly, I thought she looked better in shorts and boots. She had a short chat with the hostess, then came over to my table. Pulling out the chair, she asked, "How's your head?"

"I'll live. Where's Cromwell, the great white hunter?"

"He left early. Mind if I join you here?"

"Woks for me."

"Please, no more woks."

"Okay. Why the dress? We going dancing?"

"To see the big boss. Grant Griffin—he's the producer—is flying back to Tucson this morning after a meeting in Los Angeles. Justin is meeting Mr. Griffin at the airport and driving him out to Old Tucson. We're to meet them there at ten thirty. Can you drive?"

"You're willing to ride in the Edsel?"

"The jeep's a bit too drafty for this get-up."

"Yeah. It might expose your weapon."

She laughed ... but she also blushed.

We saddled up the Edsel at ten o'clock and headed out to Old Tucson, fifteen miles away. I took the shortcut through Gates Pass to give Sugar a thrill; there are some interesting curves as the road snakes its way through the Tucson Mountains just west of town, and loose gravel sometimes adds to the excitement.

Columbia Pictures built the Old Tucson movie set on the western shoulder of the Tucson Mountains in 1939. It was constructed for the movie *Arizona* starring Jean Arthur and William Holden, but it was still used by a lot of film companies in the '50s. Most of John Wayne's best films were shot there, and Gene Autry's Flying-A Productions made TV westerns on the set. So did some fly-by-night outfits. I wasn't sure about Paradise Pictures.

It was first built to simulate a walled-in pueblo about the size of a modern city block. Some of those 1939 adobe walls still stood, as did a few of the low-slung adobe buildings.

The current version consisted of a short, sandy street flanked on the west side by a dozen or so adobe and wood buildings pretending to be a frontier town.

On the east side of the street was a large wooden-pole corral capable of holding the film's *remuda* of horses or, sometimes, a small herd of cattle that had been driven through the faux town for a film. Off to one side of it was a small tack room that housed the saddles and other horse gear. Behind it, a stack of modern hay bales hid from the cameras.

Thirty yards farther east, backed by film-worthy mountains, was an adobe church of Spanish mission architecture. The most imposing structure around, it was centered between two tall towers with square footprints. The church's front entrance was huge and made of suitably aged wood. High above the door was a bell tower with a functioning bell.

Of course the place wasn't anything like the real Tucson of 1860, but it did look like what the 1950's public expected of a frontier Arizona cow town.

I parked the Edsel in the dirt lot located out of sight a hundred yards behind the fake street. We had to wait a few minutes while the Paradise Pictures crew filmed a stagecoach rolling into town, its driver cracking his whip. He and the pretend shotgun guard both looked pretty realistic, and I gave credit to good old Justin Cromwell, maker of documentaries.

Once the dust lay down, a pretty woman stepped out of the stagecoach, popped a little umbrella over her head, and strode into the faux hotel. An assistant director called "cut" and everyone shifted back to real time.

Sugar pointed at a large adobe building sporting a multi-colored saloon sign, suitable faded for reality, and we headed over to meet the film's producer.

Grant Griffin turned out to be a bullet of a man, from his big feet to his bald head. He should have been a wrestler, a truck driver, or maybe a butcher. There were two things he definitely should not have been: ballet dancer and Hollywood producer. I bet he surprised a lot of dainty people on his way up. He surprised me.

"Brannigan," he bellowed when I walked into the fake saloon where we were to meet. "I've heard about you." He shook hands like a bear grabs a salmon. "Justin says you're working for us now. That right?"

"Whatever Justin says." I glanced at good-old Justin to see if he'd insist on being called "Mr. Cromwell" in front of Griffin. Justin didn't say a word.

"Good," Griffin said. "Let's get down to business." He put a large hand on Sugar's shoulder and bent over until they were face to face. "Justin tells me you've already found some good spots to film. Great. The rest of us have work to do here, Sugar, but I want you and Brannigan to go back out and pick the best place to shoot that marsh stagecoach heist. Test the ground. We'll be—"

A dark man in faded Levis and a dusty red shirt stepped into the open doorway and paused there. Judging by the dried manure on his worn boots and the black grime hiding his brown hat's sweatband, he had to be a genuine cowboy. No actor ever looked *that* real.

Griffin stopped in mid sentence. "Yes?"

"That's Curtis Niyol," Justin interjected. "The horse wrangler."

Niyol pulled off his hat and curled the brim as he spoke. "There's a man out here wants to talk to you, Mr. Griffin. Says he owns that sorrel mare in the corral. Wants her back."

"Like hell," Griffin said. He bulldozed his way out of the surrounding clutch of employees and strode toward the door.

Sugar and the rest of us followed.

The large wood-pole corral stood about twenty yards away. It contained half a dozen horses watching us with some interest and one beautiful copper-red one nuzzling a young man leaning over the rails.

An elderly Chevy pickup truck and a well-used horse trailer stood nearby.

Pushing himself away from the corral rails, the young man met Griffin half way. He stuck out his hand and said, "My name's Jubal Pearce, and that sorrel mare in the corral belongs to me."

"Oh, really?"

"Yes, sir. I know you gave my pa a thousand dollars for her, all legal and such. But he didn't have the right to sell her to you. She's *my* horse."

"Well now," Griffin said, "I look at it this way. I paid for her, and I own her now. Whether your dad had the right to sell her or not is none of my concern."

"I'll buy her back," Jubal said. "I've got a little over eleven hundred dollars saved up. It's in that truck over there, and I'll give it all to you for Sienna."

"Sienna. That the horse's name?"

"Yes, sir. She's named for her color."

"I see." Griffin leaned back on his heels and looked at Justin Cromwell. "How much of her do you have on film?"

"A whole can," Justin said. "A lot of it's close-up stuff with Miguel."

"He's riding her?"

"Just some still shots and them walking down the street so far. Niyol here says he has to teach the horse to neck rein before we try to film anything more complicated."

"What in hell is neck reining?"

"The horse turns in the opposite direction when a rein presses against the side of its neck."

"Ah." Turning back to Jubal, Griffin said, "Sorry, kid. We've got too much invested in her. She's not for sale."

Jubal stared at Grant Griffin for several long seconds, then spat out, "I'll get a lawyer and take you to court. The horse is mine." He turned and made long strides toward the pickup truck.

"Okay," Griffin called after him. "But I got a signed bill of sale from your father. Any lawyer will tell you she's my horse now."

Griffin turned back to his employees. "Well, that's that. Okay, Niyol, lets see how that mare is coming along. I need her ready for Miguel to do some real riding next week."

"Yes, sir." The wrangler trotted over to the corral and slipped between the bars. A leather halter with a length of rope attached was draped over one of the corral poles. Niyol took the halter and, talking softly, slipped it over the mare's head. Then he tried to lead her across the corral to where a fancy silver-studded Mexican saddle sat on the top corral rail.

But Sienna balked. She dragged Niyol back to the corral fence, stuck her neck across the top rail, and nickered at Jubal.

Yanking on the halter, Niyol snapped Sienna across the butt with the rope's free end.

Sienna reared and fought the rope.

Swearing, Niyol swung the rope at her again, slapping it down on her rump—hard.

Jubal Pearce vaulted over the corral's top rail and landed close behind the wrangler. Spinning Niyol around, Jubal hit the man once in the gut and once across the chin.

Niyol went down, gasping for breath.

Standing over the prone wrangler, Jubal screamed, "You ever hit Sienna again, and I'll kill you!"

Spinning to face Grant Griffin, Jubal snarled, "I'll be back, Mr. Griffin. One way or another, I'm coming for my horse."

Then he climbed through the rails and jogged toward the truck.

The pickup started as Jubal leapt into the cab, then it peeled away, leaving a thick trail of dust behind.

Griffin clambered through the rails into the corral and helped his wrangler stand up. Turning to the crew arrayed along the outside edge of the corral, he shouted, "Somebody call the sheriff. I want to file assault charges against that man … Pearce."

Sugar tugged at my sleeve. "That's just not right," she said. "Wouldn't you have done the same thing?"

"You mean decked the wrangler?"

"Yes."

"Only if it was my horse."

"Let's go," Sugar said, shaking her head. "We have our orders."

We drove back to the hotel, where I waited while Sugar changed into her working togs. Then we took Sugar's jeep out to the *cienega* area east of town and spent the rest of the day looking for hard ground where a camera crew could film a running stagecoach hold-up. She had a meeting with Cromwell that evening, so I went home.

The sun's final rays for the day had just washed over the movie set when Jubal came back for his horse. He was on foot.

Sienna knew. She raised her head, ears cocked forward, and

nickered. A moment later, she trotted over to the corral fence and waited.

Looking around, Jubal came out of the gloom. Reaching through the corral bars, he spent a minute rubbing the mare's blaze face and nose. Then, slipping between the long poles that made up the enclosure's horizontal bars, he entered the corral.

Sienna almost pushed him over as she nuzzled him.

Laughing quietly, Jubal slid the halter he'd brought over Sienna's head. Then he led the mare toward the gate.

A man appeared just outside the corral.

Jubal stopped.

Curtis Niyol, the horse wrangler, opened the gate a few feet and stepped into the corral. "You goin' somewhere, young fella?"

"I'm taking my horse, like I said. What's it to you?"

"They pay me extra to be the night watchman."

"You planning to stop me?"

"Guess not. My chin still hurts from our last meeting. But you got to know the law is gonna come down all over you for this."

Taking an envelope out of his hip pocket, Jubal handed it to the wrangler. "I told Mr. Griffin I'd give him eleven hundred dollars for Sienna. It's in this envelope. Can I trust you to give it to him?"

"Reckon so. I ain't no thief."

"Neither am I. Now step aside, we're leaving."

Two dark shadows in the night, Jubal led his mare out of the corral, across the fake street, and half a mile down a seldom-used dirt road.

Becky was there, waiting with the truck and horse trailer. She opened the back end of the horse trailer and asked, "Any trouble?"

"Nope. That wrangler caught me, but he didn't want a re-match. I gave him the money and told him to give it to Griffin."

"Oh, Jubal. Aren't you afraid that cowboy will steal it?"

"I don't—"

Crack. A gunshot sounded, somewhat muffled by the thick growth of desert mesquite that surrounded them.

"Sounds like that came from the movie set," Becky said.

"Probably that wrangler killing a rattlesnake. Let's go." He led Sienna into the trailer and patted her affectionately on the rump before he raised the ramp.

Next morning I was to meet Sugar at Old Tucson early. I arrived there about seven and found Sheriff Virgil Branson's patrol car in the parking lot. I figured he'd come out to personally take Griffin's complaint about Jubal Pearce belting his wrangler. I was wrong.

The sheriff was in earnest conversation with Grant Griffin and a couple of other men over by the corral when I walked onto the set. Soon as he saw me, the sheriff came over. "Hello, Brannigan. I hear you're working for Paradise Pictures now.

You know anything about this killing?"

"What killing?"

"Huh. Guess you don't. There's a dead man lying in the corral over there, shot once in the back. Name of Niyol. You know him?"

"I've seen him. He's the film company's horse wrangler."

"So I hear. Griffin said Niyol was also the night watchman, and one of the company's horses has been stolen."

"A sorrel mare named Sienna?"

"You got it. She valuable?"

"Apparently. Any clues?"

"No. But there's eleven hundred dollars cash money in an envelope lying under the body."

Griffin came over, put his big hands on his hips, and leaned into the sheriff. "What are you going to do about getting my horse back?"

Bad move. The sheriff leaned right back into Griffin's face. "Look, Mr. Griffin, I have a murder on my hands, and I'm going to track down the killer. When we find him, or her, I figure we'll find your horse. From what you've told me, that young man and his girlfriend are the logical suspects, and we know where his folks live. I'll put out an APB and also ask the sheriff up there to pay a call on the Pearce ranch. This won't take long."

Turning to me, the sheriff said, "Dan, when do you see the doctor for clearance to come to work?"

"November."

"Good. I'm still short-handed and can use you." Then he turned and walked toward his car. From a few yards away, over his shoulder, he said, "I'll keep you informed, Mr. Griffin."

Grant Griffin and I watched the sheriff reach inside his car and pick up the radio mike.

Looking at me, Griffin asked, "You fit to ride?"

"Yeah. Why?"

"I want you to go after my horse."

"Hey, the sheriff—"

"Sheriff my ass. I heard him, he's short handed. He'll put out his APB and wait for something to turn up. I hear that Niyol was shot from long range, which means in daylight, so he's been dead at least twelve hours. If I were Jubal Pearce, I'd be far up in some friendly mountains by now. That truck and trailer rig is likely hidden in some dead-end cañon and the two killers are on the run. Sugar tells me you've been a cop, so you're qualified. What are we paying you now?"

"Fifty a day plus expenses."

"That much?"

"I'm worth it."

"Then prove it. The Pearce ranch is south of a little town called Show Low at the eastern end of the Mogollon Rim. I figure Jubal Pearce is headed for home territory. I'll have Sugar drive you up there in the jeep. There's a bonus if you bring my horse back uninjured.

"I'll need operating funds."

84

"What for?"

"Horses. Equipment. Maybe bribes. I'll have to pick up a good tracker."

"Jesus." Griffin reached into a pocket and pulled out a roll of bills. Here's a thousand. That enough?"

"Should be, Mr. Griffin."

"I sure as hell hope so." He pulled a little receipt book from his hip pocket and wrote the amount in. "Sign here."

"No problem." I signed the receipt and took my copy. "I'll bring back the change."

"Just bring back my horse. She's the star of our film."

November 1957 – Tucson

Darcy yanked two menus from a holder at the butt end of our booth. "I'm hungry," he said. "Let's order." He slid one of the menus toward me. "What do you like here?"

I pushed the menu back. "The chicken fajitas. Cajun style."

"Cajun? That mean extra hot?"

"Just spicier."

"Okay. I'll try it." He set the menus back into their holder, then craned his neck to look for our waitress. "How long did it take the sheriff to zero in on Jubal Pearce as the likely shooter?"

"Bout as long as it takes a rattler to strike."

Chita appeared at a nearby table, and Darcy motioned her over.

Hip-swaying her way over to our table, she asked, "Another

round?"

"No," Darcy said, obviously appreciating the show. "Time for dinner. We'll both have the chicken fajitas." Then, grinning broadly, he added, "Cajun style."

She laughed. "*Que hombre.* You want something to drink with that?"

"Why not? How about some wine, Dan?"

"Sure. I like cabernet."

"Good enough. You have a Napa Valley cabernet, Chita?"

"*Si.* We have two of them."

"Bring us a bottle of the more expensive one. Okay?"

"*Bueno.*" Chita gave me a conspiratorial grin and shoved off.

Darcy finished off his expensive scotch and looked wistfully at the empty glass. "You know where Jubal went that night?"

"Yeah. I found out later."

September 1957 – The Mogollon Rim

Dawn's late rays filtering in through the tops of tall pines woke Jubal. He remained still, eyes open, listening to the quite sounds of Sienna munching grass a few yards away. Rolled in a horse blanket, head on his saddle, Jubal lay at the edge of a small mountain glen in the Apache-Sitgreaves National Forest. The pickup and horse trailer were parked a dozen yards away, with Becky asleep in the truck's cab.

Sienna must have sensed that Jubal was awake; she walked

over and nuzzled his face, leaving warm breath and a trace of green saliva on his cheek.

Laughing, Jubal gently pushed the mare's nose away and wiped his face with a sleeve. Then he rolled out of the horse blanket and stood. Strolling to the edge of the clearing, he turned his back to the truck and peed into the woods. Buttoning up, he walked over to the truck and rapped on the door.

A face wreathed in tousled hair popped up in the window.

"Come on," Jubal said. "Time to roll. We'll stop for breakfast in Eagar and be at your dad's place by lunch. If that Griffin guy comes looking for Sienna, he sure as hell won't find her there." He banged on the door.

"Wait," Becky said, sitting up. "I have to pee." The truck door swung open and she jumped out.

Jubal tried to kiss her, but she evaded his grasp and ran, giggling, into the woods.

"Just as well," Jubal called after her. "You probably have goat breath."

By the time Becky returned, Sienna was in the trailer and Jubal was slouched in the truck's passenger seat. She made a face at him as she climbed into the cab. "There's breath mints in the glove compartment," she said. "Hand me one, and take two for yourself."

"Smartass," Jubal snorted, but he reached for the glove compartment.

Becky started the truck, then turned on the radio while she

let the engine warm up.

The announcer forecast another beautiful day in northern Arizona, then went to the news. "This just in. A horse wrangler working at the Old Tucson movie lot was murdered yesterday evening and a valuable horse stolen. The sheriff's office says they are on the lookout for a man and a woman in a Chevy pickup truck towing a horse trailer. The pair are believed to be headed for northern Arizona."

"Oh my God," Becky said. "That's us."

"Strangely," the radio newscaster went on, "the horse thieves left behind an envelope containing eleven hundred dollars. It was found lying under the body. In other news—"

Hands trembling, Becky turned off the radio. Then she stared at Jubal. "You didn't ..."

"No way," Jubal said, pounding a fist against the dashboard. "The man was alive and well when I left there with Sienna. Honest to God."

"But—"

"Hell, Becky, how many shots did you hear last night?"

"Just the one right after you came back."

"Well? And did I have a gun with me?"

"You're right, Jubal. I'm sorry. But the money?"

"Yeah," Jubal said. "A lot of people heard me offer that producer eleven hundred dollars for Sienna. And now they've found it on the body."

"And that's why they think you did it."

"That and the fact that Sienna is gone. But they should stop and think; if I shot the wrangler, why in hell would I leave the money?"

"It doesn't sound like they stopped to think."

"Sure doesn't. So they're coming after me, for sure. I've got to hide someplace until they figure out who really did it."

"But they know who you are, Jubal, where you live." Tears formed in Becky's eyes. "And they're after me too. Where can we hide?"

"Let me think."

"And … how will they find the real killer if they're looking for us?"

"I don't know, Becky, I just don't know." Jubal banged a fist against the truck's dashboard again. "We can't go back to the ranch, that's for sure. The local sheriff will be waiting for us there."

"What about my dad's place," Becky said.

"Not now. People know we've been dating. It won't take the law very long to come up with that. They'll soon be all over your home too."

"Then what do we do?"

"Look, we passed a little ranch a few miles back with several horses. We'll borrow another horse there and take to the mountains."

"Why in the world would they loan us a horse?"

"We'll leave the truck and trailer for collateral."

"Yeah, right," Becky said, rolling her eyes. "Listen, the law already knows who you are, but it'll likely be several hours before they link me to you. You stay here with Sienna. I'll go into town and buy what we need, including another horse. Then I'll meet you back here."

Jubal scratched his head. "I only have a few bucks left, Becky. I gave just about everything I had to that wrangler."

"That's okay, Jubal. The banker in Eagar knows me. He'll cash my check."

"I'm not sure about this, Becky. It's—"

"It's the only way, Jubal. If we're going into the mountains, we need a lot more gear than we've got. Another horse and saddle for starters."

"Okay, Becky. Guess you're right. While you're at it, you better get ammo for that .30-30 in your truck. We may have to live off the land for a while. And salt. Get some salt."

Three hours later Becky drove the pickup back into the clearing, the horse trailer bouncing along behind.

Sienna raised her head, tested the breeze, and nickered a welcome to the new horse, still unseen.

Becky stopped the truck and watched as Jubal rode Sienna around the clearing, showing off, before reining her in alongside the trailer. She clapped and said, "Guess that wrangler was wrong when he claimed Sienna didn't neck rein."

Laughing, Jubal said, "Sienna wasn't ready to do it for *him*.

She picked right up on it this morning, no problem. Of course it'll take a while to get her really used to it, but she's coming along. You get everything we need?"

"Yep. Bought a good buckskin quarterhorse only five years old. And I picked up some stove-up cowhand's rig at the outfitter's." She hopped out of the truck and marched to the rear end of the trailer. As soon as she lowered the ramp, a tan horse backed out and stood quietly next to Becky.

"Good looking horse," Jubal said. "Where'd you find him?"

"The rodeo grounds. Some calf roper lost him to the owner on a bet."

"He have a name?"

"Yeah, Buck. What did you expect?"

"Could be worse. Where's the food and ammo?"

"In the truck bed. I packed it in two sets of saddle bags and bought us each a bedroll."

"Two of each, huh. Won't take the law long to figure out we're leaving together."

"Oops."

"No mind. Let's get moving before someone finds this place."

Five minutes later the two riders disappeared into the dark shadows of the pine forest.

Chapter 6

September 1957 – The Mogollon Rim

Martha turned away from the kitchen window. "Aaron, there's a county sheriff's car pulling up outside."

"The sheriff must be up for re-election this year. He's come to beg for votes."

"Uh-uh. That's next year. You don't think he's here about Jubal, do you?"

Aaron struggled up from the kitchen table and stumped his way to the door. "Only one way to find out."

Taking off her apron, Martha followed.

A deputy sheriff was on the bottom step leading up to the porch when Aaron pushed the door open and came out.

Pausing in the open doorway, Martha stood behind Aaron.

"Mornin'," the deputy said. "I'm Palmer West. Your boy here?"

"Oh God," Martha whispered.

"No, sir," Aaron answered. "Why do you ask?"

"There's a movie set out west of Tucson. Last night the

watchman there was killed and a horse stolen."

Grabbing the door for support, Martha slid down onto her knees.

"What's that got to do with my son?" Aaron demanded, gripping one of the porch roof supports.

"Sorry to have to tell you this, Mr. Pearce, but your boy is the prime suspect. Seems the stolen horse used to be his."

"Sienna?"

"Yes, sir. And—"

"Jubal didn't do it."

"How do you know that, Mr. Pearce?"

"I know my son."

"Do you know where he is right now?"

"I reckon he's still in Tucson. You want to look around?"

"No, sir. The sheriff said your word is good. But if Jubal shows up here, you better convince him to contact us right away. Otherwise he might get hurt."

"We'll keep that in mind, Deputy."

"Yes, sir." Deputy West tipped his hat toward Martha and retreated back to his car.

Aaron turned and helped Martha get up. "Come on, girl, let's go inside. It's chilly out here."

"What are we going to do, Aaron?"

"We're goin' to pray."

By late afternoon, Jubal and Becky were well into the high

country southwest of Eagar, working their way single file along a narrow trail that lay more or less along the lowest terrain within a steep-walled canyon. Oak, aspen, and maple trees, already turning autumn's colors, lined the trail, a tell that water lurked somewhere below ground or at least had passed through regularly. Between the narrow strip of aspens and the canyon's rocky walls were thick stands of ponderosa pine. Then, as the riders approached the tree line at eight thousand feet, the pine thinned out and rocky slopes dominated.

Sienna, in the lead, picked her way along a trail made by generations of deer going to water.

Riding easy on the mare, Jubal ducked under a low branch and asked, "You figure we'll find any running water up here?"

"There's a spring a couple miles farther up the canyon. Dad says it runs most of the time."

Jubal twisted around. "You've been here?"

"Yeah. A couple of years ago. Dad brought a small party of bear hunters up here and took me along."

"You mean you just sat back there on that buckskin horse and let me lead when you actually know your way around here?"

"I thought you were doing okay. Once you picked the canyon, there's not a heck of a lot of navigation involved."

"But you let me pick the canyon."

"It's what we women do; we lead from behind."

"*Sheesh.* This place got a name?"

"Dad called it Bear Canyon."

"Because there's bears?"

"Duh. That's why dad brought the bear hunters up here."

"Oh, that's just great." Jubal yanked the .30-30 from its scabbard, jacked a round into the chamber, and set the rifle's butt on his hip.

Snickering, Becky asked, "You planning to shoot something?"

"Only if one of your bears gets nasty."

"Don't worry, they don't want anything to do with us; they're busy eating. It's almost time for them to hole-up somewhere for the winter."

"I feel better already."

Sienna stopped, ears cocked forward. Her neck stretched out, she peered at a thick clump of brush a dozen yards away.

Jubal lowered the rifle, letting its muzzle swing down toward whatever it was in the brush that Sienna found so interesting.

Pawing the soft ground, Sienna snorted.

A mule deer bolted from behind the brushy barricade and dashed away through the trees, its antlers apparently no handicap.

Becky tittered as Jubal put the rifle butt back on his hip.

Reacting to a soft squeeze of Jubal's legs, Sienna moved on down the trail. The mare did, however, keep an eye on the brush pile until she was well past it.

Half an hour later, Jubal heard the soft bubbling of a spring. "I hear water," he said. "You were right, Becky."

"You'll need to get used to that."

The two riders emerged from the shadows into a small glen. A thin stream of water trickled out of a crack in the canyon's opposite wall, then ran down the rocky face to pool briefly on the grassy floor before sinking out of sight.

Unbidden, the horses waded through the muddy apron right up to the pool, then sank their noses into the clear water and drank.

Leaning back in his saddle, Jubal took in the high walls towering above them. "Pretty as a picture. We'll camp here tonight."

"Might as well," Becky said. "If memory serves, it's a good day's ride to the next spring."

Shaking his head, Jubal turned Sienna away from the water and rode her over to a dry patch of dirt. He jammed the rifle back in its scabbard, then winced when he swung down from the saddle. "Damned if I'm not saddle sore. Guess I forgot; it's been two years since I last sat on a horse for any distance. How about you?"

"Not a problem," Becky said, dismounting. "It's no different than riding mules. You know, I read that Roy Rogers once challenged Gene Autry to a riding contest. The two would ride all day, and the one who wasn't saddle sore at sunset would be the winner."

"Who won?"

"Far as I know, Autry never took up the challenge."

"Just as well," Jubal said. "I doubt either of them could have walked away from their horse. I'm having enough trouble." He did an exaggerated bow-legged walk over to the pool, where he lay down on a slab of rock and lapped up water. "Damn," he said, finally sitting up. "That's sweet and cold."

Turning, Jubal saw Becky disappear into the woods, a roll of toilet paper in one hand. "Watch out for bears," he shouted.

Not hearing an answer, Jubal unsaddled the horses and arranged the two saddles as pillows on opposite sides of a tall aspen at the edge of the clearing. Then he untied their bedrolls and spread them out next to the saddles.

Meanwhile, the horses took up grazing on the lush grass that surrounded the pool.

Camp made, Jubal lay back on his bedroll and gazed at the small slice of visible sky. *What now cowboy? What do you do if the law comes to get you? Shoot it out?*

He heard rustling in the shrubbery on the other side of the clearing and glanced over, expecting to see Becky returning. Instead, a stag emerged from the shadows and stood, head up, apparently assessing the risks. After a moment, he moved carefully past the horses and drank.

Jubal watched, not wanting to frighten the deer before it finished, feeling a sudden kinship with the hunted animal. *Drink up, amigo.*

The stag's head jerked up and the animal came to attention. Then, whirling, he bounded back into the forest as Becky stepped into the clearing.

"You missed it," Jubal said.

"Missed what?"

"A stag came and drank."

"You're kidding."

"Nope. Guess they don't see many people up here."

"You could have shot him. Then we'd have meat for a few days."

"Never occurred to me. Besides, a shot might attract attention. There could be a posse on our trail, you know."

"I doubt it. We're probably all alone up here."

Jubal rolled onto his side. "Yeah, lady. You're up here all alone with an outlaw. Aren't you afraid?"

Becky laughed. "Some young women dream of being carried off by an outlaw. Didn't you know that?"

"No. That's kind of dumb. You have dreams like that?"

"Not until last night."

"Yeah. I'm sorry, Becky."

"It'll be okay, Jubal. They'll find out it wasn't you that shot that man. Then this will all be over. Now, what do you want for dinner?"

"Got a menu?"

"Today's specialty is canned Spam and dehydrated biscuits."

"Spam?"

"Yeah. You want it cold or hot?"

"Do you have any idea how much Spam I had to eat in the Army?"

"Stop whining. You want it cold or hot?"

"Hot."

Nodding toward the trees, Becky said, "Then you better get some firewood." She pulled a small metal pan from one of her saddle bags and held it up for Jubal to see. "I'll get some water for the biscuits."

Standing up, Jubal asked, "Will I have to rub two sticks together to start the fire?"

"You can if you want. But I'd recommend you use one of the wood matches I brought."

Shaking his head, Jubal walked toward the trees. "Guess we'll have to risk a shot tomorrow," he said. "Eating Spam is gonna get old real fast."

Night came upon them in a blink. One moment the thin clouds hovering in their little patch of sky flared pink and orange, then flamed out; a moment later it was dark.

Jubal pushed one end of a three-foot stick into the fire and watched as a whirlwind of sparks flew up and became stars.

"A penny for your thoughts," Becky said. "You look as if your mind is far away."

"Just thinking how nice it is ... being here with you."

"Like dad says, the way to a man's heart is his stomach."

"You did manage to make canned meat and dried bread fairly tasty. You do much cooking?"

"Matter of fact, I do. I'm the only woman around our place, you know. Dad does a pretty fair job, but he's gone a lot."

"What about your brothers?"

Becky laughed. "They couldn't fry an egg."

The horses went on alert. Heads up, ears cocked, they moved closer to the humans and stared into the trees on the far edge of the clearing.

Jubal froze. "Something ... or someone, is out there," he whispered. Moving slowly, he stood and glanced at the Winchester lying in its scabbard a dozen feet away.

A large, black bear trundled out of the darkness and stopped. Sniffing for scents, the bear rocked left and right, swaying his huge head.

"Don't run," Becky whispered.

Turning his face toward the sound, the bear reared upright onto his hind legs and made a *huffing* sound.

The horses moved farther away, wary of the new arrival but apparently not quite ready to flee into the dark forest.

Then, dropping back onto all four legs, the bear lumbered toward the humans.

Grabbing the cool end of a burning stick, Jubal ran toward the bear, waving the flaming end in front of him.

Growling, the bear slid to a stop in the mushy grass, then

turned and galloped back to the trees. Crashing brush told of his continued departure.

Suddenly weak in the knees, Jubal knelt. The branch sputtered in the marshy grass and flickered out.

After a moment, Jubal struggled to his feet and turned.

Becky was standing by the fire, the .30-30 at her shoulder, its muzzle pointed toward the hole in the darkness where the bear had vanished.

The fire was low and crickets were calling when Jubal stretched and said, "Time for bed." He sat on his bedroll and proceeded to pull off his boots.

Becky dragged her bedroll around the tree and placed it next to Jubal's. "You know," she said, these bedrolls are kind of special. You can zip them together to form a double bed.

"Oh, really," Jubal said. "You mean for the two of us to share?"

"If you want."

"You scared of the dark?"

"No, you nutcase. I'm in love."

November 1957 – Tucson

The wine arrived, and Darcy made a grand show of sniffing the cork, inhaling the fumes, and swishing a small sample around in his mouth. He finally swallowed, smiled at Chita, and said, "That's good stuff."

"*Bueno*," Chita said, filling our glasses. "Your fajitas will be a bit slow in coming; Manuel is having trouble catching the chicken." Then she strolled away, hips swaying.

Watching her, eyes narrowed, Darcy asked, "Is she serious about the chicken?"

"I don't think so. Chita has a wicked sense of humor."

"Ah. How about the rest of her?"

"You'll have to guess."

Apparently satisfied with that response, Darcy held his wine glass up to the light. "Wine improves with age, you know; the older I get, the better I like it."

"Spoken like a writer."

He sipped and swallowed. "More like a plagiarist, I'm afraid. But back to business. Setting his wine glass aside, he scribbled something in his notebook. "So, Jubal and Becky were already in the mountains by the time you were sent to track them down. How did you plan to do that?"

"Well, I'm not much of a tracker, so I figured what I needed was an Indian scout. Fortunately, I knew one. I'd—"

"Wait." Darcy said, scooting around on his bench seat and writing faster. "An Indian scout. Oh that's great color." He suddenly looked up. "Okay, go ahead."

"Yeah, well, I'd met a fellow called Tres at a high school reunion where he distinguished himself by telling better lies than the white guys. Curious, I checked up on his background. One of the more interesting things I found was that he sometimes helped the US Border Patrol track smugglers across the Pima Indian reservation southwest of Tucson. That big old swatch of desert straddling the Arizona-Mexican border serves as a conduit for drugs moving north and guns going south. I figured a man who could track down criminals in a wasteland like that might be the man to find Jubal Pearce and his horse. So I called him."

September 1957 – Tucson

Tres answered on the first ring. "*Ya-te-he.*"

"That's a Navajo greeting, Tres. And you're not Navajo. Why are you using it?"

"You palefaces expect it."

"How do you know I'm a paleface?"

He laughed. "A statistical probability, and you just confirmed it. Your statement about the Navajo also tells me you're a native Arizonan with a decent education. That eliminates almost everyone I know. Let me think. You're either a reporter from the Tucson Citizen whose name I don't remember, or you're an ex-cop named Dan Brannigan. Am I close?"

"You're amazing," I said. "I'm Brannigan. How did you do that?"

"I have a good ear for dialect, and not many people know that my nickname is Tres."

"By the way, how in hell did you get that name?"

"A Mexican doctor presided at my birth. After he cut the umbilical cord, he hoisted me up by the ankles and said, "*Mire. Tres cojones.*"

"You have three testicles?"

"Yes, I am so honored."

"It's an honor?"

"Absolutely. My mother was so proud ... she invited all the women on the rez to come see my accomplishment. Word spread. By the time I was thirteen all the rez girls called me *Tres*. Then they'd giggle. My condition causes me to exude great virility."

"Uh huh. Does all that virility work with other women too? The ones off the rez?"

"That, Mr. Brannigan, is a secret. What can I do for you?"

"I've been hired to track down a pair of possible killers with a stolen horse who are probably hiding out up on the Mogollon. I need a tracker ... and thought of you. Twenty dollars a day and meals. I'm guessing three days."

"You're asking a Pima Indian to go into Apache land?"

"Yes. That a problem?"

"No. We Pima fought against the Apache as US Army scouts. Whipped their ass, too."

"So you're interested?"

"Hell yes I'm interested. Times are tough on the rez. I can bring six more men almost as good as me. Want them?"

"Nope. Just you."

"When and where?"

"Meet me at noon. The Santa Rita Hotel. Bring your saddle and a mountain kit."

"You got it, *kemosabe*."

I needed a couple of things from my apartment, and had no desire to leave my Edsel sitting around the Old Tucson parking lot, so I drove home.

Sugar followed in her jeep.

Rosie's saddle horse was missing from the corral, which meant she was out in the mesquite someplace, so I left a note on her door.

With Sugar helping, I transferred saddle, blanket, bridle, and rifle from the trunk of my car to the back of the jeep. Then I headed up the stairs to my little apartment above the garage. My snub-nose Colt .38 was waiting in its nest under the bed, a small safe with its lock broken.

Being partial to hidden weapons, I strapped on an ankle holster, slid the revolver into it, and pulled my pant leg over the boot. Now ready for action, I grabbed a small bedroll from the closet and trotted down the steps to Sugar's jeep.

When we drove up to the Santa Rita, Tres was waiting on the hotel steps, the object of much gawking by several tourist types. Leaving his gear on the steps, he strolled out to meet us.

The hotel guests got out of his way and continued to stare.

Tres wore moccasins, leather leggings over old Levis, and a grease-stained leather vest. The bare skin under his vest was shiny with sweat and revealed a complete lack of chest hair. The handle of a large Bowie knife protruded from a sheath attached to his belt, and he carried a Winchester rifle. A bandolier of ammo hung like a sash across that bare chest, and a bright red headband set off the ensemble. At about six-two and two hundred pounds of mostly muscle, Tres could make an impression.

"Oh, my God," Sugar whispered. "Is he for real?"

"More than you know."

"*Ya-te-he*," Tres said, putting one foot up on the jeep's front bumper. He used two sad, brown eyes to give Sugar a one-eyebrow-up look.

Sugar began to breathe heavily. "Hi," she said, her voice suddenly hoarse. "I'm Sugar Holliday."

"I am called Tres," the Indian said. No snicker, not even a facetious smile. He looked dead serious.

And so did Sugar. "Tres? Isn't that *three* in Spanish?"

"Yes. I am the third son," Tres said, flashing a sudden grin at me.

"Load up your gear," I ordered. "We're ready to roll."

"It shall be done, *kemosabe*." He turned and trotted back toward the steps, where a small pack, a large bedroll, and a well-worn saddle lay waiting.

"He's magnificent," Sugar whispered. "Where did you find

him?"

"At a liar's convention."

I had Sugar stop off at the sheriff's office; I wanted to let him know what I was up to and also get an update on the situation. Hell, it was possible the law had already caught up with our fugitives.

The sheriff saw me through his open office door and motioned for me to come in. Grinning, he asked, "You ready to come to work?"

"Sorry. The doc still says November. But I do have a job; Griffin hired me to bring back his horse. Got any idea where she is?"

"About. Just got off the phone with Sheriff Begay."

"Apache county?"

"Yeah. A banker in Eagar called him about Becky Welch, the gal with Jubal Pearce. Seems she went to his bank first thing this morning and cashed a large check." He shook his head. "The banker didn't know we were looking for her until after she left town."

"Eagar, huh. That's a bit out of the way if Pearce was heading home."

"They must have gone up the back way, through Clifton. Less chance of being spotted."

"What else have you got?"

"Begay sent a couple deputies to check it out. They found

where she bought a horse. That led them to check out the local outfitter where she picked up a used saddle and bridle, two sets of saddle bags, and two bedrolls."

"Two bedrolls. She and Jubal are going camping."

"There's more," the sheriff said. "I called the Pentagon and got some info on Jubal Pearce's Army stint. You better watch your ass when you find him."

"Why?"

"The Army taught him a skill: he's a sniper."

"Oh now that's just great. Did Becky happen to buy a high-powered rifle with a scope?"

"No. but she did load up on cartridges. Thirty-thirties."

"What was Niyol shot with?"

"A thirty-thirty. The coroner dug the bullet out of Niyol's body, and we found the casing about three hundred yards away."

"That's a pretty long shot for a thirty-thirty."

"Probably not for a trained sniper."

"Yeah." I stood up. "Any idea where the two are going?"

"Nope. But those deputies in Eagar are still scouting around. Call me when you get there. Maybe they'll have found the truck and trailer by then."

Back at the jeep, I found that Tres had moved off the back bench onto what I considered my reserved seat next to Sugar. He was leaning close to her, and she was not leaning away.

"Indians ride in the back," I said, pointing with my thumb.

Rolling his eyes, Tres responded with, "Our day will come, paleface." But he did lurch up from the shotgun seat and plunk himself down on the jeep's hard back bench. He then stuck his long legs between the front seats and crossed them at the ankles.

The man reminded me of a dog I once had that was not allowed on the carpet but always slept with one paw touching it.

Sugar wrinkled her nose at me and asked, "Which way, boss?"

"North," I said. "Take highway seventy-seven to Globe, then highway sixty up to Show Low and over to Eagar. Jubal and Becky were in Eagar this morning."

Leaning forward, Tres tapped me on the shoulder. "You know where they're headed?"

"The woman bought a horse, saddle, and camping gear in Eagar. My guess is they've abandoned the truck and trailer somewhere near there and are going into the Mogollon on horseback."

"And we go in after them?"

"You got it."

"That's big country. How you expect to find them in there?"

Turning, I grinned at Tres and said, "That's why I hired an Indian tracker."

He grinned back. "Then I am the indispensable man on this trip, correct?"

"Well … I suppose so."

"Then *you* ride in back, *kemosabe*."

"You're kidding."

"Not if you want me to scout for you."

"Jesus, Tres. I'm paying you to scout."

"Not enough. I understand how labor unions work. You want me to scout, you let me ride in front."

I told Sugar to pull over, then I swapped places with Tres. Now sandwiched between two saddles and our travel kits, I could see why Tres had rebelled. To compensate, I sat on his bedroll and stretched out my legs between the front seats.

September 1957 – The Mogollon Rim

State Route 77 wound along the quiet little San Pedro River, flanked on the west by the five-thousand-foot Tortilla Mountains and on the east by the somewhat lower Mescal Mountains.

After a pit stop in Globe, we climbed to the Natanes Plateau, crossed the Salt River Canyon, then clawed our way up steep switchbacks to the pines and Show Low. After that it was a pleasant but chilly run east through tall stands of pine alternating with large swatches of high-country meadow. Since this leg of the trip was relatively flat, Sugar let her inner race-car driver emerge, and we made what must have been record time.

Nevertheless, it was almost dark by the time we pulled into the Old Apache Inn on the outskirts of Eagar. The place looked a tad run-down, but it advertised rooms and a cafeteria, which is all we needed right then. I booked three rooms for the night, although I suspected that two would have been enough, then led the way into the dining room.

While Sugar and Tres shared a menu, heads close together, I found a pay phone in the lobby and called Sheriff Virgil Branson's office back in Tucson. I expected a deputy to field the call, but the sheriff himself answered. "Branson."

"This is Dan Brannigan. We're here. Any news?"

"The Apache County deputies found the truck and trailer in a little clearing down a dirt road that cuts off highway two-sixty about three miles south of Eagar. Horse tracks led off to the southwest."

"They leave the rig there?"

"Yeah, with a bar-lock on one of the truck's wheels. It ain't goin' anywhere soon."

"Thanks, sheriff. I'll buy a couple of horses in the morning and we'll get on their trail."

"We?"

"Me and my trusty Indian scout."

"You aren't talking about that Pima who works for the Border Patrol sometime, are you?"

"You mean Tres?"

"That's the one." The sheriff laughed. "Good luck. Call when you can."

A *click*, and the line went dead.

Sugar and the Indian were gone by the time I got back to our table in the cafeteria. A note lying on my menu read, *Not hungry. See you in the morning.*

After a good dinner of Apache tostadas made with spicy ground-up meat perched on fry bread, I tried to talk the night manager into giving me a refund for one of the rooms. He refused with a smirk, citing the fact I couldn't identify which room nor turn in the appropriate key.

Fortunately, the place had a small bar, and a couple of Dos Equis moderated my resentment.

Chapter 7

September 1957 – The Mogollon Rim

My two colleagues were already seated at a table when I entered the motel cafeteria for breakfast early the next morning. One of them looked sheepish, the other one looked like a large Indian.

Keeping her eyes on the menu in front of her, Sugar managed a weak, "Good morning."

Tres grinned at me and said, "What's up?"

Yanking out a chair for myself, I told him. "Some deputies found the truck and trailer southwest of town. Jubal and his girlfriend are headed into the mountains on horseback, as I figured."

"And we'll follow them?"

"That's why you're here."

"Ah yes," Tres said, picking up his menu, "the indispensable man."

Claiming to now be hungry, Tres and Sugar ordered copious amounts of bacon, eggs, and toast. I settled for fruit juice and an

Alka-Seltzer.

Turned out the only person around with horses for sale was the guy who owned a small rodeo-stock operation on the east side of town. We pulled up alongside his main corral at six-thirty, about the time the sun was peeking through a fringe of tall pine a mile to the east.

I expected a man with livestock to be up early, and he was. His animals turned out to be half a dozen Brahma bulls for bull-riding events, about twenty short-horned steers for roping competitions, and four decent-looking cowponies.

A gaunt man who's butt was so small he needed suspenders to keep his Levis up strolled out to meet us. He looked us over carefully, then said, "Howdy."

"Howdy," I answered. "I'm looking to buy a couple horses ... if the price is right."

"What fer?"

Waving one arm toward the mountains to our west, I said, "The Indian and I are going for a long ride."

He gave my Indian companion a long look, then spit a brown wad of tobacco juice into the dirt and peered into the distance. "You the law?"

"No."

"Good. Thought maybe you was goin' after those two I heard about on the radio. Sold that pretty gal one of my favorite horses yesterday." He turned toward his corral. "Well, there they are. Pick two and we'll dicker some."

Picking up a pebble, I chucked it at the nearest horse. He jumped away and trotted around the corral, head up, mane and tail flying. The others followed, excited by the novel change of routine. After watching them move, I said, "I'll take the tall bay with the blaze face ... and the pinto."

Turning to Tres, I asked, "The pinto okay for you?"

Tres shrugged. "The white man's idea of a traditional Indian pony. I'm beginning to worry about your sensibility toward other races."

"You want him or not?"

"She looks okay."

"Great." I leaned on the top corral pole alongside the seller and we dickered some before I paid an outlandish price for them. I might have tried harder, but it wasn't my money.

Tres and I rode into Eagar side by side, me on the tall bay gelding and he on the smaller pinto mare.

Sugar followed in the jeep, swerving once to avoid running over a trail of fresh green "horse apples" provided by the pinto.

As we clip-clopped onto the town's main street, the few pedestrians around stared at us. A small boy tugged on his mother's sleeve and shouted, "Look, Ma. It's the Lone Ranger and Tonto."

Fortunately, the Indian kept his voice low, and the boy couldn't hear what Tres had to say about that comment.

Reaching over, I gave Tres a pat on the back and a broad grin. He did not seem to appreciate the reward.

The local outfitter provided what limited supplies we needed plus a detailed list of Becky Welch's purchases. Then we headed out of town, still side by side, Sugar's jeep in trail.

We found the truck and trailer about nine thirty. I checked the vehicles while Tres strolled around the clearing, sniffing the air, looking for tracks, whatever Indian trackers do.

Sugar hovered at the Indian's side, seemingly fascinated.

"They spent one night," Tres finally announced. "The man slept over here." He paused. "Alone." He pointed to a small patch of grass that looked a bit flatter than the rest.

"Becky's father will be pleased to hear that," I said. "What else?"

"Truck and trailer left empty, then came back with one horse."

"How in hell do you know that?"

Tres gave me a pained look. "How else would the woman go into Eagar and bring back a horse?"

"Wonderful. Anything else?"

"Still looking."

I called Sugar over. "You can go back to Tucson. Let Mr. Griffin know we're on the trail."

"Or I could hang around Eagar," Sugar said.

"Up to you. But we'll likely come out of the mountains someplace else."

She pulled a map out of the jeep's glove compartment and studied it for a minute. "I'll wait in Show Low."

"Okay," I said. "Try the Baboquivari Bed and Breakfast. It's old but clean. I'll call you there when we come out."

"Here," Tres called out. "Two horses. Tracks a day old, but clear. They rode southwest." He waved in that general direction. "You ready, *kemosabe*?"

From the jeep Sugar called out, "Hey Tres, I've always wanted to know; what does *kemosabe* mean?"

"Depends," Tres said. "Some people think it's Ojibwe Indian for *trusted scout*. Others think it came from the Spanish *qui no sabe*, which translates as *he who knows nothing*."

"Like clueless? You mean Tonto may have been calling the Lone Ranger *clueless*?"

"That's nothing," Tres said. "*Tonto* is Spanish for *stupid*. Chuckling to himself, he mounted his pinto and rode into the trees.

Swinging into the saddle, I turned the bay horse to follow my Indian scout.

Sugar started the jeep, waved once, then drove back up the little dirt road.

I soon put aside what had been growing doubts about my exaggerated Indian. He really was a tracker.

About a mile into our trek, Tres pulled up and pointed at a bit of moss lying against a rock. "That's in the wrong place," he said. "Too sunny." He leaned over from the saddle and picked it up. "See, it's been dislodged from over there." He pointed at another rock, which sported a bald spot in the middle of a plate-sized patch of green. Feeling the bit of moss he'd picked up, Tres announced, "One day old."

"How do you know? Moisture?"

He laughed. "Has to be. They are one day ahead of us."

"Smartass."

"Maybe, but it tells me they took this trail, not the one that forked off a hundred yards back."

"Point taken, *amigo*. Lead on."

Late that afternoon we came upon a little glen with fresh water bubbling out of a crack in the rock wall. Tres held his horse back from the water and, without dismounting, studied the muddy terrain around the small pool. Then, pointing at the remains of what had been a small fire, he said, "They spent their second night here. Must have been exciting."

"Why"

"Bear tracks. A big one. The *oso* walked into the clearing, charged across it, then turned and ran away." He pointed as he narrated the story.

Once Tres pointed out the sequence of events, I could see how the tracks told a story. "I'm impressed."

Finally letting his horse approach the water, Tres asked, "We camp here?"

"No. We have daylight left." I let my gelding drink. "But we better fill our canteens here, it may be a long ride before we find water again."

We both dismounted, drank from the pool, and filled out canteens. As we climbed back on our horses, I asked, "You saddle sore?"

"Of course not. Why do you ask?"

"You walked a little funny just now."

"Oh, just a case of sore testicles."

"All three?"

Tres ignored my jibe. Then, as we rode past the little pool, he stopped the pinto and pointed. "The two slept close together over there. See the wide patch of grass pressed down?"

"Did they make love?"

"None of your business." Tres picked up the deer trail leading west, and we rode on.

November 1957 – Tucson

Our dinner arrived. Manuel apparently had caught the duty chicken without undue effort. Chita set Darcy's plate in front of him and said, "*Quidado, señor, la plata es muy caliente.*"

"No problem," Darcy replied. "I like spicy food."

Chita laughed. "No, *señor*, I meant the plate is hot. Do not burn your fingers."

"Oh. What's the word for spicy?"

"*Picante.*"

After serving me, Chita set a third plate in the center of the table. This one contained a tall stack of flour tortillas with diameters almost as big as the dinner plate upon which they sat. Then, smiling at me for a change, Chita asked, one eyebrow raised, "Anything else?"

"I'll let you know, Chita. *Gracias.*"

This time Darcy focused on his plate instead of the departing Chita. I guess food is something else that becomes more important with age.

Our plates contained small slices of lightly charred chicken that had been well seasoned with garlic powder and various spices, then cooked at high temperature with bits of peppers, onions, and tomatoes. The meat was surrounded by piles of rice, lettuce, shredded cheese, guacamole, sour cream, and salsa.

"Okay," Darcy said, looking up at me. "How do I attack this?"

"Like so." I picked the top tortilla off the stack, tore it in half, and cupped one of the halves in my left hand. Using my spoon, I put a couple of chicken slices on the tortilla half, then smothered it with bits of everything else on the plate except the rice. I'm not overly fond of rice. Rolling the tortilla around the result, I bit off one end of the cigar-shaped roll and chewed with gusto. By the time I swallowed, Darcy was busy creating his own edible delight.

Gentleman that he was, Darcy allowed me to finish my meal and refill my wine glass before he stopped eating long enough to say, "Let's get back to your story. How long did it take you to catch up with the two desperados?"

"The better part of three days. My smartass Indian scout proved to be a darn good tracker. He picked up on all sorts of sign that I missed: that bit of moss scraped off a rock, a bent twig, an overturned dead branch. We had to backtrack twice, but still made good time. I began to think either Becky or Jubal had to be familiar with the terrain, because they camped near fresh water every night. We didn't have time for such luxury, so we just filled our canteens when we could and pressed on. We dry camped when it got too dark to follow the sign."

"See any wild animals?"

"Mostly mule dear and the usual forest critters like squirrels and rabbits. Saw bear scat a couple of times, but never caught sight of the reclusive *oso negro*."

"*Oso* what?"

"Black bears."

"Ah. What about wolves?"

"They howled a lot, and a few came close at night."

"Weren't you afraid they'd attack the horses?"

"Yeah, and us. We kept a fire going all night and took turns on watch. A couple of times I saw amber eyes reflecting the firelight, but they never came right into camp."

Motioning with his fork toward his almost empty plate, Darcy asked, "What did you eat?"

"Beef jerky, salt biscuits, and canned peaches."

"Sounds rather tedious. What about your horses?"

"Didn't eat *them*."

Sighing, Darcy said, "Please don't *you* be a smartass too."

"Sorry. The horses grazed whenever we stopped, and we packed in some oats to boost their energy. Fresh grass and oats was probably better than they'd had in a long time. The down side was the oats gave the horses gas, and I rode close behind the pinto."

Darcy pushed his plate away and hoisted his wine glass. "Colorful. I'll have to include it in my story."

"Aren't you going to write that down?"

"I'll remember the image. What happened when you found Jubal and Becky?"

"Trouble."

September 1957 – The Mogollon Rim

It was late in the afternoon. We were making our way down a deer trail that meandered along the bottom of what looked like an ancient river bed sandwiched between two low ridges a couple hundred yards apart. The ridges were mostly bare rock, but the valley between them was chock full of aspen near the river bed and mature pine trees farther out. Some of the pines were so mature they lay on their side, long dead.

The Indian suddenly pulled up and raised one hand.

I reined in alongside.

His voice low, Tres said, "I smell smoke."

Head raised, I sniffed the cool air and said, "I don't smell anything but pine."

Tres grinned at me. "Paleface spend too much time in smoggy cities. Lose olfactory ability." He swung down off the pinto and wrapped the horse's reins around a nearby branch. Motioning for me to stay put, he crept forward, staying on the trail. He was back in a few minutes.

"They're about a quarter mile ahead, camped out in a clearing with a spring bubbling out of the ground. Looks like they have meat on a spit slow-cooking over a small fire." He grinned, "Very little smoke."

"Uh huh. I salute your nose." Dismounting, I handed him my horse's reins. "Stay here with the horses."

"You going in alone?"

"Yeah." I pulled my Winchester from its scabbard and levered a round into its chamber. "I'm going to sneak up and take Jubal by surprise. Make sure the horses don't spook and run away if there's shooting."

"Are you real sure about this?"

"It's what I'm trained for, *amigo*. You just keep the horses under control."

"Be careful, *kemosabe*." The Indian wasn't smiling this time.

As Tres had done, I stayed on the deer trail. The ground under the trees was littered with dead branches, and I figured to minimize the chance I'd step on one and make a noise. The canyon wasn't very wide, so any sound would likely bounce off the walls. I really hoped to take Jubal without a gun fight; a trained sniper just had to be the better shot.

After I'd gone a couple hundred yards, I finally picked up a whiff of that smoke. Good. The breeze was still in my face; those horses up ahead wouldn't smell me and give an alarm.

Continuing on, I soon heard bubbling water, then spotted an open space through thinning trees. Moving carefully, I crept forward, then paused when I saw the camp itself.

Two saddles and a pair of sleeping bags were stashed under an aspen at the edge of a round clearing about thirty yards across. The only weapon in sight was a lever-action rifle leaning against the aspen next to the sleeping bags.

Jubal was bent over a small campfire about a dozen feet away from their equipment. His back to me, he was either tending the fire or turning the spit.

The sorrel and a buckskin horse were grazing on a patch of green grass at the far side of the clearing. Neither animal was tethered. Jubal obviously wasn't worried his mare would run away, and he probably figured the buckskin could be counted on to stay near her.

Becky Welch was nowhere in sight, so I waited. A minute went by, then another. A wolf howled somewhere in the distance.

Then the sun slid behind some clouds hovering over western mountains, and the breeze shifted. The sorrel raised her head and looked in my direction. The buckskin did the same.

Reacting to the horses, Jubal stood, then turned toward me.

I couldn't wait any longer and stepped into the clearing. "Stay away from the rifle, Jubal, and nobody gets hurt. Where's Becky Welch?"

There was a *swish* close behind me, and I ducked. Something hard glanced off my right shoulder.

CRACK.

My rifle fired as I staggered forward and fell. The bullet glanced off the rock wall and *whirred* away into the trees, the sound whipping through the canyon. Rolling over, I levered in another round as I came up in a crouch, assessing the situation.

The two horses were charging away through the trees on the far side of the clearing, fleeing from the sudden noise.

His arm stretched out, Jubal was diving for the rifle.

And Becky was close alongside me now, swinging a thick stick at my arms again, trying to knock away my gun. She scored a good hit, and the Winchester flew out of my hands.

Jerking the stick away from Becky, I pushed her down and reached for my rifle.

CRACK.

A bullet plowed into the dirt next to my fingers, and a harsh voice said, "Leave it!"

This was followed by a loud *click-clack* as Jubal levered another round into the chamber of his own rifle .

Standing slowly, I glanced again at my rifle lying just out of reach in the grass. *Too damn risky.* Reluctantly, I raised my hands and said, "Take it easy, Jubal."

In answer, he stalked toward me. The muzzle of his rifle made tiny circles as if it were independently considering where to plant a bullet in me. Jubal's eyes were hard. I'd seen this look before—on the face of men making difficult decisions.

"Easy, Jubal," I said. "There's a posse back up the trail. They'll be here any minute."

"I doubt it, cowboy. I don't see a badge. You a bounty hunter?"

"Sort of. I was hired to bring back the mare."

Jubal stopped, and the gun muzzle lowered a bit. "Griffin sent you?"

"That's right."

"Ah, I remember you now. You were at the movie set when I slugged that wrangler."

"Yeah. My name's Dan Brannigan."

Moving to Jubal's side, Becky asked, "What are we going to do, Jubal?"

"We're going to catch our horses, find his, then get the hell out of here. There's a couple of piggin' strings in my saddle bags. Bring one of 'em here. We'll tie Mr. Brannigan to a tree. When we're ready to leave, I'll cut him loose but keep his horse. It'll take him a few days to walk out of here."

As Becky turned away from their saddles, a piggin' string in hand, she suddenly stopped. "Jubal," she shouted, "there's someone in the trees behind you."

Jubal spun around, his rifle coming up.

Stepping forward, I yanked the .38 from its holster inside my right boot. As Jubal aimed his rifle at Tres, I placed the revolver's muzzle near the back of his head and cocked it.

Like most revolvers, mine makes a small *click* when you cock it. Jubal undoubtedly recognized the sound. He froze.

I heard a muffled scream from Becky, but ignored it. "Now," I told Jubal, "Point that rifle at the ground, uncock it, then drop it."

The man did as he was told.

"Good," I said. "Now you and Becky go sit on those bedrolls."

Shaking his head in defeat, Jubal went.

Becky sat down next to Jubal, then buried her face in her hands.

Tres pushed some branches aside and strolled into the clearing. "Heard gunfire," he said. "Thought you might need help."

Picking up Jubal's rifle, I said, "You don't follow orders very well, do you, Tres?"

He shrugged. "It's my nature. What can I say?"

"Well, you came real close to getting shot." I uncocked my revolver and stowed it back in its holster. Walking over to retrieve my own rifle, I asked, "Where'd you leave our horses?"

"Tied to a tree back where we separated. After two shots, I figured the noise-making was over and they could take care of themselves."

Several wolves howled farther up the canyon, and Jubal became visibly agitated. "Look," he said, "our horses ran off in the direction those wolf cries came from. I need to go after 'em."

"Yeah," I said, handing Jubal's rifle to Tres. "I don't think Griffin would like it if wolves ate his horse."

"She's *my* horse, damn it. But we're wasting time."

"Okay." I turned to Tres. "Bring our horses into camp. And keep an eye on Miss Welch over there. Jubal and I will go after their horses. I don't think they'll have gone far."

"I know this canyon," Becky said, looking up. "The timber thins out just a bit west of here. If you go up on that ridge to the south, you should be able to spot the horses pretty quick."

"Sounds like a plan," I said. "Come on Jubal, you go first."

It took us about five minutes to get up on the ridge and walk west. Becky had been right. A bit farther up the canyon, the timber thinned out revealing a rocky bottom. The wolf cries became frequent—then excited.

Jubal broke into a run along the ridge, and I followed close behind.

Then we saw them. The two horses were trapped in a small *cul de sac* jutting into the north wall of the main canyon.

Lunging and snarling, five wolves were taking turns darting in at them, trying for a kill.

Their backs to the rocky wall, rearing and pawing, the two

horses fought for their lives.

"Shoot the wolves," Jubal yelled.

"Can't. I might hit the horses. They're all too damn far away."

"Not for me," Jubal said, holding out his hand. "I'm an Army-trained sniper. Give me the rifle."

"Ah ..."

"Give me the damn rifle," Jubal ordered. "I'll hand it back when I'm done. My word on it."

Taking a deep breath, I handed him my .30-30.

"Sit on that boulder," Jubal ordered, pointing at a large, rounded rock. "I need your shoulder for a gun rest."

I sat.

Jubal levered a new round into the rifle's chamber, then rested the gun on my right shoulder. I put my fingers into my ears, knowing what was coming next.

A soft exhale from Jubal, then ... *CRACK.*

One of the wolves yelped and limped to one side. Lying down, it chewed at a hind leg.

Another round, another exhale, and ... *CRACK.*

This shot knocked one of the remaining wolves ass over teakettle. The animal lay still where it came to rest.

Giving up their attack, the other three wolves broke and ran up the canyon, dashing for cover among scattered boulders.

The two horses bolted past the wounded wolf and ran back down the canyon, toward camp.

Jubal watched them go, then turned to me. "Nice weapon," he said, handing it over. "But it shoots about two mils to the left."

Chapter 8

September 1957 – The Mogollon Rim

With the sun now well down over the western horizon, daylight was fading fast by the time Jubal and I made our way off the ridge and back into camp. All four horses were grazing peacefully in the little meadow, the wolves apparently a distant memory. My bay horse and the pinto had been hobbled, but Sienna and the buckskin remained free. Sienna raised her head and nickered a greeting to Jubal as we came out of the woods.

Her back to us, Becky was leaning over the fire, tending whatever was cooking on the spit. When she heard Sienna nicker, she spun around and ran to Jubal. After kissing him hard on the lips, she asked, "You all right?"

"I'm fine," Jubal said. "But I don't know about Sienna. Wolves damn near got her and the buckskin." He broke away from Becky and strode over to the mare.

Sienna stopped eating long enough to poke her nose into Jubal's stomach, then she went back to grazing.

Jubal ran his hands over the mare, then did the same to the

buckskin. Smiling, he came back to the fire. "They're okay. Just a few scratches. Probably scrapes from branches while they were running. Damn lucky." He looked around. "Where's the Indian?"

"Good question," I muttered. "I told him to stay here."

"He's getting more wood," Becky said. "He thinks we need to keep a big fire going tonight to scare off the wolves."

A dead branch cracked, and Tres strolled into camp carrying three thigh-sized logs and his rifle. "I heard shots," he said. "What happened?"

"The wolves," Jubal said. "They had the horses cornered. I shot two, and the others ran off."

"*You* shot them?"

"Yeah," Jubal said. "Brannigan figured the range was too far for him, so he lent me his rifle."

Tres dropped the logs near the fire. "And you just handed it back?"

"I'd given him my word."

Becky turned to me. "And people think this man committed murder. That is just so damn dumb." She bent over the fire again, poked whatever was cooking, then turned the spit. "Jubal snared a rabbit," she said. "Looks like there's enough for four."

"*Ya-te-he.*" Tres said, squatting under the tree where our saddles and blankets lay. Grinning, he began digging though our saddlebags for something to contribute.

Easing down next to him, I whispered, "I don't see Jubal's

rifle. What did you do with it?"

"Didn't want the woman to get her hands on it, so I took it with me. Left it in the woods where I picked up the firewood. I'll get it when we leave."

When Becky declared the rabbit suitably roasted, she and Jubal slid the charred body off the spit onto the smooth side of a large slab of aspen bark.

"Aspen bark good for burns," Tres observed. "And for reducing fevers. Works like aspirin."

I shook my head. "How in hell do you know that?"

"I'm Indian. We know stuff like that. You never read about native cures, ethno medicine?"

"This may come as a shock to you, Tres, but the answer is *no*."

Tres and I watched while Jubal cut up the rabbit and dropped the warm pieces into Becky's metal bowl. The meat appeared to be cooked clear to the bone, juicy inside and crisp on the outside, probably the way I'd like rabbit.

Becky had rounded up three smaller slabs of aspen bark and now set them out as plates. She doled out the rabbit bits, a few small pieces on each slab of bark, then used the bowl as her own dish.

Muttering what sounded like some ancient Indian chant, Tres passed around our remaining salt biscuits and canned peaches.

The rabbit turned out to be tasty, and sopping up the juice with our salt biscuits made even those dry creatures seem kind of fresh. Tres ate his share of the meat with such gusto that Becky slipped him an extra piece before taking her bowl over to the spring to clean it. Finished with the rabbit, the Indian licked his fingers and belched.

With much slurping, we finished off the cans of sliced peaches in warm syrup. Then, while Tres stoked our campfire, I leaned back against a nearby tree and got Jubal started on his story.

After a few minutes, Becky and Tres came over. She sat close to Jubal and listened. Tres hunkered down nearby and proceeded to sharpen his knife with a small whetstone.

"That's about it," Jubal said twenty minutes later. "I did *not* shoot that man. Yes, I took Sienna, but I left eleven hundred dollars to pay Mr. Griffin for her. Becky can tell you, we were well away from the place when we heard a shot, likely the one that killed the wrangler."

Leaning forward, I gave him my best listen-to-me look. "You have to go back, Jubal. I believe you ... I do ... but you need to give yourself up. If you don't, someone else will come for you, and they won't be as nice as Tres and me."

"You gonna make me a prisoner?"

"Not unless I have to."

He turned and stared into the fire.

Becky reached over, put one hand on his shoulder, and whispered, "He's right, Jubal. Brannigan believes you, so will others."

After a long pause, Jubal shrugged and said, "Okay, we'll go out in the morning, together."

"Good," I said.

Tres stood and asked, "What's the plan for tomorrow?"

I looked at Becky. "You seem to know your way around this canyon. What's the best way out to civilization?"

She pointed west. "About a mile farther up, there's a cutoff toward the north. Half a day's ride that way and we'll come to an Apache village near running water. Last time I was there, they had trucks, and there's a U S Forest Service road leading to the highway and Show Low."

"Sounds like a plan," I said. "We'll head out at dawn."

"I'll take the first watch," Tres said. "You've had a busy day."

Then a rough voice from the darkness said, "*And it's about to get a mite busier.*"

Startled, my muscles tensed. I suppose the others were equally surprised; the four of us froze while the interloper strode into the firelight.

The man was big, like a TV wrestler is big, but dressed pretty much like any working cowhand—except for the hardware. The carved butt of a large-caliber revolver stuck out of a slick holster angled and tied down for a left-handed cross draw, and a sheathed hunting knife was strapped to his right leg just above the boot. But what grabbed my attention was the sawed-off, double-barreled, 12-gauge shotgun he held in his right hand, It was pointed at us. The gun had a short, angled grip, intended to be held as he did, with one hand, like a pistol. I recognized it as something akin to what Italians called a *Lupara*, the weapon of choice for Mafiosi.

"You," the man said, glaring at Tres, "get rid of the knife."

Tres turned slowly and stuck the knife into a nearby tree.

Stepping a little closer, the man peered at Tres. "You sure don't look Apache. What kind of stinkin' Indian are you?"

Standing tall, Tres said, "I am Pima."

The man laughed. "Ah, a lousy bean eater." He looked around. "Now I see a couple rifles. I want the woman there to pick 'em up real slow and bring 'em to me. Any trouble and my shotgun here goes off. And when she does, it ain't real pretty."

Transfixed, Becky just stared.

His shotgun quivered. "*Now!*"

As if in a trance, Becky rose, collected the two rifles, and carried them toward the man.

"Keep out of the way," he snarled. The shotgun's muzzle motioned a strong hint that Becky shouldn't get between it and the rest of us.

Obediently, Becky stepped to one side, then inched up to the man and waited.

Keeping his eyes on the rest of us, the man asked her, "Can

you work the levers on them rifles?"

"Of course," Becky snapped.

"Then do it. Empty 'em out, then cram dirt into their breeches and leave 'em on the ground. And you better not let any gun muzzle swing my way."

One at a time, Becky did as instructed, temporarily incapacitating the two rifles. Then, stepping back, she demanded, "There. Now who in hell are you and what do you want?"

"The name's Trippy. People around here call me Big Al Trippy, and I want money, little lady. The insurance company that covers Paradise Pictures posted a reward for the man who shot their wrangler, stole a movie horse, and set their production back a heap. I'm here to take that man in and collect the reward. Now, which one of those two pretty white studs perched over there is Jubal Pearce?"

Becky hesitated, then pointed at me.

Before Jubal could react, I put a hand on his knee and then stood. *What in hell is she up to? Protecting Jubal, of course; he might do something stupid. Just so I don't.*

"How'd you find us?" I asked.

Trippy motioned for Becky to go back to the bedrolls, then he grinned at me. "I know these mountains. Found out where you went in and figured where you'd come out. Been waiting up here for two days. When I heard shots a while ago, I knew right where you was at. Now, you move real careful and saddle up a horse. You and me are goin' for a ride."

Turning away, I winked at Jubal, then walked over to the grazing horses. *Okay. If Big Al gets ornery, there's the gun in my boot, and if he turns me in as Pearce, the jokes on him.*

The bounty hunter didn't seem to care which horse I took, so I picked the bay gelding I'd been riding. I led him over to my rig and saddled up.

My companions stayed right where they were: Jubal seated on the ground, Becky close beside him, Tres standing nearby. Their attention remained focused on the bounty hunter.

As I tightened the cinch on my saddle, Becky asked, her voice a little quivery, "What do you plan to do with the rest of us?"

Trippy laughed. "Don't you worry, missy. You behave and you'll live to ride out of here. But remember, the law says a bounty hunter can blow away anyone interfering with him doin' his duty. *¿Savvy?*"

Nobody answered.

I led the saddled horse over to a spot near the man and waited. My hand itched to grab the revolver in my boot, but that looked like a real bad idea just then.

"All right," Trippy said, looking at me. "You walk up that deer trail heading west. I'll be right behind you. After a short walk you'll come to a horse. That'll be mine. At that point we'll both mount and ride on. Me and the shotgun here will be right behind you all the way. If you try anything, I'll blow you away.

If your friends try anything, I'll give you the first barrel and them the other one."

"Wouldn't killing me lose you the bounty?"

"Nah. Insurance companies don't care. They're just trying to send a message, make a point. I'll just say you was trying to jump me. Maybe I'll just do that anyway—"

One of the logs on the fire gave a loud pop that sent a flurry of sparks soaring skyward. Startled, my horse swung around to face the noise—and bumped into Trippy. For an instant, the bounty hunter was off balance, his shotgun pointed at the ground.

Apparently seeing an opportunity, Tres grabbed his knife and began a throwing motion he would never finish.

Trippy's right hand didn't even try to bring the shotgun up, but his left hand blurred as he drew his revolver and fired.

His arm still raised, the knife poised to throw, Tres grunted and collapsed backwards. blood oozing from a hole in his right shoulder. The knife fell to the ground.

The bounty hunter holstered his revolver. "Well now, y'all saw that knife in his hand. He was gettin' set to throw it, and I shot in self defense. Anyway, tendin' to him will give y'all something useful to do while me and my prisoner ride out." Motioning toward me with the shotgun he said, "Get moving, Pearce."

Jubal and Becky bent over Tres as I turned to walk up the dark trail.

November 1957 – Tucson

Darcy smacked the table with one hand loud enough that it startled some of the nearby customers. "That's one damn trigger-happy bounty hunter. They all like that?"

I shook my head. "Don't know. He's the only one I ever met."

A gleam in his eye, Darcy asked, "You ever been in a real gun fight?"

"A few."

"What are they like?"

"Scary as hell."

"You've obviously survived. Got a trade secret you can share?"

"Are you going write an article on how to live through a gunfight?"

"No. Just curious."

"Shoot first."

"Huh?"

"Grandpa Brannigan claimed to be the last of the old-west gunfighters, and he shared his secret with me when I was just a boy. He said if you're facing a man and you both go for your guns, shoot first, even if you miss."

"Why?"

"The shot will rattle the other guy so he misses too. Then you nail him with your second shot."

"And this works for you?"

"Sort of. I'm one for two."

I nursed my wine while Darcy scribbled in his notebook.

After a bit he looked up. "What did they do with the Indian?"

September 1957 – The Mogollon Rim

"Oh my God," Becky sobbed. "Is Tres gonna die?"

"Maybe not. The Army taught me a few things about bullet wounds. Get me some of that moss growing by the spring. It's not the medicinal kind, but it might plug up the holes and slow the bleeding. Hurry."

Becky ran to comply and came back a few seconds later with a gob of the moist stuff, green water oozing between her fingers.

Taking a piece the size of a walnut, Jubal crammed the moss into the bleeding hole in Tres's shoulder.

The Indian's eyes snapped open and his jaw clenched. A moment later he relaxed enough to say "*Ya-te-he*" through clenched teeth.

"You've been shot," Becky told him.

"No ... shit."

"I'm going to sit you up now," Jubal said. "This will hurt."

Tres merely nodded and closed his eyes.

Grunting from the effort, Jubal lifted the Indian's broad shoulders and propped him up in more or less a sitting position.

Pulling Tres's leather vest out of the way, he exposed the exit wound. "Well," Jubal said, "it could be worse. At least that bounty hunter isn't using hollow-points." He stuffed another hunk of moss into the gaping wound behind Tres's shoulder blade.

"Here," Becky said, handing Jubal the flank cinch from one of the saddles. "It's the only thing around here long enough to reach around his chest."

"Good thinking," Jubal said. He wrapped the long leather strap, essentially a belt with buckles on each end, around Tres's chest so it covered both wounds and held the moss in place. Pulling the two buckle ends of the cinch toward each other on the Indian's chest, he said, "I'm gonna need a piggin' string."

"Right here," Becky said. She leaned over Jubal and laced the rawhide thong through the opposing buckles a couple of times. Then, while Jubal tugged the buckles together, Becky tightened and tied the thong.

With the leather strap held in place, Jubal lowered Tres back down. Then, looking up at Becky, he asked, "Why in hell did you tell that bounty hunter that Brannigan was me?"

"Easy. I love you, and the odds you survive the trip out of the mountains are a lot better with me than with some beady-eyed killer named Big Al Trippy."

"Aren't you worried about Brannigan?"

"Course I am. Just more concerned about you." She bent over and put her face close to the Indian's. "Tres is awful quiet,

Jubal. Is he dying?"

Tres's eyes popped open again. "Not yet," he whispered. "Rifle. Woods."

Leaning in close, Jubal asked, "Where?"

"Dead tree. Firewood."

"Where you got the firewood?"

"Yeh."

"I know the direction," Becky said. She pulled a partially burning branch from the fire and, holding it aloft as a torch, ran into the woods.

"For God's sake," Jubal called after her, "don't start a forest fire."

She emerged from the darkness two minutes later carrying the rifle and the now-flickering torch. "Okay," she said. "We have some protection beside the fire."

"We won't have that fire long," Jubal said. "We got to get Tres to some serious medical care *pronto*."

"Travel at night?"

"Have to," Jubal said. "We'll be okay. Horses can see pretty good at night. Better than we do anyways. Guess we'll have to pack Tres out like a dead deer."

"We could make a *travois*."

Jubal slapped his knee. "You are a blooming genius, Becky. We can cut a couple holes in the bottom of a sleeping bag and run two aspen saplings through the bag and out the holes. When we lash the poles to the pinto's saddle, one on each side, we'll have a *travois*. We'll put Tres on top of the bag and haul him out of here in real Indian fashion."

Twenty minutes later, Becky used her metal pot to pour water on the fire, then the little caravan set off down the darkened trail. Sitting tall in the saddle atop the sorrel mare, rifle butt resting on his right thigh, Jubal led the way.

The pinto followed, dragging the makeshift *travois* with an intermittently conscious Tres lashed to the bedroll strung between two long aspen poles. The dirt-filled rifles lay by his side.

Becky followed on her buckskin, alert for any sign of some predator that might be lurking in the dark.

An hour later a rising moon helped them spot the cut leading north, and they began their trek down the mountain.

At dawn, when they paused to check on Tres, Becky asked, "We haven't heard any shots. You think Brannigan is okay?"

"Don't know," Jubal said. "He's got that gun in his boot, and he just might try to use it."

"You figure he's fast enough to take that bounty hunter?"

"Not a chance."

"Anything we can do to help him?"

"Maybe. Think you'll be okay without the rifle here?"

"Should be. It's daylight now. What do you have in mind?"

"You lead the pinto and stay on this trail. I'm going on ahead. Maybe I can catch up with them."

"Be careful, Jubal. I want you back."

November 1957 – Tucson

Darcy held the wine bottle up to the light. There's a wee drab left. Want it?"

"It's all yours."

"Thank you kindly, sir." He tipped up the bottle and emptied it into his own glass. "So the Indian lived. Where is he?"

"Back on the reservation."

"With Sugar?"

I had to grin. "You should see her. She spends her days scouting locations for good old Justin Cromwell and her nights keeping Tres happy in an old adobe hut on the reservation."

Shaking his head, Darcy said, "I just cannot picture that."

"Neither could I, but she sure smiles a lot."

"How is the Indian?"

"Pretty well mended. He spent a week in the Flagstaff hospital, then was released to physical therapy. Sugar drove him home, and now he rides along with Sugar on her little scouting expeditions. She takes him into town for ongoing therapy once a week."

"So love conquers all."

"Well, I wouldn't know about that. Haven't done too well in that category."

"Is there a sad story?"

"I survived."

"Ah, but you excel at survival. How did you get away from that bounty hunter?"

"Frankly, I didn't."

September 1957 – The Mogollon Rim

Mid morning found the bounty hunter and me riding single file down a narrow switchback trail with a cliff on one side and a sheer drop to white water on the other. We rounded one of many sharp turns and saw a rider coming up the trail toward us.

Trippy finally broke the silence he'd maintained since we left camp. "Pull up. Rider coming."

"I see him."

We waited while the man, a middle-aged Apache, rode up and reined in his horse about twenty feet away.

Not wanting to be between the bounty hunter and anybody, I nudged my own horse over to the uphill side of the skimpy trail.

The Apache looked us both over, then spoke. "*Ya-a-teh*, Trippy." I notices that his greeting was slightly different than the Navajo one favored by Tres.

"*Ya-a-teh*, Gregg. You hunting?"

"Yeah. Who you got there? Some famous outlaw?"

"This here is Jubal Pearce. Killed a man in Pima County. Stole a horse. Good reward."

"I don't think so."

"What in hell do you mean?"

"Deputy came by our village yesterday. Brought wanted

posters. Good picture of Pearce from the Army. This not him."
Laughing, the Apache slapped his leg. "Looks like you screwed
up, Trippy. My brother will laugh his ass off when I tell him.
Hoooah."

"Son of a bitch," Trippy yelled. "No stinkin' Indian laughs
at me." The shotgun reared up and roared. Nine double-aught
pellets struck the Apache in the chest and knocked him off his
horse. The Apache's pony spun around and bolted back down
the trail.

Our two horses danced around some, but both were easily
controlled.

Then the shotgun swung toward me. "And if you're not
Pearce, just who in the hell are *you*?"

"My names Brannigan. I was sent to bring back the horse."

"Like a bounty hunter?"

"Sort of." I slouched low in the saddle and let my right hand
drift down my leg. *Gonna have to try for the boot gun real
soon. Real soon.*

"So," Trippy snarled, "the woman lied, and the bastard I
want is still up on the mountain."

"That's about it."

"Well, you've had your fun with me, *chingado*, now have
your fun in hell." Trippy aimed the shotgun at my head.

I ducked and went for my boot gun.

Smack.

Rock chips exploded from the cliff face next to Trippy and

slammed into his horse's flanks. Squealing, the animal lunged sideways, then struggled for footing at the edge of the trail.

Pieces of dirt spun away from the lip and fell toward the canyon floor two hundred feet below.

As horse and rider teetered there, Trippy's shotgun fired. The buckshot missed everything, but the gun's kickback helped push the bounty hunter a few inches closer to eternity. With a surprised look on his face, Trippy and the horse leaned out into space, pitched over the side, and cartwheeled down toward the rocks and rushing water below.

Turning slowly, the shotgun flew wing on them.

Revolver finally in hand, I watched Trippy fall until the flat sound of a distant rifle shot drifted over me. Looking up, I stared in the direction from where it came ... and saw Jubal sitting on his sorrel horse a long way back up the trail. His Winchester was propped up on one hip.

Jubal waved, then turned and rode away.

After holstering my gun, I checked on the Apache. There was nothing I could do for the man. But at lest he'd died laughing.

When Jubal's little caravan arrived about an hour later, I walked over to the *travois* and looked down at what I hoped would not be another dead Indian.

"*Ya-te-he*," Tres whispered. "Where's Trippy?"

"In hell."

"Good."

I grinned down at him. "You took a damn fool chance back there, Tres."

"My... nature." He closed his eyes and seemed to go back to sleep.

Turning to Jubal, I said. "Thanks. That was a pretty lucky miss."

"What makes you think it was a miss?"

"Well," I said, "you sure didn't hit Trippy."

"You were directly behind him. If my bullet had gone through the man, it would have hit you."

"So you did a bank shot?"

"Like you said, we got lucky."

Chapter 9

November 1957 – Tucson

Darcy's mouth was open. He finally used it to say, "A bank shot?"

"That's pretty much what it was. Those flying rock chips scared Trippy's horse right off the ledge."

"Christ. You had a close call."

"Like Winston Churchill said, *There is nothing so exhilarating as being shot at without result.*"

"I've heard that one before. You often quote Churchill?"

"He's one of my heroes."

"Any others?"

"Roy Rogers."

"That figures." After a sip of wine, Darcy gave me an eyebrow-up look. "Far as I know, Jubal hasn't been charged with the bounty hunter's death. Why not?"

"Cause all his rifle shot hit was the cliff."

"But ..."

"Like I told the sheriff up in Show Low, Trippy fired two

shots with that blunderbuss. The first one killed the Apache and spooked the horses; the second one missed me because Trippy's horse slipped over the edge and took the bounty hunter along for the ride."

"I see." Darcy studied his wine glass. "Another case where the facts don't quite add up to the truth. Didn't the sheriff up there question your story?"

"No reason to. He called the sheriff's office here in Tucson, and Sheriff Branson vouched for me. Besides, Big Al Trippy was not very popular around Show Low."

"As can be imagined. You sure the bounty hunter was dead?"

"Had to be, at least if he was lucky."

"Lucky? What do you mean?"

"I saw a couple of bears sniffing around the man as we left, and I reckon they ate him before sundown. He was probably fertilizer by noon the next day."

Mouth open again, Darcy stared at me for a few seconds. Then he downed the last of the wine and said, "I need a real drink after that story. Lets go over to the Santa Rita Hotel and have a nightcap at that Mountain Oyster Club down in the basement."

"I'm not a member."

"No problem," Darcy said. "They made me an honorary member."

"Now *that* is impressive. They don't do that for just

anybody."

"Like I told you, I'm a likeable old coot." He waved at Chita and made motions as if writing on his palm.

She apparently understood, showing up a minute later with our tab on a little tray.

Darcy pulled a fat roll of bills from a pocket, ladled several on top of the tray and handed it back to Chita. "Keep the change, darlin'. I'll see you tomorrow."

Beaming, Chita tweaked Darcy's beard. "*Gracias, Señor. Hasta mañana.*"

"You are a generous man," I said. "You always tip like that?"

"Only when I've been drinking. Lets go, I'm getting thirsty again."

Pima County Deputy Sheriff Earl Castillo smiled at Pilar across mostly empty plates on a dimly lit restaurant table and said, "Tell me about yourself."

She sipped some wine before answering. "You just making conversation ... or are you interested in me?"

"I want to know about *you*. You're a beautiful woman."

"Is beauty what motivates you?"

"Mostly."

The waiter salvaged their conversation by bringing the dessert course: Mexican flan.

When the waiter left, Earl said, "Let's start over. What do

you think of the trial?"

"Well, I think Jubal Pearce is innocent."

"Oh really. Why?"

"Instinct. I've been around some bad people, and he doesn't seem like one."

"Bad people, huh. Where was that?"

"Far away from here." Pilar attacked her flan and left Earl to do the same. They ate in silence, although the deputy took time out to smile at his dinner date occasionally. They were not returned.

Leaving some of the flan untouched, Pilar pushed her plate away and reached for her wine glass. "Do you like being a law man?" she asked.

Caught with a mouth full of dessert, Earl merely nodded affirmative.

"Why? You like locking people up?"

"If they're bad people," Earl said, his mouth now free. "Like the ones you knew. Far away from here." Then he put his spoon down, choosing to talk rather than eat. "My instinct says you don't particularly like me, Pilar. Is it my obvious lack of charm?"

Pilar laughed for the first time that evening. "I'm sorry, Deputy. It's not really you. To be honest, I accepted your dinner invitation in order to find out some more about this Dan Brannigan guy. Since he's an ex-cop I thought you might know him. He seems to know you."

Earl blinked and his attempt at a smile failed. "I see. You went out with me in order to learn about another man. This has to be a low point for me."

"Don't feel sorry for yourself. My interest is protecting the man I work for: Mr. Darcy O'Rourke. He's a nice old goat who's writing about the trial. But this Brannigan guy is getting real tight with Darcy, and I want to know what he's up to."

"What do you know so far?"

"Just that he's an ex-cop who chased down Jubal Pearce up on the Mogollon Rim."

"I know him as an honest man, who was a good city cop. If you want more, you'll have to get it from him." Earl raised his hand and signaled the waiter to bring their check.

"Thank you for dinner," Pilar said as they left the restaurant.

"My pleasure."

She laughed again, and this time Earl joined in.

Darcy and I left Carlotta's Cantina and walked south toward the handful of modestly tall buildings that marked downtown Tucson. We made it all of a block and a half before our trip was, as they say, rudely interrupted: two men stepped out of a dark alley and stood in our way. One of them held a revolver pointed at me. The other was Billy Joe Dupree.

Dupree's Bowie knife appeared in his right hand, and he grinned, teeth flashing in the moonlight. "Lo, Brannigan. Seems you got more than one life. Sorta like a cat."

"I like it that way, Dupree." I motioned for Darcy to move away from me. *And the .38 is in the Edsel instead of my boot. Damn courthouse rules.*

Darcy shuffled sideways and put his back against the adjacent brick wall. "This the man who shot at Old Blue?" he asked.

"Yeah."

Yanking a white bandana from a hip pocket, Dupree tossed it to me.

It felt slick and cool. "Silk?"

"That's right."

"Didn't figure you for a dandy, Dupree."

"Tell you what we're goin' to do with it, Brannigan, we're goin' to have us a real Cajun knife fight. You right handed?"

"Yeah."

"Then wrap one end of that hanky around your left hand and get a good grip on it."

Not seeing any good alternative just then, I did it.

"That's it," Dupree said. "Now hand me the other end."

I held out my left hand, the free end of the bandana dangling.

Grabbing it, Dupree took a firm grip on his end and twisted it around his left hand.

We were now bound together by pride, if not by silk. Since I'm not a particularly proud man, I considered dropping the stupid rag and running, but then there was Darcy to consider ...

and the other man's gun. "Do I get a knife too?"

"Sho nuff. Toss him your pig sticker, Yancy."

Dupree's buddy pulled a standard-issue hunting knife from a scabbard and tossed it to me.

Snatching it's handle out of the air, I went into a defensive crouch. I expected Dupree to lunge, but be merely laughed.

"Now the rules of Cajun knife fightin' are simple," he said. If you let go of the scarf, Yancy shoots you. Savvy?"

"Oh yeah. I saw the movie and—"

Dupree exploded into action. Lunging forward, he swung his big blade at my head.

Now I don't know a hell of a lot about knife fighting, but I am a big fan of surprise. So when Dupree lunged forward, I sat down.

The Bowie knife's blade swished over the top of my head, and Dupree's forward momentum carried him right into me. He tripped over one of my legs, rolled over me, and went *splat* on the sidewalk. He landed on his back close by, so I reached over and put the blade of my knife against his throat, right under the Adam's apple.

"Shoot the bastard," Dupree wheezed, somewhat out of breath.

"Nope," Yancy said. "Wouldn't be right. He's still got aholt of your bandana."

I put a little pressure on the knife and said, "You want to call it a draw?"

He thought about that, then gurgled an answer.

"That a yes?"

"Yeh."

"Good. Now hand your knife to that nice old man with the beard. And do it slow and easy."

Dupree raised his Bowie knife, may have thought about using it, but then held it out at arm's length.

Darcy hesitated, then stepped forward and took the knife. Moving quickly back to the wall, he held the blade well away from his body, as if it might bite.

Just then two people turned the corner half a block away and strolled toward us: Pilar and her dinner date, Deputy Sheriff Earl Castillo.

With the hunting knife still pressed against Dupree's neck, I called out a warning: "Careful, Castillo. There's a man here with a gun."

As expected, Castillo stepped in front of Pilar and drew the snub-nosed revolver he always keeps holstered in the small of his back.

Yancy looked over his shoulder, saw that someone else had a gun, and melted back into the alley.

I leaned close to Dupree. "There's an armed deputy about fifty yards away. I'm going to let you up now. When I do, you and your friend in the alley are going to get the hell out of here before someone gets hurt. Agreed?"

"Yeh. What about my Bowie knife?"

"You know the drill. You can pick it up at the sheriff's office tomorrow." I lifted the knife away from Dupree's neck. "Now git."

Struggling to his feet, Dupree snarled something nasty at me, then joined his buddy in the alley. Their footsteps echoed down that dark corridor as the two men ran away.

An adrenaline aftermath was taking charge of my body, so I decided to stay where I was until my legs stopped quivering. I was still there when Pilar rushed up to Darcy.

Castillo stopped next to me. Looking down, he asked, "You tired?"

"Just resting."

"What's the knife and hanky for?"

"Cajun knife fight."

"Really? Who won?"

"Guess I did. That's why I'm resting. Winning took a lot out of me."

"You about ready to get up?"

"Probably." I held up the hand with the bandana, and Castillo pulled me upright."

"Okay," Castillo said, "Time for me to act like a deputy. What happened here?"

"A man named Billy Joe Dupree and—"

"That guy who tried to shoot Old Blue?"

"The very same. Anyway, he and a sidekick named Yancy came out of the alley over there and stopped us."

"*Us* meaning you and the old man by the wall?"

"Yeah. He's Darcy O'Rourke. Pilar knows him."

"Oh yeah. She told me about him. Then what?"

"While Yancy held a gun on us, Dupree pulled out that Bowie knife Darcy's holding and challenged me to a Cajun knife fight."

"And you agreed?"

"You know me, always ready to try something new."

"Sure."

"At any rate, Dupree provided the handkerchief, Yancy tossed me his hunting knife, and we went at it."

"Well I don't see any blood. Hard to have a knife fight without blood."

"It didn't last long. Dupree fell down, and we agreed to call it a tie."

"I see. And they left you this stuff as souvenirs."

"Actually, I told them Deputy Earl Castillo was coming, and they ran for their lives."

"Really? You willing to repeat that lie down at the office?"

"Sure. Why not. You'll be even more famous than you are now." Turning to Darcy, I asked, "You okay?"

"A bit excited," Darcy responded. "You really handled that well. You been in knife fights before?"

"No. But I did have to take out a drunken soldier coming at me with a broken beer bottle once."

"My God. When was that?"

"I was an MP in Japan during the Korean War. Some of the GI's back from the killing fields got carried away." I winked at Pilar. "But mostly it was just *geishas* and *hotsi baths*."

"I can imagine," she said, wrinkling her nose as she turned away and asked, "You ready to go back to the hotel, Darcy?"

"I think so. It's been a busy day." Darcy looked at me. "Sorry, Dan. I'll get you into the Mountain Oyster Club some other time." He handed me the Bowie knife.

"No problem, Darcy. Thanks for the dinner and drinks."

Castillo cleared his throat. "I'll escort Pilar and Mr. O'Rourke back to their hotel. Danger seems afoot tonight."

"Yeah, and other things. What about that threat to a juror?"

"Turned out to be ambiguous bar talk. A waitress heard two cowboys talking. She picked up the words *kill* and *courthouse*, told the bartender, and he called the police. The cowboys were gone by the time the city cops got there. You know, it could have been Dupree and his buddy talking about you."

"Could be. This is the second time he's tried to cut me up."

"You better file a report with the city law. They'll want to know about Mr. Dupree."

"*Mañana, amigo.* I think I'll go home now."

"Sweet dreams," Castillo said, turning away to take Pilar's arm.

"Fat chance."

Midnight came and went as I spent a restless night fighting

my pillow. Something was gnawing at my subconscious. Something Dupree had said. *Seems you got more than one life. Sorta like a cat.* That seemed like an odd thing to say. *Like a cat. Cats have nine lives. More than one life. As if I'd been killed before ...*

I leapt out of bed.

Fortunately, easy-going Charley Lopez was on duty and answered my phone call. "Sheriff's office. Deputy Lopez speaking."

"Charley, this is Brannigan. I need a quick favor."

"Nothing illegal I hope."

"Not this time. Pull the file on Niyol's murder and tell me what he was wearing when he was shot."

"No harm in that I guess. Wait a minute."

As expected, I had to wait three.

"Got it," he finally said. "Red shirt, Levi's, cowboy boots, and a brown Stetson."

"That's it, Charley. Thanks. Now one more thing."

"Oh yeah? What?"

"Call the sheriff and ask him to meet me at his office in an hour. Tell him it's very important."

"It's real early, Dan."

"Just do it. Please."

Hanging up the phone, I felt good about myself for the first time in weeks. Soon as I was dressed, I picked up the Bowie knife and trotted out the fence post that had a bullet in it.

Dupree's bullet.

Sheriff Virgil Branson was leaning back in his chair, feet up on the desk, eyes closed, when I rapped on his office door. He opened bleary eyes, rubbed the stubble on his face, and waved me in. "Okay, Brannigan, what in hell is so all fired damn important?"

"How about if I can prove Jubal Pearce didn't kill the wrangler."

The sheriff sat up, and his boots slammed onto the floor. "You shittin' me?"

"No, sir. You have the bullet that killed Niyol, but haven't been able to match it to a rifle, right?"

"That's right. The slug didn't come from the .30-30 Pearce had when you caught up with him. We figure he used a different rifle and ditched it somewhere."

"I think it was a different rifle all right. Look, a man called Billy Joe Dupree has attacked me twice with a knife. The second time was last night. In the course of our brief conversation, he said something about me having more than one life. Like a cat."

"Like the proverbial nine lives?"

"Yes, sir. I got to thinking, maybe at one point in time he thought I'd been killed."

"That is really shaky thinking, Brannigan."

"It gets better. When Dupree and I had our original

confrontation up in Oro Valley, I was wearing Levis, a red shirt, and a dirty brown hat. When Niyol was shot, he was wearing Levis, a red shirt, and dirty brown hat."

"So?"

"The way I figure it, Dupree found out I was working with that outfit filming at Old Tucson, and he went there looking for me. About dusk he saw this wrangler almost three hundred yards away, back to him, and the guy's clothes look familiar. He shoots the man in the back and leaves thinking he's killed me. He finds out later it was Niyol."

"An interesting theory. What about proof?"

I pulled a bullet out of my shirt pocket and laid it on the sheriff's desk. This round was fired by a .30-30 belonging to Dupree. I'm betting the markings on this one match the markings on the slug pulled out of Niyol."

The sheriff picked the bullet up and played with it. A wicked smile replaced his frown. "Wouldn't that shake up the trial."

"Yes, sir. How long you figure it will take your lab techs to see if there's a match?"

Glancing at his watch, the sheriff said, "About as much time as we have before the trial resumes." He picked up his phone and dialed a number.

Judge Randall was giving some additional guidance to the jury when Sheriff Branson pushed the courtroom's big doors open and strode up to the low barricade separating the participants from the audience.

I was right behind him.

"Your honor," the sheriff called out, "May we approach the bench?"

"For what purpose, Sheriff?"

"Mr. Brannigan here has uncovered new evidence."

"New evidence? In this case?"

"Yes, your honor."

Both attorneys stood up.

Nodding, Judge Randall said, "Approach." Then he looked down at the two lawyers and added, "You boys better come up here too."

All four of us merged into a scrum in front of the judge's podium.

"Keep you voice down," the judge ordered.

Speaking softly, Sheriff Branson explained. "Your honor, Mr. Brannigan here recently had occasion to fire a round from a .30-30 rifle into a fence post out at Rosalinda Correa's ranch." He set the bullet I'd dug out of the fencepost in front of the judge. "This round."

Peering at it, the judge said, "So?"

"The rifle that fired it belongs to one Billy Joe Dupree. This morning, having reason to believe that Dupree might have shot Niyol, Brannigan dug the round out of the fencepost and brought it to me."

"For a ballistics match with the bullet taken from the body?"

"Yes, sir."

And did they match?"

"Identical markings. Dupree's rifle killed Niyol."

"Holy shit," the prosecutor whispered.

"There will be a ten-minute recess," the judge declared in a booming voice. "Bailiff, take the jurors to the jury room." Standing and looking down on the four of us, he added, "In my chambers, gentlemen. Right now."

Ten minutes later, the sheriff and I came back into the court room and found seats along one side of the gallery.

After a few more seconds, the two attorneys returned and took up their assigned places. Jubal looked confused, but his lawyer wore a Cheshire-cat grin.

"All rise," thundered the bailiff as the judge strode in.

Judge Randall took his seat, then reconvened the trial and ordered the bailiff to bring the jurors back into the box.

Once the jury was seated, the judge looked over the people assembled before him and said, "Does the prosecution wish to make a statement?"

Rising, the county attorney said, "We do, your honor."

"Proceed."

"Due to new and compelling evidence, the county recommends that the charge of murder against Mr. Jubal Pearce be dropped."

"So be it," the judge said. He banged the bench in front of him with his wood gavel.

The courtroom erupted. Some laughed. An old woman cheered.

I looked at the defendant's table. Becky was leaning over the bar, her arms wrapped around Jubal from behind. He looked sort of dazed. His parents were hugging each other a few feet away.

Darcy O'Rourke was in his place under the clock in the back row, beaming like Santa Clause.

Pilar had risen from her seat next to Darcy and was applauding. She caught my eye and flashed me a huge smile.

The judge let the tumult go on for a couple of minutes, then banged his gavel again until quiet was restored. "Order in the court," he bellowed. "We still have the felony charge of horse stealing to deal with. This court will recess until after lunch and reconvene at one o'clock."

I ran to the Edsel and beat my personal best time driving from downtown to the Old Tucson movie lot.

Grant Griffin was there, watching as a Hispanic rider wearing a huge *sombrero* and *vaquero* gear cantered Sienna past the cameras. The movie hero was seated on a silver-tipped Mexican saddle with a typical oversize, flat-topped horn and long leather *tapaderos* dangling from the stirrups. Horse, saddle, and rider all looked spectacular.

Good old Justin Cromwell called "Cut" when horse and rider were well past the cameras.

Trotting over to the producer, I said, "Excuse me, Mr. Griffin, I need to talk to you."

He raised an eyebrow. "I already gave you a bonus for bringing Sienna back in good shape. This isn't about more money, is it?"

"No, sir."

"Okay then." He got up from his little yellow folding chair and led me over to the canteen tent. We both poured cups of black coffee, then took seats at a table well away from the others. Giving me his tough-guy look, he said, "Well?"

"Jubal Pearce didn't kill your wrangler. The murder charge has been dropped."

"So I heard. Somebody called here from the courthouse."

"I'm pretty sure the killer was after me, not Niyol."

"Lucky you. Look, I really don't have a lot of time. What did you want to talk to me about?"

"Dropping the horse stealing charge against Jubal Pearce."

"Why should I?"

"For starters, that allegation means the trial will go on, but now it will be focused on the sorrel mare, how you acquired her, what she's worth, and how Jubal tried to buy her back. The newspapers will love it. I can see the headline: *Hollywood bigwig screws soldier while he's off defending our country.*"

Griffin set down his cup and stared at me.

"You want that kind of publicity, Mr. Griffin?"

He took a sip of coffee before he answered, "Of course not."

"Furthermore," I said, "Niyol never did get Sienna ready for your *vaquero* over there to ride, did he?"

"No."

"But Jubal Pearce did. He had the mare for four days, and look at her. She's in better shape than ever and handles well in front of your cameras. You need a good horse trainer, and I know just where you can get one. Cheap."

"Pearce would be working for Cromwell. Minimum wage, a dollar an hour. And he has to stop talking to the press about that damn horse. Will he agree?"

"Count on it."

"Okay. I'll make the phone call."

Chapter 10

November 1957 – Tucson

Next morning I did an unusual thing; on my way into the Santa Rita Hotel's coffee shop, I bought a copy of the *Tucson Daily Citizen*. It carried the story of Jubal's acquittal on the front page, above the fold, and featured a large photo of Sienna nuzzling Jubal. The caption read *New equine star is valuable asset for Paradise Pictures.*

When Sheila came over to take my order, I put the paper aside and asked, "How's good old Justin Cromwell this morning?"

A soft rose bloomed on her cheeks as she said, "I don't know what you're talking about."

Suspicion confirmed. "Oh, well then just bring me black coffee and a bagel with cream cheese."

"Yes, sir."

Brrrrr. She left a chill in the air that lingered.

To my surprise, Darcy came in about the time my breakfast arrived. He waited for Sheila to do her thing, then he stepped up to the table and asked, "May I join you?" He sat down without waiting for my answer.

"Seems we've done this routine before," I said.

"I remember."

"You come here for breakfast often?"

"Never. I was looking for you and remembered that you frequent this place. Something to do with the female staff here no doubt."

Sheila reappeared and took Darcy's order: black coffee and two English muffins with honey on the side. I was surprised to learn that they served English muffins.

When Sheila left, Darcy leaned across the table and said, "You did a fine job yesterday, clearing young Jubal. I guess the detective in you came out."

"If you hadn't taken me to Carlotta's, I wouldn't have run into Dupree and gotten that clue tossed into my lap."

"Ah yes, that old devil chance." He glanced at the newspaper lying on the table, photo up. It's none of my business, of course, but did Grant Griffin ever pay you that bonus for bringing Sienna back safely?"

"Yeah, he did. You putting that in your article?"

"Not if you don't want me to. Worried about the taxes?"

"Hadn't thought about it. He gave me cash."

"You sign a receipt?"

"Of course. Why?"

"That means there's a paper trail. Griffin has to report all company expenses to an accounting firm in Los Angeles. They compile the information and report it to the film's financial backers. Eventually the information gets to the IRS."

"So I better declare it on my tax return. Point made."

Sheila brought Darcy's coffee and the muffin with honey on the side. I resisted the urge to make a wisecrack about her muffins.

Darcy smiled up at Sheila. "Thank you, my dear. I won't forget your excellent service."

Blushing again, Sheila retreated.

After sipping his coffee, Darcy started to spread some honey on one muffin. "I'm curious about that cash payment," he said, looking up. "When you were escorting Sugar Holliday around the countryside, were you also paid in cash?"

"You really are a nosy old coot."

"But I'm a lovable one. Look, I won't get too specific in my article, but it would be useful background to know how film companies operate out here in the desert ... including how and how much they pay the local help."

"Fifty a day and expenses. Cash."

"Wow, that's a lot. You sign a receipt?"

"Always."

"Interesting. I always thought these film companies threw their money around willy-nilly." The notebook came out and Darcy scribbled away.

"Thought you said you weren't going to use that in your

article."

"I won't if you don't want me to."

"Ah, go ahead. Maybe it'll establish a pay scale for movie company fixers."

"Want me to double the amount?"

"Hell no. The IRS would probably want taxes on whatever you wrote. Which leads me to the subject of spending it. I'm throwing a dinner party for Jubal tonight at my dad's restaurant, The Inferno. Seven o'clock. You and Pilar are invited."

"Why thank you, sir. We'll be there."

"You sure about Pilar?"

"Oh yes. She changed her mind about you sometime in court yesterday."

Right after breakfast I called the company that insured Paradise Pictures. A woman answered, "Great Western Insurance."

"This is Dan Brannigan. I'm calling to see if your company has reached a decision about paying me the bounty for bringing Jubal Pearce in."

"Just a minute, sir."

Five minutes later a man's voice came on line. "Mr. Brannigan?"

"Yes, sir."

"We all had a good laugh when we received your request for payment. Good joke."

"Beg your pardon."

"Mr. Pearce was armed with a loaded rifle when you and he walked into the Navajo County sheriff's office in Show Low. It's debatable who brought in whom."

"Then you won't pay the reward?"

"You *do* catch on quick. You must be smarter than we thought. Good day, sir." He hung up.

Just as well, taking the money would have made me feel guilty.

Since Sugar was now using Tres as an escort while she looked for scenery, I was unemployed again. Thus inspired, I called the sheriff's office and asked them to set up an appointment with the county's contract doctor to get my go-to-work physical.

Then I drove over to dad's restaurant and made arrangements to host a dinner party at seven. Getting the gang together for a celebration seemed like a good way to spend some of that bonus money Griffin gave me for getting Sienna back. It could also serve as a going-away party for Darcy. He was undoubtedly leaving soon.

The party started well. Tres wore real clothes, all the women were beautiful, and Darcy was ebullient as ever. Pilar surprised me by choosing to sit next to me. This was attributable, I think, to her perception that I'd switched sides at Jubal's trial. She was now showing good judgment, and she smelled nice. The two of us were just getting into some deep after-dinner conversation when my dad came over and tapped me on the shoulder.

"Sorry to interrupt," he said, not looking at all sorry, "but you've got a phone call at the bar."

"Ah ... can you take a message?"

"You better take the call. It's the sheriff's office."

"Huh." I excused myself, went behind the bar, and took the call. "This is Brannigan."

"Dan?"

"Of course. Who's this?"

"Charley Lopez. I got the duty tonight, and *you* have a problem."

"Oh yeah? How so?"

"A man named Grant Griffin called from Old Tucson. Said to tell you that someone clobbered their new night watchman and stole a horse."

"Shit. It's the sorrel, isn't it?"

"You got it. Any idea where Jubal Pearce is?"

"He's here. Tell Griffin we're on the way."

"One other thing, Dan. There's a ransom note. It says you're the man who has to deliver the money."

Jubal, Tres, and I drove out to Old Tucson in my Edsel. Between the wine I'd consumed at the party and our desire to get there quickly, it turned out to be an exciting drive. Tres, acting the stoic Indian, took it all in stride, but Jubal clung to the arm rest as if it might save him when we rolled over.

It was almost eleven o'clock by the time we pulled up to the corral where Deputy Earl Castillo was in animated conversation with Grant Griffin. The deputy seemed relieved to see me and came right over. "Looks like you're back in the horse-retrieval business."

"So I hear. Who called it in?"

"The watchman, soon as he came to. He's got a concussion, but he'll live. We sent him to St. Mary's in an ambulance and then called Mr. Griffin."

"The thief take anything besides the sorrel mare?"

"Yeah. An expensive silver-inlaid saddle and bridle used in the movie."

"You mean the thief just saddled up and rode away?"

"Not hardly. Tracks indicate two men used a pickup with a horse trailer. I've notified the border patrol."

"Think they're headed for Mexico?"

Earl handed me a piece of dirty tablet paper that turned out to be the ransom note. Everyone clustered around while I examined the words scrawled on it in pencil.

"Come on, Jubal pleaded. "What's it say?"

I read it out loud. "Griffin, if you want to get that expensive mare back, have that asshole Dan Brannigan bring five thousand dollars in unmarked hundred-dollar bills to the big wash just east of *Tres Bellotas*, then go south along the wash for three miles. Tell Brannigan to be there at noon tomorrow, alone and unarmed. If anything goes wrong, we shoot your horse." I looked up at the group. "It's not signed."

"Yeah," Earl said, "but someone who doesn't like you very much wants *you* to bring the money. It's got to be a trap."

"No doubt," I said. "And it has to be Billy Joe Dupree." I read the note again. "Where in hell is *Tres Bellotas*?"

"Mexico," Tres said. He pointed his chin south. "It's a dot on the map just across the border. Means *three oaks*. Must be about seventy-five miles from here as the crow flies. Not much there."

"You know the place?"

"Yeah. I was born near there."

"Ah," Earl said. "So that's why they call you Tres."

Tres grinned at me. "Could be."

"Oh sure," I snapped. "Three testicles. Third son. Now it's because of three trees. What's next?"

"No need to get nasty, *kemosabe*."

"Okay, okay. How in hell do I get there?"

The Indian waved his good arm in the general direction of Mexico. "Take the Nogales highway to Arivaca Junction. There's a rough road out of there heading southwest toward the village of Arivaca in the reservation. After a while you'll see a big wood sign saying *Bellotas Road*. It's just two ruts going south, but it'll take you right up to the border. The Mexican government never saw fit to extend the road into their country and the sand gets too deep for wheels. You'll have go the rest of the way on horseback."

"Can a truck and horse trailer handle those roads as far as the border?"

Tres shrugged. "If you go slow."

"What are you thinking?" Earl asked.

"There's a movie company pickup truck with a horse trailer in the parking lot. I'll sleep here tonight since there isn't a watchman, then in the morning I'll load up one of these movie horses, haul the critter down to the end of the road, then ride it into Mexico."

"Oh good," Earl said. "They'll kill you on the other side of the border. That'll save us a lot of paperwork."

"Thought you'd like it."

"And where are you going to get the five thousand dollars?"

All of us turned toward Grant Griffin.

He tried to stare us down, but finally folded. "Damn it to hell, I've got to get that horse back. Okay, I'll put up the money." He leaned in and stuck his nose in my face. "Make damn sure you bring her back in one piece."

"Do I get another reward?"

Griffin reared back and screamed, "Jesus!"

"Okay," I said. "This one is on the house, but I'll need to borrow that pickup, the horse trailer, and one of those ponies in the corral."

"We'll need two horses," Jubal said. "I'm going with you."

"The note says I'm to come alone, Jubal."

"But she's my horse."

"No," Griffin snapped. "She's *my* horse."

"Quit arguing," Earl ordered. "No one is going."

Now we all stared at the deputy. "Look," he said. "Sienna's a pretty horse, but she's not worth your life, Dan. We both know it's Dupree. He and his buddy tried to kill you the other night, and they'll sure as hell finish the job once you ride into Mexico unarmed."

"I have an idea," Tres said. "Maybe ..."

We looked at him as if an oracle were about to speak.

"Look," he finally said, "Jubal here is a sharpshooter, and I know the land down there. The two of us will get down there at dawn and find a good spot on high ground. You know, someplace where Jubal can set up one of those high-powered sniper rifles on a tripod. When you ride in at noon, we'll have you covered."

"And just what does that mean?" I asked.

"Anything goes wrong, Jubal shoots Dupree."

Earl looked at Jubal. "You have a rifle like that?"

"No, but I saw a sniper rifle with a high-power scope at a gun shop in Tucson. It's the same weapon I trained on in Germany. Think we can get it tonight?"

"I'll get you into the shop one way or another," Earl said. "However, I still think you're all crazy."

The Indian bounced on his toes. "You got a better plan,

Deputy?"

"Guess not," Earl admitted. "But we better get moving; dawn is only seven hours away. I'll provide the truck and trailer to get you both and your horses down to the border."

A minute later, Earl and Jubal took off in the patrol car on their mission to get the gun. Despite his stated misgivings, Earl now seemed real eager to help me ride into trouble. I wondered if Pilar had anything to do with it.

Soon as the dust raised by Earl's car blew away, Grant Griffin and I walked over to the corral to pick out some horses. Tres fell in behind.

Griffin's movie horses didn't look like anything to brag about; most were the scruffy kind you see the posse ride. On the other hand, we wouldn't be riding them very far or fast.

Using my standard technique, I picked up a pebble and tossed it at the rear end of the nearest nag. He lurched away and led the others in a fast trot around the corral's large perimeter. The exception was an intelligent-looking buckskin that stood his ground, watching me. I'm partial to buckskin horses, and I liked this one's attitude.

The buckskin eyed me warily as I walked up to him. Then he stretched out his neck, greeted me with a low nicker, and wiggled his lips. He was obviously interested in the possibility of food; somebody had spoiled him with apples or sugar cubes. I don't approve of such bribes, but it's always good to know what motivates man or beast.

I put one hand on the buckskin's neck and led him over to where a halter and lead rope hung from a corral post. He walked along peaceably, then tossed his head toward Tres, apparently still hoping for a snack.

Tres watched while I haltered the buckskin. "You know," he finally said, "that's the horse I was going to pick."

"There's a pinto on the far side. More your style."

"Ah yes." Tres turned to Griffin. "I'm typecast, you see. The faithful Indian companion who must always ride a spotted horse." He stepped up onto the bottom rail of the corral in order to look over the remaining stock. "Think I'll take the white one; he looks somewhat like the Lone Ranger's famous steed."

"You and Jubal better take dark-colored horses. You're sneaking in remember."

"Screw it. I'll take the gray horse for Jubal and the pinto for me."

"Suit yourself," Griffin said.

I led the buckskin around the corral a couple of times to make sure he didn't limp, then grabbed a hunk of mane and swung up on his back. The horse responded well to any touch on his neck, promptly turning the other way, and he had a good gate when I urged him to trot, then gallop around the corral. Satisfied, I slid off and turned him loose with a friendly slap on the rump.

"I'll take him," I told Griffin. "What's his name?"

"Beats me."

"Think I'll call him Winston."

"Why in God's name call him that?"

"The eyes. They remind me of Winston Churchill."

My watch said one o'clock when Earl drove up in what I recognized as his personal pickup truck. An empty horse trailer bounced along behind. The deputy was wearing civvies.

Jubal stepped out of the truck carrying a long canvas gun case and wearing a bandoleer of ammo that looked like .30-06 rounds. "Got the rifle," he said. "Earl here is a smooth talker."

"So I've heard. That gonna be enough ammo?"

Grinning, Jubal said, "If I need more than one or two rounds, it likely won't make a bit of difference to you."

"Yeah. My thought exactly."

Earl strolled over and tapped Tres on the shoulder. "You and Jubal better grab some gear out of the tack room and get your horses loaded. It's time to move out."

"You loaning them your rig?" I asked.

"Not exactly. I'm driving them down. They can get a little sleep on the way."

Moving close to Earl, I whispered, "You could lose your job if you cross the border."

"Oh I don't intend to. But you three will have a friend on this side of the fence."

"Goody."

As Earl's rig rolled away with three men and two horses,

Griffin yawned and asked, "Where do you plan to sleep?"

"On those hay bales behind the tack room."

"Okay, I'll meet you at Arizona Bank's downtown branch at nine-thirty. That'll give me time to draw out the five grand."

"Gonna have me sign a receipt?"

"Does a bear crap in the woods?"

"That's what I figured. But right now I'll need the truck keys."

"Come on over to my office." Griffin turned and led the way toward the adobe building pretending to be an old Spanish mission. "We don't do any filming inside here," Griffin said over his shoulder, "and it's cool in there. A good place for my office."

"Doesn't it make you uncomfortable scheming to make money while you're inside a church?"

He gave me an odd look. "The money's real. The church is not." Inside, Griffin fumbled through a desk drawer and came up with the keys to the truck. "Here. Drive slow, the tires are old."

"On the truck or the trailer?"

"Both. See you at nine-thirty." A moment later he was on his way to a comfy hotel room.

I went behind the tack room, broke open one of the hay bales, and made a bed of it. Then I took off my boots and chuckled at the irony as I lay down, *hitting the hay*.

* * *

When faint light touched the crowns of the Santa Catalina mountains, I snorted alfalfa dust out of my nose and struggled upright. The horses watched with some interest as I rinsed my face in the water trough and then peed on a corral post. Morning duties done, I prepped for the mission.

My saddle and bridle went from the Edsel's trunk to the bed of the Ford pickup. Thinking ahead a bit, I detached the scabbard that held my .30-30 to the saddle and hid it under the truck's bench seat. Then I hooked the horse trailer to the pickup, loaded Winston into the trailer, and headed for Rosie's place. I needed a shave and some equipment.

Mutt and Jeff must have heard us rattling down the dirt road because the two dogs charged out of the house and met me as we rolled into the ranch yard.

The screen door banged a couple of times when Rosie came out onto the porch to see what was causing the ruckus.

Once the pickup's motor died, she shouted, "What in hell are you up to?"

"Got a small job on the border, Rosie. Could you whip up a quick breakfast while I shave?"

"Sure." She gave me one of her looks. "That party last night must have been a doozie; you're driving somebody else's rig."

"I'll tell you later."

Upstairs in my apartment over the garage I shaved, changed into my working togs, and strapped on my ankle holster. Then, with a bit more care than usual, I checked my .38 and slid it into the holster. When I pulled my boots on and slid the pantlegs over their tops, I had a surprise for Dupree.

Rosie had a plate of scrambled eggs, hash, and toast set out for me alongside a cup of hot coffee. I glanced at my watch and went for the food.

"You in a hurry?"

"Yes, ma'am."

"This hurry have anything to do with that stolen movie horse?"

I nodded affirmative, my mouth being busy eating.

"The radio said there was a ransom note. You the one taking the money?"

Nodding again, I finished off the hash and slugged down the coffee. As I stood up, Rosie handed me a thermos.

"Coffee," she said. "It's a long way to the border. And remember, when you cross into Mexico, the rules change."

"Thank you, Rosie. For breakfast and the advice."

"I'm fixing pot roast for dinner," she said. "Don't be late."

Grant Griffin came out of the bank right on time, escorted by a tough-looking *hombre* wearing a .45 and a scowl. Grant slid into the truck's passenger seat and closed the door; the guard leaned against the door and looked around nervously.

"Got the money?" I asked.

"Right here," Griffin said. He slid a tape-wrapped packet out of his inside coat pocket and handed it to me. "All

184

hundreds."

"If I'm going to sign a receipt, I need to count the bills."

"I decided to trust you."

"I'm flattered."

"Just get that horse back, understood?"

"Yes, sir."

Tres was right about the roads. Bellotas Road was someone's highly optimistic viewpoint; Bellotas Goat Path might have been more descriptive. But I drove slowly, maneuvered with care, and arrived at road's end at eleven thirty.

Earl's truck and trailer were parked to one side under a huge mesquite tree, but there was no sign of the deputy. He emerged from the bush as I was unloading the buckskin.

"Tres and Jubal went across at dawn," Earl said. "No sign of the bad guys. They must have crossed earlier or someplace else."

"There are options?"

"It's a long border."

Putting a sugar cube in the palm of one hand, I held it out to Winston. His big lips snatched it up, and he chewed it with obvious enjoyment as I slapped a saddle blanket down on his tan back and set my rig on top of it. I ignored his pleading lips while I tightened up the cinch and the flank strap, but I gave him another cube before I slid the bit into his mouth and set the bridle over his ears. Then I took the packet Grant Griffin had given me out of the truck's cab and stuffed it into one of the saddle bags.

Earl put hand on my shoulder. "You sure you want to do this?"

"Yeah."

"Why?"

"That's a damn good question, Earl. I've asked it myself. All I can figure is that Jubal saved my ass a few weeks ago, and I owe him."

Stepping back, Earl gave me a languid salute and said, "Good luck, *amigo*. I'll be here waiting."

"Thanks." I swung up on the buckskin and turned him south, toward the border.

Chapter 11

November 1957 – Mexico

Mexico's border was marked by a three-strand, barb-wire fence intended more to keep cattle in their own country than to discourage human traffic. The wires strung across the large wash I was to follow were currently of no use for either purpose—they'd been cut. The tracks of several southbound horses led through the gap, almost obliterating the numerous footprints of people walking north.

Pausing there, I stared into the future ... then looked over my shoulder at the past. After a moment I patted Winston on the neck and squeezed my heels into his flanks just enough that he got the hint and walked on ... into Mexico.

The dry wash was fairly flat, about thirty yards wide, with a narrow, sandy streambed running along the western edge. The terrain told the story pretty well. Most of the year there was no water in the streambed, unless you dug down a few feet, but when the rains came up north, water did run, but only in the streambed. Then, when there was a summer gully washer, raging water jumped over the low banks of that narrow streambed and cut the wide, shallow path that made up the broader wash. Random patches of now-dry salt bush and stunted mesquite trees were testimony to the existence of those periodic gully washers.

Prone to take the easy path, I stayed on the right-hand side of the wash and rode down the sandy streambed. The banks on either side were about level with my stirrups, and it occurred to me that they offered a place to dive for cover if I had the need—and the chance.

I wasn't sure just where this *Tres Bellotas* was, off to my right someplace, but I figured Dupree would let me know when I was three miles south of it. I was right.

"Halooo, Brannigan," eventually rang out from somewhere in front of me.

Reining in the buckskin, I tried to spot the man. The terrain there made it difficult. Rocky outcroppings some forty or fifty feet high formed a narrow canyon up ahead that yoked the wash down to a narrow pass where the streambed, flanked by mesquite, filled most of the canyon floor. The rocks also forced the streambed to turn west, out of sight, once it was in the canyon.

Squinting against the noonday sun's rays, I scanned the higher rocks. Dupree had to be up there, watching me.

"Keep coming, Brannigan."

Then I saw him. Partially obscured by a patch of scrub

brush, Dupree was perched on a shelf halfway up the rocks to my right, his legs dangling over the side. He looked peaceable enough, except for the rifle lying across his lap.

Glancing left, I hoped that Jubal and the Indian were on the opposite hunk of tall rock, with that sniper rifle aimed at Dupree. But there was no sign of a human, which was undoubtedly what Jubal and Tres intended.

My gut told me I was about to do something stupid, and my gut hardly ever lies, but I pressed my heels into Winston's buckskin flanks, and we moved on. Trying not to be too obvious, I looked around for Yancy, but saw no one besides Dupree.

"That's the way," Dupree called out. "Ride right up the wash. You bring the money?"

"Of course," I shouted back.

"Show me."

Pulling the packet out of the saddle bag, I held it over my head and yelled, "Where's the sorrel horse?"

Dupree laughed. "Waiting for you, Brannigan. Just around the bend." He stood up on the ledge and waved me into the canyon as if it were a toll road.

I put the packet back in the saddle bag, then reached down and patted the buckskin's neck. "I don't like this, Winston old man. Not one damn bit. Jubal had better have us covered."

When I rode around the rocky corner, there was the sorrel, her flaxen mane and tail glistening in the bright light. Silver conchos fastened to her bridle sparkled in the sun, as did the silver on her saddle. It was quite a sight—so was her rider.

A stocky Mexican *vaquero* slouched in that silver-inlaid saddle, his upper torso shaded by the broad brim of his *sombrero*. A bandoleer of ammunition was draped across his chest and he held an unusual rifle propped up on one hip. He moved the weapon as if to make sure I saw that he was armed.

Two other Mexican cowboys, also armed with rifles, sat on horseback nearby, their attention focused on something under a nearby mesquite.

As I rode closer I could see what held their attention: Jubal was seated on the ground, his back to the tree, both legs sprawled out in front of him. His arms had been pulled behind the tree trunk and his wrists tied together. His head hung forward, chin on chest. He appeared to be dead.

The buckskin stopped of his own accord a few yards from the other horses.

Ignoring the three Mexicans, I dismounted and walked over to Jubal. Kneeling next to him, I whispered, "Jubal?"

His head came up, tentatively, revealing a face that had taken a beating. One eye was swollen shut, and both cheeks were badly bruised. Dried blood was on a cut above his good eye. That eye widened when he saw me, and he gasped out, "Sorry, Brannigan. We blew it."

"At least you're alive," I said. "Where's Tres?"

"He got away."

"Well, that's—"

Something that felt like a gun muzzle jabbed me in the back, and Dupree's voice followed. "That's enough chit chat. Where's that damn Indian?"

"I have no idea," I said, standing up. "Probably aiming a high-powered rifle at your back."

Dupree laughed. "I think not, Brannigan. Señor Lopez over there on the sorrel has the fancy rifle. I thought you might try something sneaky, so I hired some local talent, as you can see. They spotted your two friends a couple of hour ago. You cheated, Brannigan, you were supposed to come alone."

Jubal spit, then said, "The Mexicans snuck up behind me while I was sighting-in the rifle. Tres was scouting a ways off and got away clean. That guy Yancy is out looking for him."

"Okay," Dupree said, stepping back. "Let's get down to business. Give me the money."

"It's here," I said. "Tell that Mexican sitting on Sienna to get his fat ass off the horse and lead her over to me."

"Oh I can't do that," Dupree said. "Señor Lopez and I have a business deal. He gets the horse and that silver-studded rig; I get the money. Now hand it over and you just may live."

Fat chance. Walking over to Winston, I made sure to put the horse between me and Dupree. I reached into the saddle bag and ...

"Careful," Dupree said. He aimed his rifle at my face. "If that hand comes out with a gun, you're dead meat."

Moving slowly, I pulled out the taped packet and held it over my head.

Keeping the rifle pointed at me, but talking to the Mexicans, Dupree said, "Watch him, he's a sneaky bastard."

Lopez looked eager for me to do something so he could initiate his fancy new weapon. The other two fondled their rifles and moved around just enough to acknowledge receipt of their orders.

"Okay," Dupree said to me. "Throw me the package."

Holding my breath, I tossed it onto the soft sand in front of Dupree.

Keeping his eyes on me, Dupree bent and picked it up. Then, putting the rifle in the crook of one arm, he started to rip the packet open.

I looked at Jubal and mouthed the words, "Three ... Two ... One."

Kapow.

The packet exploded in a spray of red powder intended to temporarily blind whoever triggered the detonator. In the three seconds that followed, a slew of other things happened in quick succession, all of them seeming to take place in slow motion.

His face covered with red blotches, Dupree staggered backwards. "Shoot him," he screamed, as he regained control of his rifle and swung the muzzle toward me.

Ducking down behind Winston, I reached into my boot and yanked out the hidden revolver.

Jubal let out a piercing whistle that brought Sienna lunging toward him. Unprepared, Lopez fell off the sorrel backwards, losing his grip on the sniper rifle before landing on his backside in the sand.

Dupree fired at me, but the round hit Winston.

As the buckskin collapsed, I stood upright and shot Dupree right between his greedy, bloodshot eyes.

Slow to react, the other two Mexicans finally got their rifles pointed at me—just as Yancy's limp body came hurtling down from the rocks above. It landed with a *thud* between the Mexican's horses, causing those two startled animals to whirl away from the impact. This unseated one of the riders; the other one stayed on his mount as both animals fled down the dry wash.

I pointed my .38 toward the two Mexicans lying in the sand, and they slowly raised their hands.

Down from above came the cry, "*Ya-te-he.*"

November 1957 – Tucson

Sheriff Virgil Branson's coffee cup slammed down on his desk, splattering bits of dark brown fluid onto the hardwood surface. In the strained voice of one who is seldom surprised, he said, "They did *what?*"

"Yes, sir," Darcy O'Rourke responded. "The three of them rode into Mexico on horseback. Jubal Pearce and that Indian went ahead to set up some kind of protection for Brannigan, who was carrying the ransom money." Darcy glanced at his wristwatch. "They should be dealing with the horse thieves right about now."

Branson turned and yelled through the office's open doorway, "Get me Castillo."

A lanky deputy seated at the reception desk shouted back. "No can do, Sheriff. Castillo checked out at midnight when his shift was up. Said he'd be out of reach for a while."

"Out of reach? What in hell does that mean?"

"Away from a phone, I guess. But he said he'd be back in time for work tonight."

"Jesus." The sheriff turned back to Darcy. "Don't tell me that Castillo went into Mexico too."

"No," Darcy answered. "The women said he was just hauling the horses for Pearce and the Indian down to the border."

"Women? What women?"

"Pilar, she's my assistant, Becky Welch, and Sugar Holliday, the Indian's, ah, girlfriend. The three spent the morning drinking coffee and worrying over at the Santa Rita's coffee shop. I happened to bump into them there a few minutes ago, and they filled me in. I figured you should know."

"Damn right." The sheriff's fingers beat a rapid tattoo on his desktop for several seconds, then he yelled at the deputy again. "Get me *Commandante* Martinez at the Sonora State Police Headquarters."

"In Hermosillo?"

"Of course in Hermosillo. You think Sonora's capital city has been moved?"

"No, sir. I'll get right on it."

November 1957 – Mexico

I frisked Lopez and the other Mexican for handguns and knives, finding two of each. I threw everything I found into a patch of cholla cactus. Then I cut Jubal free and handed him the sniper rifle. He rubbed circulation back into his wrists while I poured sand into the breaches of the Mexican's rifles. Then those guns also went into the cholla patch.

Somewhere during that time, Winston shuddered and died.

Kneeling in the sand next to the poor critter, I stroked his neck and let the adrenaline drain out of my system. Winston's visible eye, glassy now, stared at me with faint reproach.

"Sorry, Winston," I whispered, "you were good company." I pushed his eyelid down over the accusing eye, then chased away the blowflies that had already begun to gather.

Looking up, I found that Jubal was upright and glaring with his one good eye at Lopez, who'd taken a comfortable seat in the sand.

Lips curled back, teeth showing, Jubal leaned in close to the man. "*¿Comprende Inglés?*"

The beefy Mexican sat up straighter, grinning. "*Seguro.*"

Jubal came over, handed me his rifle, then stomped back to

Lopez. "Stand up, you *hijo de un perro*. We're going to have a fair fight this time."

Losing his grin, Lopez asked, "*¿Luchar?*"

"*Si.*"

While Lopez climbed to his feet, his eyes flicked around, perhaps looking for an escape route.

"If he runs," Jubal called out, "shoot the bastard."

"*Con much gusto,*" I answered.

With a snarl, Lopez rushed at Jubal, arms wide, apparently trying for a bear hug. But footing in the soft sand was not helpful, and he staggered.

Stepping aside, Jubal gave Lopez a left to the nose, followed by a stunning right cross to the jaw.

As Lopez sank to his knees, Jubal blackened both of the man's eyes with a flurry of punches. Jubal turned away then, as if to leave, but he spun back with a kick to the Mexican's chest that sent the man sprawling.

I held up the sniper rifle. "Happy now, Jubal?"

"Very," he said, taking the gun back. "Where's Tres?"

The Indian called down from the rocks above. "Up here, *kemosabe.*" Then, "What next, Brannigan?"

"We get the hell back across the border," I said. "Where are your horses?"

"In a mesquite grove half a mile from here. That thug Yancy made the mistake of trying to find them. I was waiting for him."

"*Bueno.* We'll meet you there, Tres."

With Jubal leading Sienna, we walked back up the streambed and around the bend.

Just beyond the canyon's mouth, where the wash became broad again, were half a dozen mounted Mexican police.

November 1957 – Tucson

Sheriff Virgil Branson said *"Gracias, Commandante"* and hung up the phone. He stared at nothing for a moment, then said, "That is really odd."

Darcy O'Rourke leaned forward and put his hands palm down on the sheriff's desk. "What's odd?"

"The *commandante* in Hermosillo got an anonymous tip early this morning that a criminal event was about to take place a few miles southeast of *Tres Bellotas*. He dispatched a sergeant and several policemen from Nogales, Sonora, to ride over there on horseback and check it out."

"How far a ride?"

"Hmmm. Maybe thirty miles."

"Then perhaps they got there in time to prevent trouble."

"Or to cause it."

November 1957 – Mexico

We stopped. The Mexican police posse in front of us didn't look too threatening, at least not yet. Off in the distance I could see another mounted policeman leading our two movie horses toward us.

A tall policeman with stripes on his sleeve smiled and said, "*Buenos tardes.*" Then he motioned with the .45 caliber revolver in his right hand, and the five riders with him aimed their rifles at us.

Jubal and I both raised our hands.

"*Bueno,*" the tall man said. "You are trespassing on private property. What have you to say?"

"We thought it was public land," I ventured.

"Really. What a quaint defense. But there must be more villainy; I heard gunfire a few minutes ago. Perhaps now we will get to the bottom of that. You and your *amigo* turn around and go back where you were. We shall see what you have been up to."

Señor Lopez was waiting for us. "*Sargento,*" he shouted, "these *gringos* stole my horse. Arrest them."

"She's *my* horse," Jubal muttered.

The tall man looked over the carnage we'd left behind: two dead Americans and one dead animal. He glanced from one body to another, then fixed his eyes on Lopez. "Who killed the man with the red face?"

Lopez pointed at me.

And who killed the other *gringo*?"

"An Indian, I think."

"Oh? Where is this Indian?"

Pointing, Lopez said, "He was on the rocks up there."

The police sergeant issued orders that made two of his men

dismount and clamber up the cliff.

Turning back to Lopez, the captain asked, "Who shot the horse?"

Lopez pointed at Dupree's body.

"I see. The gringos had quite a gunfight here. Why?"

"They fought over money, *Sargento*. Five thousand dollars."

"Oh really? Where is it?"

"*No sé, Sargento.* I do not know. And then they tried to steal my horse."

"Bullshit," Jubal snapped. "She's *my* horse."

The sergeant laughed. "And a pretty one too. But that is a Mexican saddle, as is the bridle. So you are clearly lying, *gringo*; the mare must belong to a Mexican. Bring the horse to me."

"But she is *mine*," Lopez pleaded. "I fought for her. Look at my face."

"Yes, I see. Your face is uglier than the last time I saw it, Lopez, when you were locked up in the *cárcel*. There is no way a *canalla* such as yourself could own such a magnificent animal. So, since we are on land belonging to *señor* Alejandro Morales, I will take the horse to him. He has many such fine horses on this *rancho*. He will know what to do with this one."

Looking up at the mounted police sergeant, Jubal handed over Sienna's reins. "Take good care of her, Sergeant. I shall claim her soon."

A shout from above interrupted the conversation. The

sergeant talked with the two men on top of the rock for several moments, then he turned his attention back to Jubal. "My men have been unable to find your Indian *compañero*. Who is he?"

Jubal hesitated, then said, "A man called Tres."

"Tres? The big Pima Indian who works with *la migra*?"

"So I hear."

"Interesting." The sergeant shouted more instructions at the two men on top of the rock.

"What did you tell them?" I asked.

The sergeant grinned, wickedly. "I said if they have to kill the Indian, be sure to bury the evidence."

"I see. And what are your plans for us?"

"First *señor*, who are you?"

"Dan Brannigan," I answered. "From Tucson. My friend with the swollen face is Jubal Pearce, a rancher up on the Mogollon."

"Well, *señor* Brannigan, we will start by searching everyone here for that five thousand dollars Lopez mentioned. Both of you, empty your pockets and take off your boots. You too, Lopez."

Five minutes later, the police sergeant stood in front of me with my .38 in his hand, my watch on his wrist, and a disappointed look on his face. "So, there is no money. Too bad. Perhaps we could have made some, ah, arrangement." He looked up at the sun. "Our horses are tired and it is a long ride back to Nogales; we will take you to the *rancho* of *señor*

Alejandro Morales. It is only about ten kilometers south of here. We will lock you both up there until a police van from Nogales comes for you sometime tomorrow."

"What charges?" I asked.

"*Señor* Lopez over there will testify in court that your *amigo* assaulted him and tried to steal a valuable horse. Meanwhile, you murdered the man with the red face. You will both be found guilty and spend the rest of your days in a Mexican prison."

November 1957 – Tucson

Darcy O'Rourke treated the three worried women to dinner at Carlotta's Cantina, but he established a rule that they couldn't talk about what might be going on in Mexico. That lasted until Deputy Earl Castillo, back in uniform, found them halfway through their dessert course.

Becky was the first to spot the deputy as he made his way toward them through the dinner crowd. Half rising, she shouted, "Where are they?"

Shaking his head, Castillo dragged a vacant chair over and sank into it. "I thought I'd find you—"

"Where are they?" Becky demanded again.

"They've been arrested," Castillo said.

Setting aside his dessert spoon, Darcy leaned forward. "In Mexico?"

"Yeah. I waited as long as I could for the guys to return, then I drove back here to make my shift. The Mexican police commandant in Hermosillo called Sheriff Branson a few minutes ago while I was checking in. The commandant said a police patrol picked up Jubal and Dan this afternoon and are holding them prisoner at a ranch about ten miles south of the border."

"Wait a minute," Darcy said. "The sheriff told me there was no communication between that sergeant's patrol and the commandant. No radio."

Earl shrugged. "The ranch where the police posse took Jubal and Dan has a CB setup. The sergeant in charge used that to call in a report."

"What are they charged with?" Becky asked.

"Jubal's charged with stealing a horse."

"Again?"

"Yup. And the same horse."

Pilar leaned in. "What about Brannigan?"

"Dupree and his pal Yancy are both dead. The Mexicans are charging Dan with Dupree's murder."

"Oh shit."

Chapter 12

November 1957 – Mexico

I got a brief look at the *hacienda* before they locked Jubal and me up. Like all the other structures I could see, the main house, the *casa grande*, was made the Mexican way, stucco over sun-dried adobe blocks. Its whitewashed walls were capped by a red-tile roof, and a broad porch appeared to circumnavigate the house. The building was shaded by tall oak trees obviously transplanted nearby for that purpose. The house faced south, toward the warm winter sun.

What figured to be a two-minute walk to the west, nestled in a natural grove of mesquite trees, was a large bunkhouse of similar construction. The common policemen would undoubtedly bunk there with the ranch's *vaqueros*. The police sergeant would probably be a guest up at the big house.

Nearby was what looked to be a separate cookhouse where the *cocinero* would prepare and serve several meals a day to whoever occupied the bunkhouse. A windmill and storage tank situated on high ground behind the cookhouse provided water for the ranch headquarters.

After looking around, Jubal muttered, "It must be good to be a wealthy *ranchero*."

We were brought in on the east side of the complex. There, a hundred or so yards away from the nearest building—and presently downwind from the house—was a corral and horse stable. The stable was a long, low-slung affair that faced north, probably to keep the summer sun out of the stalls. It appeared capable of housing a dozen horses in individual stalls, each stall equipped with Dutch doors. With one exception, the top section of the two-piece doors was open. Fine-looking horses stared out of several, no doubt curious about the horses in the posse.

As we soon found out, the last stall at the end nearest the ranch house had been converted to a storeroom. A window had been set in the top half of that Dutch door, likely to allow fresh air and light into the space when the door was closed, its normal position. But the opening had been covered with steel bars and wire mesh, no doubt to keep out marauding pack rats and other hungry vermin.

When the police, accompanied by *señor* Alejandro Morales himself, locked us in the storeroom, it contained thirteen hay bales, two large wooden bins for oats, and a bucket of warm water. The water, it was pointed out, was for us. A courtesy from *señor* Morales.

"*Gracias*."

The accommodations weren't too bad, and that evening the *cocinero*, accompanied by four grim policemen, brought us a huge plate of tacos for dinner.

"*Tacos*," the cook said, smiling. "*Comer con las manos.*"

Yeah, good point. We could eat tacos with our bare hands. No utensils required. No knives. "Ha ha."

Sunset brought out a bright moon in a clear sky, and we rearranged some hay bales to form cots. Then, being both tired and full of tacos, I was ready to sleep.

Not Jubal. He wanted to talk. "You ever kill a man before today?"

"Yeah."

"How many?"

"I don't want to remember."

"Oh. Does it get easier?"

"No. For God's sake, Jubal, you're the sniper. Haven't you ever shot anyone?"

"Never."

"Lucky you. Go to sleep." I lay down, closed my eyes, and immediately drifted off. I awoke much later to a soft noise; Jubal was standing at the window trying to work the bars free.

"You're wasting your time," I said.

Turning toward me, Jubal said, "Horse feed is apparently expensive here. They go to great lengths to secure it."

"It's a long haul up here from farm country," I said. "You sleep at all?"

"No."

"The moon gone down yet?"

"About ten minutes ago. Why?"

"It's the only way I can tell time since that sergeant took my watch."

"How very resourceful," Jubal snapped. "What time does the moon set this morning?"

"Six thirty. Dawn is about half an hour away."

"Really? And how do you happen to know that?"

"Because I checked before leaving Tucson."

"Jesus, Brannigan. You had some intuition you might need that piece of obscure information?"

"Just being thorough. We now have about half an hour of darkness."

"To do what?"

"Escape."

"How?"

"Tres will come now that it's dark. That guard still out there?"

"Haven't seen him for a while. Maybe he's taking a crap."

The padlock securing both halves of the Dutch door rattled quietly.

Easing up from my hay bed, I moved close to the door.

Jubal came away from the window and stood next to me. We both waited, tense but hopeful.

With a soft squeak, the door swung open a few inches. A dark face peered in and said, "*Ye-te-he.*"

"What took you so long?" I whispered.

Tres grinned as he slid into the dark room. Speaking softly he said, "Waiting for that moon to go down, *kemosabe*, so I could move around." He eased the door closed behind him. "There are three hound dogs lying on the porch up at the main house, but the breeze is blowing from them to us, so we should be okay. Just keep it quiet. Let's get out of here."

"There was a guard," Jubal whispered. "What happened to him?"

"I put him to sleep. Got his key and a *pistola* too." He grabbed the butt of a revolver tucked into his belt, yanked it out, and handed it to me. "For your boot."

"Good job," I said. "You bring a rifle?"

"Right outside." He turned toward the door and said, "Come on."

"Wait," Jubal whispered. "Where's Sienna?"

"With the two movie horses. They're in a small corral at the other end of the stable."

"Any guards there?"

"Didn't see any."

"Okay," Jubal said. "Let's get the horses and make a run for the border."

"Can you ride bareback?" Tres asked.

Nodding, Jubal said, "Of course."

"Good. Cause they took that silver-studded rig inside someplace."

"You're the Indian," I whispered. "Why don't *you* ride bareback?"

"Sore testicles."

"Again?"

"What can I say?"

"Where are the movie saddles?"

"On the top rail of the corral."

Jubal twirled two fingers over his head and pointed at the door. "For Pete's sake, let's get the hell out of here."

Tres opened the door a crack and looked around. Then, nodding for us to follow, he went out, grabbed the rifle leaning against the stable wall, and led the way.

We moved quietly along the front face of the long stable. Several of the horses stuck their heads out, no doubt hoping the passing humans were bringing food.

The corral holding our three horses was only a few yards beyond the end of the stable, but we ran across the open space hunched over, as if short shadows were more difficult to see than taller ones. Maybe they are.

Sienna nickered a soft greeting to Jubal and trotted over to meet him.

While Tres and I saddled our horses, Jubal found a short

piece of rope and fashioned a crude hackamore that he slipped over Sienna's head.

When we finished, Tres opened the corral gate, and—"

Owoooh! Owoooh! At the corner of the stable, a rangy hound with floppy ears had commenced wild baying. A chorus of yelps and howls from the main house joined in.

"Let's ride," Jubal shouted as he swung up on Sienna's back.

"Go northeast," Tres yelled, leaping into his saddle. "Keep the north star just off to your left."

A man shouted, *¡Alto!* Gunshots rang out.

We galloped out of the corral and turned northeast, racing across scrub grassland dotted with salt bush, creosote, and an occasional mesquite tree. Somewhere ahead lay the sandy-bottomed dry wash that would lead us north.

Several baying hounds chased after us until we were well away from the *hacienda*.

Sienna stretched out and seemed to float over the rough terrain. Of course she wasn't burdened with an extra forty pounds of saddle.

Behind, riding side by side, Tres and I urged our reluctant horses to greater effort. The stars provided enough light so we could see each other and follow Jubal's dim form up ahead. The darkness presented no problem to our horses; they have a higher ratio of rods to cones that gives them superior night vision.

"Maybe we should have stolen a couple of those fancy horses in the stable," Tres shouted.

"Now you think of it. That sergeant will probably put some armed *vaqueros* on them."

Tres swung his horse wide around a patch of prickly pear, then pulled back alongside. "Yeah, and they'll likely catch us too. These plugs aren't going to outrun anything."

"How far to the border you figure?"

"About seven more miles," Tres said, looking over his shoulder. "But I think we have a problem."

"What's that?"

"As we rode away I spotted a jeep parked behind the house. It occurs to me that a jeep could outrun a horse in this terrain."

"You're right. What made you think of it?"

"I hear a motor."

"Oh shit."

A moment later, headlights blossomed behind us just as we reached the wash and turned to follow it north. Up ahead, Jubal reined in Sienna and waved at us to hurry.

Zut.

Something buzzed past my ear a split second before I heard the sound of a rifle shot. Instinctively, I bent low over my horse's neck and begged him for more speed.

Galloping alongside, Tres yelled "I'm going to stop that damn jeep then fade into the desert. *Vaya con Dios*." He reined his horse to a sliding stop, then leapt off and took cover behind a rock outcropping.

Surprised, I pulled up my horse and stared at Tres.

Tres whipped off a shot at the approaching truck. The headlights stopped advancing, then blinked out. More rifle rounds zipped past, some of them ricocheting off the rocks. Tres fired off another round, then yelled, "Go, dammit. Go."

Realizing my revolver was useless at this range, and I'd be a drag when Tres ran into the desert, I called out *"Buena suerte, amigo,"* then urged my wheezing horse back into a gallop.

Jubal was waiting a hundred yards up the wash. Without any urging, Sienna leaped alongside my galloping horse and we ran side-by-side up the streambed.

Leaning toward me, Jubal shouted, "What happened to Tres?"

"He's taking out a jeep load of police."

¡Que hombre!

November 1957 – Arizona

"Car Seven, what's your twenty?"

Deputy Earl Castillo, plucked the mic off the dash, keyed it, and said, "North side of Amado."

"This is the sheriff. Get down to the border by *Tres Bellotas*. We've been monitoring the CB frequency used by that rancher where Brannigan and Pearce were being held. They escaped on horseback a few minutes ago and are making a run for the border."

"Any pursuit?"

"Yeah. Right now its a jeepload of police."

"Right now? There's more?"

"A Mexican Army helicopter from Cananea has been ordered to intercept them before they get to U.S. territory."

"Mexico has helicopters?"

"The commandant said they've got two UH-12s on loan from Hiller Aviation for evaluation."

Castillo paused, then clicked his mic and said, "Kind of hard for a horse to outrun a chopper."

"Ten-four."

November 1957 – Mexico

We thundered past the scene of our earlier battle, scaring hell out of a pack of coyotes devouring poor Winston's remains. Then we were on the home stretch, only three miles to go. Then two. Then one.

A mile is a short distance. I can walk it in twenty minutes, easy. And that's about how far we were from the border when dawn's first light arrived. Moments later we heard the *wop-wop-wop* of helicopter blades coming at us from the southeast. That last mile suddenly seemed like infinity.

Bent low over Sienna's flowing mane, Jubal turned his face toward the sound and yelled, "You hear what I hear?"

"Yeah, a helicopter." I ripped off my hat and used it to whip my poor horse across the butt. He soldiered on, while Sienna leapt ahead, easily dodging around the ubiquitous clumps of mesquite and creosote.

The *wop-wop-wop* sound grew louder.

"I think they're coming for us," Jubal shouted.

"No shit." I could see the border fenceposts in the distance.

A minute later, we were only about a quarter mile from the border, running flat out, when something that looked like a plastic bulb with a long erector-set tail roared in and made a low pass about twenty feet over our heads.

My exhausted horse lurched sideways and fell, sending me rolling into a clump of ten-foot-high creosote bushes.

Jubal reined in and motioned for me to jump on behind him.

Leaping to my feet, I started to run for Sienna, but a spray of bullets from an automatic weapon blasted the sand in front of me, and I dove back under the bushes.

"Ride for the border!" I screamed.

Sienna danced twenty yards away. "Come on," Jubal shouted.

I yanked the Mexican policeman's revolver out of my boot and fired two rounds at the helo's canopy, now about fifty yards away. The rounds ran out of oomph and merely ricocheted off the bubble.

But the chopper reared back.

Looking past the helo and beyond Sienna, I saw a sheriff's patrol car slide to a stop just beyond the border. I fired another round at the helicopter and yelled, "Jubal! Ride for it!"

With the chopper jinking now, someone in it fired again.

Sand puffs blew up close to Sienna, and suddenly Jubal agreed with me. He whirled the mare north, and she leapt away.

The helicopter turned slightly. I could see a rifle poking out of the open side hatch, aiming at Jubal.

I stuck my revolver up through the thick branches, aimed high, and fired at the small slice of open hatch I could see. Not wanting to be around for the response, I rolled away from my clump of brush and ran zigzag toward a clump of mesquite trees about twenty yards closer to home.

That drew their fire all right. The helo spun around again. Bullets creamed the bush I'd just left, then chased me all the way until I dove under the mesquite's drooping branches and clawed my way into a shallow depression. The *whir* of a rattlesnake's tail somewhere near my feet brought me scrambling out of there and running for my life.

Sienna crossed the border at a dead run before Jubal pulled her up in a sliding stop, flung himself off her back, and sprawled on the sand near Castillo's patrol car. As he struggled up off his knees, he shouted, "You got a rifle?"

"In the trunk," Earl said. But don't bother, that helo is

out of range."

"Not for me. Get it."

Castillo tossed Jubal the keys. "I'm going into the woods to pee. I don't want to see what you're about to do." He turned and walked away. "You got a slight breeze from the northwest."

Yanking open the car's trunk, Jubal pulled a Winchester .30-06 from its holder and ran back across the border into Mexico. Kneeling behind a mesquite, he lay the barrel on a low branch, took a deep breathe, then exhaled slowly as he set the sights above and to the right of the helicopter's whirling tail rotor.

The chopper had me dead to rights. It settled to the ground about a hundred feet in front of me, its open left-side hatch facing me. A soldier strapped in the near seat pointed his rifle my way and dared me to raise my pistol. A bullhorn voice called out, "*¡Entregarse!*" The rifle's muzzle made up and down jerking motions to emphasize the surrender command.

Dropping the policeman's revolver, I raised my hands.

Then a funny thing happened. I heard a loud clang above the roar of the chopper's engine, and the helicopter began to do a crazy dance. The engine groaned as the helicopter bounced and twisted … then rolled onto its side. Its big, whirling blades shattered against the sand, sending pieces flying in all directions.

I hit the deck, face down and praying. A big hunk of metal flew past, only inches over my head. Then it was over. I picked up the revolver and walked over to the helo.

The two men inside were dazed but not seriously injured. There was no fire. I grabbed the rifle that had so recently threatened me, then walked over to see if my exhausted horse was still alive.

He looked up at me with resignation in his eyes.

"Come on," I said. "I'll walk you home." I tugged on the reins.

With that, he grunted twice and struggled to his feet.

Leading my gray horse, I saluted the two Mexicans as they crawled out of their flying cocoon, then strolled casually back into the United States.

November 1957 – Arizona

When I crossed the border, Deputy Earl Castillo was seated on the ground, his back to the patrol car, legs sprawled out in front of him. He was running a ramrod holding a cleaning patch through the barrel of his county-issued rifle. He looked up and asked, "Have a nice trip?"

"The weather was good. Got any water?"

"There's a spare jug in the trunk. Maybe Pearce left you some."

Heading for the car's trunk, I asked, "Where is Jubal?"

"Walking the sweat off his mare." He eyed the gray

horse. "You could do the same."

"Already walked him enough." I downed some water, then poured the rest into my hat and carried it over to the horse.

He stuck his nose into the hat and guzzled up all he could.

I finally pulled the hat away and plunked it on my head. The dribbles on my sweaty face felt good, even if some of them were horse slobber.

"Watching this, Castillo asked, "What's the nag's name?"

"This is no nag, my friend. He has heart. Think I'll call him *Agallas*."

"Guts?"

"He's got 'em, in spades." I stripped off the saddle and used a handful of grass to dry the horse's back.

"Pearce told me Tres stopped to take out a jeep that was following you guys. Have any idea what happened to him?"

"Nope. He said he was going to stop the jeep, then melt into the night.

"Kinda hard to melt into the night at dawn."

"*Es verdad.*"

Jubal showed up, Sienna walking behind. "Looks like that helicopter had an accident," he said, grinning. "Lucky for you."

"Yeah. Something happened to its little tail spinny thing." I turned and looked at the wreckage. "You know, that would be a helluva long shot from here."

"Every round I heard fired," Castillo said, "came from the other side of the border. Good thing, too. Otherwise we'd have an international incident on our hands." He slid the rifle with the now-clean bore into its scabbard. "And lots and lots of paperwork." Castillo reached up, grabbed the car's door handle, and pulled himself erect. "I radioed the dispatcher soon as that helo rolled over and gave him an update."

"He say anything about Tres?"

Castillo shook his head. "Get the horses loaded into that trailer you brought down yesterday and let's get moving."

Deputy Earl Castillo led the way north in his patrol car. Jubal and I rode in Griffin's truck, the horse trailer lumbering along behind.

After leaning his head against the passenger door, Jubal went right to sleep.

As we neared Tucson, a patrol car with its lights flashing appeared far ahead and came rapidly toward us. Castillo pulled off onto the shoulder, and I followed him.

Jubal sat up rubbing his eyes. "What's going on?"

The approaching patrol car stopped opposite Castillo's car, and the sheriff himself emerged. He met Castillo in the middle of the road.

"It's the sheriff," I told Jubal. "He and Castillo are having a *palaver*."

After a few seconds, the sheriff walked over to our truck. Looking up at me, he said," Come on out, Brannigan, and let Pearce drive. You'll have to ride the rest of the way with me."

"Okay." I jumped down. "What's up?"

He pulled out a set of handcuffs. "Sorry, Brannigan. I have to arrest you."

"Arrest me? What for?"

"Grand theft. The Mexican Police say no ransom money was found at the scene of your shootout with Dupree, and now Grant Griffin claims you must have stolen it."

November 1957 – Los Angeles

"It's your daughter, Mr. Holliday. Line four."

"Which daughter?"

"Sugar."

Roger Holliday reached across the expansive slab of glass that made up his desktop, punched a button, and snatched a black receiver from its cradle. "You still shacked up with that damn Indian?"

"None of your business, Daddy."

"Like hell it isn't. I suppose you caught some disease from him and need money for medical help. What have you come down with?"

"I'm fine, Daddy, but I do need your help. Did you read the newspaper clippings I sent you?"

"You mean all that stuff about a sorrel horse and that murder trial?"

"Yes, Daddy. Jubal Pearce was acquitted, but the real killer stole the horse and took it into Mexico."

"So?"

"Tres, Jubal Pearce, and a man named Dan Brannigan went across the border yesterday to ransom the horse. There was a gunfight, and the Mexican police got involved. Pearce and Brannigan came back this morning, but Tres stayed behind to slow up some kind of pursuit. I think he's in real danger."

"No shit. What do you want me to do about it?"

"Pull off one of your escapades."

"Jesus."

"I love him, Daddy."

"I see. Any idea where the Indian might be?"

"Before they escaped, the other two men were held prisoner at a ranch just south of a little place called *Tres Bellotas*."

"Okay, Sugar. I'll see what I can do. But do not breathe a word of this to anyone. Got that?"

"Yes, Daddy. I love you."

Chapter 13

November 1957 – Tucson

Dinner in the county jail consisted of dry meatloaf, soggy mashed potatoes, and severely wrinkled lima beans, all served on a cold steel tray. The meal came with no knife and no fork, just a dull spoon, but there was a paper cup of purple cool-aid. *Oh joy.*

Deputy Oscar Krulak, the jailor, was good enough to give me an almost-empty bottle of catsup that managed to replace much of the food's taste. Krulak showed up again as I was finishing off the last of the catsup-covered lima beans. He unlocked the cell door and jerked his thumb toward the front of the jail. "You got a visitor, Brannigan."

"Who is it?"

"Name's O'Rourke. Old guy. Looks like a leprechaun."

I got up from the bunk and tried to hand the empty tray to Krulak.

Backing away, Krulak said, "Leave it; I don't do scullery work."

"Congratulations." I set the tray on the cement floor and followed Krulak down the hall to the small conference room used by attorneys visiting their clients. He pressed a button on the wall, and a door to the room popped open.

A low wall topped by a steel counter separated the so-called conference room into two sections. Except for a small pass-through window for documents, steel-mesh ran from the countertop to the ceiling, making sure the prisoner stayed on his side of the room. Each side had one chair and a door. Only one of the doors led to freedom.

Darcy was seated in the chair on the freedom side of the table. He smiled a warm greeting and asked, "How's the food?"

"I've had better, and that includes last night in Mexico. You heard anything about Tres?"

"Sorry, not a word. I do, however, bring some good news. As a favor to the sheriff, the judge has agreed to proceed straight to a preliminary hearing on your case. It's tomorrow afternoon, right after the court's scheduled docket."

"The sheriff asked for it?"

"He told the judge he wants you cleared posthaste. He's short a deputy."

"Well, that is good news. I figured I'd be here a while before I got a chance to tell my side."

"And you even have an attorney to represent you."

"Phil Lazarus?"

"He says he handles all your legal peccadilloes."

"So he does. He's also my personal loan shark."

Darcy stood up. "Well, Lazarus will be by to meet with you in the morning, and I'll see you in court. I'm going to testify on your behalf."

"You'll make a fine character witness, Darcy O'Rourke. The judge's name is Hanrahan."

"I know. A proud Irish name from Leinster." He pushed a button and both doors popped open.

Deputy Krulak was standing next to my door, and he escorted me back to my cell. The dinner tray was gone.

Pima County's courthouse is a two-story, pink palace dominated by a huge dome covered with hundreds of colored tiles, mostly green. Essentially, the building is a squared-off U-shape with fourteen curved arches on its open side inviting passers-by in from the street to its central courtyard. To me, the place has always suggested some Moor's castle in Spain. Thick walls ensure that the courtrooms inside are cool and quiet, peaceful even.

The sheriff led me into Courtroom Two and closed the door behind us. Then he removed my handcuffs, so I didn't look any more criminal than usual.

I'd been in this courtroom before, but it felt different this time. I made my way through the little gate in the bar and took my place next to Phil Lazarus at the defendant's table.

Sheriff Branson parked himself in the front row of gallery

seating, right behind me.

My eyes wandered, finally coming to rest on the official seal of Pima County positioned high on the wall behind the court's elevated *bench*. The seal's centerpiece was a depiction of the San Xavier Mission, the so-called White Dove of the Desert, flanked by a couple of saguaros. Again, peaceful.

John Blessing, Assistant Pima County Attorney, and his pretty female helper swept in and took their seats at the prosecution table. They both nodded toward our table, the barest of courtesies.

"All rise," thundered the bailiff, and we all lurched to our feet.

The judge appeared quite official himself as he took his place at the bench, white hair standing out above the black robe draped over his shoulders.

Being able to see that the judge wore Levis and cowboy boots under those regal, legal robes was comforting somehow.

"Be seated."

After a moment, the judge looked up from the few documents lying in front of him. "Okay. Let's get started." His eyes wandered around the mostly empty courtroom as he waded through the boiler plate from memory. "The date is Thursday, the twenty-first of November, nineteen hundred and fifty seven. This is a preliminary hearing in the case of Pima County, State of Arizona, against Mr. Daniel Brannigan, a citizen of Pima County. The charge, initiated by complaint, is grand theft in the amount of five thousand dollars, a Class-2 Felony."

His eyes finally stopped on me. "Mr. Brannigan, the purpose of this hearing is not to determine your guilt or innocence; it is merely to find out if the county prosecutor has sufficient evidence to bind you over for trial." Turning to the prosecutor's table, he said, "Mr. Blessing, are you acting as the attorney of record for Pima County in this case?"

John Blessing snapped to attention. "I am, sir."

"Are you ready to proceed?"

"We are, your honor."

"And who represents the defendant?"

Rising slowly from his seat next to me at the defendant's table, my scrawny attorney said, "Phillip Lazarus, your honor." Phil glanced around the courtroom as if to make sure his witnesses were all here, then said, "And we also are ready to proceed."

"Very well. Please begin, Mr. Blessing."

"The county calls Mr. Grant Griffin to the stand."

Griffin rose from somewhere behind me and made his way to the witness box. He avoided eye contact with me when he turned, but he smiled briefly at the judge and then focused on the bailiff standing before him.

"Raise your right hand," the bailiff ordered.

Griffin did so.

The bailiff rattled off, "Do you swear to tell the truth the whole truth and nothing but the truth so help you God?"

"I do."

"Be seated."

Blessing stepped forward as the bailiff retreated. "Mr. Griffin, would you state your full name for the record."

"Grant Merewether Griffin."

"Now please explain to the court your occupation and why you are presently in Arizona."

"I am the producer for a Los Angeles motion picture company called Paradise Pictures. In that capacity I am much like the CEO of a major corporation, responsible for the financial, administrative, and operational functions of the company. I employ a director who is responsible for the artistic aspects. We are here in Arizona filming a western series for television called *Vaquero*."

"Thank you. Did you recently have occasion to trust Mr. Brannigan with five thousand dollars of company funds?"

"Yes, sir."

"Please explain to the court."

"Three days ago, on November eighteenth, a valuable horse belonging to Paradise Pictures was stolen." His eyes flicked around the room, no doubt looking for Jubal. "A ransom note was left demanding five thousand dollars to be delivered to a place in Mexico by the defendant, Mr. Brannigan."

"Excuse me," Blessing said, seemingly excited. "You mean to tell us that the note specified the money had to be personally delivered by Mr. Brannigan?"

226

"It did."

"How unusual."

Phil Lazarus raised a hand, "Objection, your honor."

"On what grounds?"

"Such ransom delivery specification may or may not be unusual, your honor. But the prosecutor has not established that."

"I'll allow it," the judge said. "Seems a reasonable assumption."

"Strike one," I whispered to Phil.

Blessing smirked and said, "Please continue, Mr. Griffin."

"So, at nine o'clock the next day, the nineteenth, I went to one of the banks the company uses and drew out five thousand dollars in hundred-dollar bills."

"Which bank?"

"Arizona Bank's downtown branch."

"Were the bills marked in any way?"

"No. I told the clerk the ransom note specified unmarked bills."

"Were the serial numbers recorded?"

"No, sir. I didn't think of it."

"What did you do with the money?"

"I wrapped the five grand in a plain-paper package with masking tape around it."

"How large was the package?"

"About the size of a fat checkbook."

"Did anyone witness the wrapping of the cash?"

"Mr. Franklin, the bank branch's manager, and Mr. Rivera, the bank guard on duty at the time, both observed this."

"Very well. What happened next?"

"Accompanied by Mr. Rivera, I took the package outside and handed it to Mr. Brannigan, the man seated over there." He pointed at me.

"What did Mr. Brannigan do with it?"

"He took it, got in his truck, and drove away, headed toward Mexico."

"About what time was that?"

"Nine thirty."

"Since then, has Mr. Brannigan made any effort to return the five thousand dollars?"

"No, sir."

"Thank you, Mr. Griffin. No further questions. Your witness, Mr. Lazarus?"

"Yeass," Phil drawled. "Tell me, Mr. Griffin, did you carry the package from the bank to Mr. Brannigan in your hand?"

"No. I put it in my suit pocket."

"Your inside coat pocket? The one next to your body?"

"Yes."

"How many inside pockets does that suit coat have, Mr. Griffin?

"I don't remember. One or two."

"Hmmm. I have a suit, Mr. Griffin. It has two inside

pockets. One on the left and one on the right."

"Objection," Blessing snapped. "He's badgering the witness."

"Sustained," the judge said, appearing bored with the proceedings.

"No further questions," Phil said.

"Strike two," I whispered.

Looking at Griffin, the judge said, "You may step down."

Griffin again avoided eye contact with me, which was difficult since he had to walk right past the defense table where I was glaring at him.

Blessing then turned toward the gallery section behind us. "Would Mr. Jorge Rivera please take the stand."

I turned to watch a burly man wearing a dark suit and scuffed Wellington boots come forward. His neck was a size too big for the shirt, and the skinny necktie he wore didn't do much to cover up the shortfall.

Rivera stood tall in the witness box, chin up and eyes straight ahead. He looked proud to be there.

The bailiff stepped forward and ordered, "Raise your right hand." As Rivera's large paw came up, the bailiff rattled off his spiel.

Smiling, Rivera responded with a loud "*Si*," then sat down.

Blessing got right to the point. "Please state your name for the record."

"Jorge Ruiz Rivera."

"Thank you. Now, Mr. Rivera, did you watch while Mr. Griffin wrapped up the five thousand dollars?"

"*Si.* I did."

"And did you go outside with Mr. Griffin when he took the package to Mr. Brannigan?"

Nodding, Rivera said, "He asked me to go with him."

"Finally, in English please, did you see Mr. Griffin hand the package containing the five thousand dollars to Mr. Brannigan?"

"Yes, sir."

"No further questions. Your witness, Mr. Lazarus."

Lazarus paused, then asked, "Why didn't you record the serial numbers on the bills?"

"Didn't have to. The clerk took them from a block of hundreds in the drawer. She recorded the first and last number. They always do that."

"No further questions."

"Then the prosecution calls Mr. Jubal Pearce."

Jubal strode to the witness box looking entirely too chipper for a man who'd been beaten up the previous day. Perhaps he was just glad to be on the right side of a trial.

The bailiff did his thing. "You swear to tell the truth the whole truth and nothing but the truth, so help you God?"

"I do."

"Please state your name for the record."

"Jubal Ethan Pearce"

"Were you present on November nineteenth when Mr. Brannigan handed a package supposedly containing five thousand dollars to the alleged horse thief, Billy Joe Dupree?"

"Brannigan tossed it. It landed on the ground, and Dupree had to pick it up."

"Please answer the question. Were you present?"

A sigh. "Yes, sir."

"You saw with your own eyes that the package supposedly containing five thousand dollars went from Mr. Brannigan's hand to that of Mr. Billy Joe Dupree, the alleged horse thief."

"Yes."

"What happened when Dupree opened the package?"

"It blew up. Threw some kind of red powder all over Dupree's face that seemed to partially blind him."

"Then what happened?"

The judge was leaning forward now, all ears as they say.

"A gunfight."

"Who shot whom?"

"Dupree shot at Brannigan but missed and hit his horse. Brannigan killed Dupree. One shot to the head."

"Was there any evidence at all that the package that blew up contained any money?"

"No."

"Thank you, Mr. Pearce. Your witness, Mr. Lazarus."

"No questions."

As Jubal rose to leave, the judge asked, "Just out of

curiosity, Mr. Pearce, what else happened in that fight?"

"Our Indian friend threw Dupree's accomplice off a cliff, we disarmed two Mexican's who'd been working for Dupree, and I beat the crap out of one of them in a fair fight."

Leaning back, the judge said, "Sounds exciting."

Jubal winked at me with his one good eye as he walked past on his way to the gallery.

"Mr. Blessing, do you have any more witnesses to call?"

"No, sir."

"Then it's your turn, Mr. Lazarus."

"The defense calls Mr. C. Roper Collins to the stand."

Turing, I watched my own dapper banker walk to the stand assisted by a gold-crowned cane. He nodded to the judge, as well he should have since they play poker together twice a month. C. Roper Collins then raised his right hand, took the oath, and eased down onto the chair, resting both frail hands atop the gold crown of his cane.

Lazarus finally bestirred himself and strolled over to the witness box. "Please state your name for the record."

"Charles Roper Collins."

"And tell the court your occupation, Mr. Collins."

"I am manager of Valley Bank's Tucson office."

"Now tell the court what happened at about nine forty-five on the morning of November nineteenth."

"Mr. Dan Brannigan, the defendant, knocked on my door at the bank and asked to speak with me."

"What did he want?"

"He said he'd been given five thousand dollars to ransom a horse in Mexico, and he didn't think it was a good idea to take the money there."

"Did he say why it wasn't a good idea?"

"Yes. He said the criminal would just take the money and kill the messenger."

"What did Mr. Brannigan want you to do?"

"He asked me to keep the money in a safe deposit box and help him rig an exploding package in its place."

"And did you do that?"

"No, sir."

"Why not?"

"Because when we opened the package, there was no money in it, just cut up newspaper."

Lazarus paused.

The courtroom was silent for a moment, then the courtroom's tall door behind me swished open and banged closed.

Judge Hanrahan's eyes searched for someone or something behind me in the back of the courtroom. I had to think he was looking for Grant Griffin. The judge's expression told me Griffin was gone.

Voice oozing victory, Lazarus asked, "Soo, Mr. Collins, what did you do?"

"I got my staff to prepare an exploding packet for Mr.

Brannigan similar to the ones we keep handy in case of an armed robbery. We put it in the same wrappings that the cut-up newspaper came in."

"What did Mr. Brannigan do then?"

"He took the package, thanked me, and left."

"Your witness, Mr. Blessing."

The prosecutor rose and strolled over to the witness box. "Is it possible that Mr. Brannigan replaced the money with newspaper cuttings after he got the package from Mr. Griffin and before he showed it to you?"

"Well, I guess so, but—"

"Yes or no, Mr. Collins. Yes or no."

Gripping the head of his cane tightly, Collins glowered at the attorney and answered, "Yes."

"Thank you, Mr. Collins. No more questions."

As C. Roper Collins made his way back to the gallery, the judge leaned forward, a Cheshire Cat now. "You have any more witnesses to call, Mr. Lazarus?"

"Why yes, I do, your honor. I call Mr. Darcy O'Rourke to the stand."

Almost skipping, Darcy made his way through the gate in the bar and up to the witness box. Anticipating the bailiff, he turned and raised his right hand.

"Do you swear to tell the truth and nothing but the truth so help you God?"

"I do."

"Please state your name for the record."

"Darcy Seamus O'Rourke."

"And what is your occupation?"

Grinning at me, Darcy said, "I am a licensed forensic accountant working as an investigator for the Los Angeles branch of the Pinkerton Detective Agency."

I think my lower jaw bounced off the defendant's table.

Lazarus pushed right on. "What are you doing in Arizona?"

"A major investor in the television series being filmed by Paradise Pictures here in southern Arizona recently approached the agency. The investor suspected that the film company's producer, Mr. Grant Griffin, was padding expenses and skimming the difference. I was sent here to investigate."

"What triggered this investor to contact the Pinkerton agency? What made him suspicious?"

"The story about Jubal Pearce's trial and the pretty movie horse made its way into the Los Angeles Times. It mentioned that Griffin had paid a rancher up on the Mogollon Rim a thousand dollars for the mare. That got the investor's attention; he'd recently seen an expense report that indicated the horse had cost the company fifteen hundred."

"And so he hired the Pinkerton Agency?"

"Yes."

Lazarus was clearly enjoying this. "Have you been able to determine whether or not Mr. Griffin was indeed stealing from the company?"

"Yes, sir."

"And?"

"I have not been able to check on Mr. Griffin's activities before he came to Arizona, but he's been systematically submitting inflated expense reports and keeping the difference ever since."

Can you describe Mr. Griffin's skimming operation?"

"Paradise Pictures buys and rents a great many local services on a short-term basis: a dozen horses for a month, thirty extras for a week, catering, clean-up crews, etcetera. As the producer, Mr. Griffin pays for these irregular services. In many cases he does so with cash and has the recipient sign a receipt. These receipts are compiled into expense reports sent to the company accountants back in Los Angeles."

"So how does Mr. Griffin cheat the system?"

"Simple. He uses a two-part receipt book with the original and copy pages separated by a sheet of carbon paper. The payment amount goes on a line in the upper portion of each receipt; the signature line is on the lower portion. When Griffin wants to skim some money, he puts a piece of plain paper under the upper portion of the carbon paper. When he fills in the amount, and the recipient signs for it, the carbon paper passes the signature on to the second copy, but the dollar amount is recorded only on the piece of plain paper. After the signer leaves with the correct top copy, Griffin pulls out the piece of plain paper, lays it on top of the carbon paper, and records a higher value. Thus a small contractor might leave with a thousand dollars and an accurate receipt, but Griffin's copy would show the accountants that the man was paid eleven hundred. Griffin pockets the difference."

"How do you know this?"

"I brought copies of the receipts Mr. Griffin submitted to the accountants with me. I then hunted down the actual receipts and compared them."

"Has the IRS become involved?"

"Not yet. And it's not likely under normal circumstances. If and when the IRS audits the company, the receipts are right there to back up the company ... and Mr. Griffin."

"But," Lazarus said, "wouldn't the IRS verify those receipts with the person who got paid. Just as you did?"

"They might, but there is a significant time delay. The cash is being paid out now, but the company's tax return won't be filed until next year, and it likely won't receive more than a cursory examination by the IRS until a year or more after that. And frankly, it is doubtful that two or three years from now an IRS agent will come to Tucson looking for actual receipts."

"But it seems to me, Mr. O'Rourke, that this alleged skimming would not net Mr. Griffin a whole lot of money. Do you have an estimate?"

"Yes. The total amount of cash paid to these people has been running about a thousand dollars a day, and Mr. Griffin likes to skim ten percent."

"You mean he's been clearing seven hundred a week from this little scam?"

"About. But sometimes he makes a lot more, like when he paid a rancher in a remote part of the Mogollon Rim a thousand dollars for a horse and then claimed he'd paid fifteen hundred."

"Are you aware of any other such instances?"

"I am aware of at least one other."

"Please explain."

"Yesterday afternoon I obtained a warrant from Judge Hanrahan that allowed me to check the Western Union offices in town to see if Mr. Griffin had wired money in the last three days."

"And had he?"

"On November nineteenth, shortly before noon, Mr. Griffin wired five thousand dollars to a bank account in Las Vegas."

"Do you know who owns that Las Vegas account?"

"The Pinkerton man in Las Vegas reports the bank account in question belongs to a big-time bookie and sleaze ball named Bunny Malone."

"Were you able to determine if any of the bills submitted to the Western Union office matched the serial numbers of those Mr. Griffin withdrew from his bank that day?"

"Yes. Western Union records the serial numbers of all large bills coming in to the office. The hundred-dollar bills supposedly given to Mr. Brannigan at nine-thirty were actually presented to Western Union about two hours later to pay for the wire transfer to Las Vegas."

"Your witness, Mr. Blessing." Lazarus floated back to our table and plopped down onto the chair next to me.

"Home run," I whispered.

Blessing stood. "I have only one question for the witness. It appears that Mr. Griffin is a successful man in his business. Do you have any idea why he would resort to the criminal activities such as those you describe?"

"During my visit to Western Union yesterday, I discovered that Mr. Griffin has been wiring large sums to the account owned by Bunny Malone several times a month. Griffin appears to be a serious gambler on a losing streak."

"Thank you, Mr. O'Rourke. Your testimony has been very enlightening." Then, with a come-on head nod to Lazarus, Blessing said, "May we approach the bench, your honor?"

"Absolutely."

After a whispered consultation, John Blessing turned to me and announced, "The county is dropping all charges against you, Mr. Brannigan. You are free to go."

"Sheriff," the judge called out, "you better get ready to apprehend Mr. Griffin. The county attorney will process an arrest warrant for him within the hour."

Chapter 14

November 1957 – Tucson

The sheriff grabbed my arm as I started to leave the courtroom. "You have a four o'clock appointment at the doctor's office to get your fit-for-duty exam. Come to my office as soon as you're done; I have a job for you."

"Ten-four."

It was a quarter past five when I finally waved to the desk sergeant and knocked on the sheriff's open office door.

Sheriff Virgil Branson looked up from some document on his desk, then motioned for me to enter. "Well," he said, grinning, "did you pass?"

"Fit as a fiddle and ready to rumble." I handed him the doctor's lengthy medical evaluation form.

Flipping to the signature page, the sheriff muttered "Good" and handed me the document he'd been reading when I came in. "Here's a warrant for the arrest of Grant Griffin," he said, the grin gone. "Bring him in."

"Aren't you forgetting something, Sheriff?"

240

"Oh yeah." He stood up. "Raise your right hand and repeat after me."

I held the arrest warrant in my left hand and raised my right while the sheriff swore me in as a Pima County Deputy Sheriff.

After the obligatory handshake, the sheriff reached into a desk drawer and pulled out a leather clip with one of the county's seven-pronged badges attached. "Clip this to your belt," he said. "I'll give you another one for your shirt as soon as you buy a uniform, which better be real soon."

"Yes, sir." It felt good to have a steady job again. Clipping on the badge, I grinned. It was even better being a lawman once more.

"And you might need this," the sheriff said. He opened another drawer and pulled out a walnut-handled Colt .45 revolver nestled in a hand-tooled leather holster. "It's my personal weapon, so take good care of it." He handed the gun belt to me as if it were the family heirloom. Maybe it was.

Setting the warrant on the sheriff's desk, I wrapped the gun belt around my waist, just below my pants belt, and buckled it. There were a couple of extra holes in the belt, but it fit, and the weapon rested low on my right hip, where I like it. A small rawhide loop over the hammer secured the revolver in its holster. I flipped the loop off and drew the gun.

"It's loaded," the sheriff said. "Five rounds. There's twenty more in the belt loops."

"Fits my hand real good." I slid the .45 back into its holster and set the loop over the hammer.

The sheriff picked up the warrant and handed it to me. "Time is wasting away, Deputy."

I stopped in the outer office to call Griffin's hotel. The clerk said he'd been there earlier but had checked out. No forwarding address. The clerk did, however, have the license-plate number of Griffin's Cadillac. I gave it to the desk sergeant and asked him to get out an APB.

So, Griffin must have stayed at the trial long enough to figure out the jig was up. And now he was running. *Where? Mexico?*

Calling the Border Patrol in Nogales, I asked them to alert the Mexican officers on the other side.

But maybe Griffin would stop at his Old Tucson office first. I checked out a patrol car and headed for the movie town.

November 1957 – Old Tucson

Grant Griffin parked his black 1957 Cadillac Fleetwood Brougham in the corner of the parking lot nearest the fake town. He turned off the car's ignition but stayed slumped behind the wheel for a long time, reviewing the day's events.

He'd stayed at the trial long enough to know he was in trouble. Cheating the company had been easy and safe. Even sending Brannigan off to ransom that damn horse with nothing but wrapped-up newspaper clippings had been a reasonable risk; odds were the fool wasn't coming back. And something like that had been necessary since he was dangerously late scraping together the money for another payment to Bunny Malone. But using the exact same bills to wire the cash to Vegas had been a bone-headed mistake. Downright stupid. The bills were brand new, and he should have realized they'd come from a set of hundred-dollar bills in the cashier's drawer. It was going to be easy for someone to discover their serial numbers, trace them to Western Union, and nail him for a crime.

Worse, Bunny Malone was not going to like being linked to a crime, even one that wasn't his.

Time, precious time. He'd used some of it to collect his clothes from the hotel and the cash from the various company bank accounts, but he was fast running out of time. *Now it was time to grab the evidence from the office and get the hell out of Dodge.* He almost smiled. *This place does look like old Dodge City.*

Outside, standing next to the car, Grant scanned the dirt road behind him. There was no sign of fresh dust along the route, but still ... He turned and hurried past the horse corral en route to his office in the fake Spanish mission.

It was dark and cool inside. Grant closed the door behind him, then flipped the switch that activated two dim lights hidden behind wall sconces, the only lighting beside the small reading lamp on his desk.

The heart in Grant's chest beat twice before he realized that the dark shadow behind his desk was a man ... a man dressed all in black. Then Grant's heart flopped. "Who are you?"

"A visitor ... from Vegas. People call me Fredo."

Grant moved a few inches back toward the door. His left hand felt behind him for the latch. "What do you want?"

"I want to know if you're as stupid as you seem?"

"Uh, I don't—"

"First you got careless and wound up with a detective on your tail. Then you sent the boss money that can be traced back to a crime, your crime. The whole arrangement is blown now."

"But I was late with my last payment. In a hurry. I didn't know that—"

"Yeah, Griffin, you *were* late, but that's old business; my orders now are to close your account."

Fredo's right hand came up from below the desktop , and Italian Beretta it held barked twice: *Thud. Thud.*

A look of amazement spread across Grant's face. He looked down at the two red blotches spreading across his abdomen, then he collapsed onto the floor.

The man calling himself Fredo stood and admired his handiwork. He strolled around the desk and, being careful to avoid the blood, used one foot to push Grant flat on his back. Bending over, Fredo searched Grant's pockets, pulling out a thin wallet and a set of car keys. He dangled the keys in front of Grant's bulging eyes.

"In five minutes I'll be driving your Caddy up the road.

About that time you'll be sliding down to hell. Have a nice trip, asshole."

Grant's eyes begged, but his lips couldn't frame any words.

Fredo walked to the oversize door and opened it.

A man in worn dungarees and a beat-up cowboy hat trotted up and stood there panting; a revolver dangled from his right hand. "I heard gunfire," the man said.

"So you did." Fredo shot the man in the forehead, then walked past the fallen body.

The sun was easing down behind the western mountains when I pulled into the movie set's parking lot. Even though it was well after normal working hours, there were still several cars in the parking lot, including Griffin's big, black Cadillac. *Jackpot.*

A quick glance at the other vehicles told me nothing important. My now-dusty Edsel was right where I'd left it, and the truck/trailer rig I'd driven to the border was parked nearby. The pickup Jubal had been using was there, which meant he was back on the job. I didn't recognize the rental car, but having one or more here after hours was not unusual. None of vehicles appeared to be occupied.

In a hurry, I took the direct route to Griffin's office, which meant a slight detour around the big corral.

Jubal and Sienna were close together in there, well away from the other horses, conversing in whatever language the two of them had derived. If either of them saw me, they didn't show it.

Thud. Thud.

I stopped, puzzled. *Distant gunfire?*

Off to my left, on the far side of the corral, the night watchman appeared. He was running toward the mission door, a pistol in his hand.

Something's up. I flipped the rawhide thong off my revolver's hammer.

The watchman stopped in front of the mission door as it swung open …

Thud.

The horses bolted around the corral, throwing up a cloud of dust, blocking my view. I stepped up on the corral's lowest rail and tried to see over the churning sea of horses.

There, walking toward the corral, was a stranger dressed in black—carrying a pistol. And behind him, the watchman lay sprawled on the sand, a smear of blood on his forehead.

The stranger saw me. His face twisted into a snarl as he raised his pistol.

Shoot first.

I drew and snapped off a shot without aiming. My round kicked up sand by the gunman's feet; his bullet hit nothing but air.

Then the stranger ducked down, out of sight behind the horses milling around the corral, and I had to hold my second shot.

On opposite sides of that big corral, we bobbed and weaved around for several seconds without either of us getting a decent shot at the other. I saw Jubal and Sienna off to one side and yelled, "Get away."

Then the stranger slapped a new clip into his gun and broke the standoff; he started shooting the horses.

Two horses fell, and the gunman swiveled toward Sienna.

Jubal ran in front of his mare screaming, "Nooooooo!"

The gunman shot him. Then, as Jubal fell, the man shot Sienna.

Beyond the corral, behind the gunman shooting horses, a blood-soaked Grant Griffin staggered out of the mission. Falling to his knees, he picked up the pistol lying next to the slain watchman and pointed it at the gunman's back. Without a word, he pulled the trigger—and missed.

When the gunman spun toward this new threat, I moved to one side and shot him in the head. He went down hard.

In the distance, Grant Griffin pitched face forward onto the sand, as spent as the round he'd just fired.

Three horses were down, either dead or dying. Panic stricken, the others milled around the corral, continuing to throw up a thin cloud of dust.

Jubal lay in the middle of the melee, blood staining his right side.

Vaulting into the corral, I ran to him.

Looking up at me, fear in his eyes, Jubal whispered, "Where's Sienna?"

"She's been shot," I said. "Lie still. I'll see how she is."

Sienna had fallen against the corral bars a dozen feet away. She lay still, eyes wild. Her nostrils flared, pushing little puffs of dust away. Blood oozed from a hole in her side and ran down into the sand.

As I stood there, Jubal dragged himself over. Tears streaked his dirty face. "Easy," he whispered. "Easy, girl." He lay his head on Sienna's neck and closed his eyes. "No, God. No."

There was nothing I could do for Sienna. Nothing anyone could do. I turned away and left them alone.

One of the other two horses down was still alive, barely. I recognized him as my friend from the run for the border: the gray horse I'd named *Agallas*. Sides heaving, the terrified animal was exhaling bloody froth. His eyes begged me. Stroking his nose, I told him, "*Adios, amigo.*" Then I stepped back and put a .45 bullet into his brain.

A quick check of the three men outside the corral confirmed they were all dead. I pulled the stranger's wallet out and checked his ID. From Las Vegas. That figured.

I went to the patrol car and radioed HQ. "Dispatch, this is Brannigan. I'm at the Old Tucson movie lot. I have four men down, three dead and one with a body wound. I need an ambulance *pronto*."

"You have four men down?"

"Affirmative."

"You've been a deputy for less than an hour, and you have four men down?"

"I've been busy. And send a back hoe."

"What for?"

"To bury three dead horses."

"You're kidding."

"Unfortunately, I'm not. Out."

There was a first-aid kit in the patrol car's trunk, so I carried it over to the corral.

Sienna was dead, at least to the rest of us. She'd probably never be dead for Jubal.

He'd closed her eyes, but continued to stroke her nose. The far-away look in the man's eyes was not something I wanted to remember. I knelt next to Jubal and put a hand on his shoulder. "You okay?"

He nodded.

I ran a hand under his back to see if the bullet had gone through; it had not. "I need to put a compress on your wound, Jubal. Slow the bleeding."

"Okay."

"This will hurt some."

"Good."

The ambulance got there first, followed a few minutes later by Deputy Castillo and Sheriff Virgil Branson.

Following standard police procedure, Castillo began to string yellow tape to mark off the crime scene. He paused near Sienna, then moved on.

Sheriff Branson walked around to survey the damage, then came over to me. "What happened?"

"The dude in black is from Vegas. Likely a hit man sent on an errand. He apparently shot Griffin twice in his office, then bumped into the night watchman when he came out. Shot the watchman in the forehead. I arrived on this side of the corral about that time. The hit man spotted me, and we exchanged a couple of shots across the corral."

"Who shot the horses?"

"He did. I guess he figured to get them out of the way so he could get a clear shot at me."

"And he shot Pearce?"

"Yes, sir."

"Why?"

"Jubal tried to protect his mare when the horses started falling. I guess that's all the reason a hit man needs."

"Then he shot the sorrel mare?"

"Just another horse to him, I guess."

"Yeah, sad. How'd you manage to take him?"

"Griffin staggered out of the fake mission, picked up the watchman's gun, and blazed away at the hit man. When he turned to fire back, I nailed the bastard."

Sheriff Branson turned and looked across the corral at the

hit man's body. "Head shot at sixty feet with a Colt forty-five is damn fine shooting."

"It's a good gun."

Becky's pickup truck came roaring across the parking lot about that time and slid to a stop in the sand next to the corral. She was out of the cab, through the corral rails, and on her knees next to Jubal in what would be record time if it were an Olympic event.

We watched them long enough to realize that she and Jubal were both crying. Turning away, I fought the urge to join in … and failed.

A county van pulled up next to the corral and the forensics team bailed out of it. Calm and professional, they started taking photos of everything.

"We'll have to investigate all this," the sheriff said. "Standard procedure in an officer-shooting case."

"I know."

"I'll have to take your badge and gun until this is settled." He held out his big paw.

"Yeah, I understand." I gave him the clip-on badge, then undid the gun belt and handed it over. "Am I still on the payroll?"

"Of course. We'll let the technical guys do their thing tonight. You go get some rest, or at least some good Scotch. Come back here tomorrow and snoop. Poke around Griffin's office and any other place you find interesting. See what you can dig up. There's got to be more to this story."

As I walked to my patrol car, Castillo trotted up. "The medics say Jubal should make it. Damn shame about his mare."

"Let's go get drunk."

"Can't. You have any idea how much paperwork three bodies require?"

November 1957 – Mexico

The Indian lay on a bed of hay bales. Dawn had thwarted his plan to melt into the night, and the Mexican police posse had ridden him down shortly after sunrise. After roughing him up sufficiently to please the sadistic tendencies of the sergeant in charge, they'd taken him back to the Morales *hacienda* and thrown him into the feed-storage room to await transfer to the Mexican jail in Nogales, Sonora.

For some mysterious reason, the vehicle coming to transport him had been delayed, and Tres was now spending his second night in captivity. His sleep was interrupted about midnight by a small noise.

Zzzzzzzzzzzt ... bump.

Tres opened his eyes. *Smells like burning sulphur. Am I in hell?*

With a faint squeak, the door to the storeroom swung open. A moment later an apparition moved through the dark opening and leaned over Tres. It seemed to be a man, but one from someone else's nightmare. Its face and hands were painted in hues of black and green. The clothing, head to foot, was camouflage, and there were some things on the creature's belt that looked like weapons Tres could only imagine.

Lying still, eyes wide open, Tres felt the sudden urge to pee.

The apparition put a big hand on Tres's shoulder and whispered, "Up and at 'em, Tonto. We're haulin' your ass out of here."

Relieved, Tres muttered, "Who … who are you?"

"Your best friend." The hand gripped Tres's forearm and yanked him to his feet. "There's a man outside dressed like me. Follow him close, and keep your mouth shut. Got it?"

Nodding, Tres whispered, "There are dogs."

"There *were* dogs."

Pushed through the doorway, Tres bumped into another painted apparition.

Eyes glowing in the dark, this one whispered, "Come with me," then it turned and trotted off into the darkness.

Tres followed.

For the next ten minutes, the three men jogged single file through the desert scrub. Then the leader brought them to an abrupt halt next to an oddest vehicle Tres had ever seen. It looked like a stripped-down auto chassis with four huge, balloon tires. Two rugged bench seats were welded to the frame.

"Get in the back," one of the men ordered.

As he crawled onto the rear seat, Tres asked, "What in hell

is this thing?"

"We call it a *dune buggy*. Hang on, this will be a rough ride."

Fifteen minutes later they roared through the gap in the border fence and headed up the dirt road to Arivaca. As they neared that village, the man in the front passenger seat turned to Tres and asked, "You know anyone in Arivaca?"

"Yeah."

The dune buggy slowed, then came to a stop. "Good," the man said. "It's a short walk up ahead. Don't tell anyone about us; we'll be long gone by the time you get there."

"But, who—"

"Just a couple of tourists who did you a favor. Now get down and get moving."

"Yes, sir. And *muchas gracias, amigo*."

"You can thank your girl friend."

"Shut up," the driver snarled as he hit the gas. The dune buggy roared ahead and soon disappeared into the night.

November 1957 – Tucson

Darcy came in while I was having breakfast in the Santa Rita coffee shop. He settled in across from me and asked, "Any news on how Jubal is doing?"

"Just came from the hospital," I said. "He's improving. They indicated he should be able to have visitors tomorrow."

"Great." Darcy picked up a menu, glanced at it, then spoke

to me over the its top. "I hear you had a short but busy career as a deputy sheriff yesterday."

"Fortunately, I'm still on the payroll."

"Oh good, then you can buy breakfast."

"I haven't been paid yet, Darcy. But you, I expect, are on an expense account. Am I right?"

"But isn't this is my going-away party?"

"That was the other night. You just haven't left yet."

He sighed. "Okay, I'll buy."

Sheila was either off duty or avoiding me; a honey-blonde waitress with blue eyes came over to our table. "You Dan Brannigan?" she asked.

"Guilty."

"Thought so. Sheila warned me about you. What would you like?"

"For breakfast?"

A pained look went with her response. "Of course."

"Short stack, orange juice, and black coffee."

She turned to Darcy. "And you, sir?"

"The same, but add some cream for my coffee."

"Be right back."

As she turned to leave, I wasted no time getting after Darcy. "Why the big charade pretending to be a writer?"

He laughed. "It gave me a good reason to poke around without arousing Griffin's curiosity. Besides, I've always wanted to be a writer, and this looked like a really good story. I called a friend of mine at *Life* magazine. He said they'd take a look at what I wrote, and maybe put it in the magazine."

"What about that book in the library? The one Carlotta read?"

"Part of my cover story. We have the necessary permissions, and it was easy to print up a new version featuring my name. We've used it before."

"You are obviously a scoundrel," I said. "But what about Pilar?"

"Like I told you, she's my assistant. I got here a few days before the trial started, and spent time on the set nosing around, using my cover as someone writing about the horse and the trial. My second day out there, Pilar came up to me and offered her services as a translator."

"Why?"

"Pilar told me she'd heard me trying to talk, without much success, to one of the Mexican crew. She explained that a lot of the crew working out there are in the country illegally, and they were reluctant to talk with a stranger. She said she could help. So I hired her."

"Then Pilar must have learned what you were really up to."

"I don't think so. She helped me get to know a few of the Mexican crew, but I didn't ask them questions about their pay and receipts when she was around. I'd send her on some errand first. At any rate, my research on the set was about done, and the trial was to start the next day, so I moved over to the courthouse to see what the trial testimony might disclose."

A flurry of raised voices across the room drew our attention just as a booming voice called out, "*Ya-te-he.*"

And there came Tres. Shirt gone, trousers torn, and sporting several streaks of dried blood, he looked like a war refugee. He dodged around several tables manned by open-mouthed, touristy-looking diners and then planted himself at our table. Picking up a menu, he asked, "Who's buying?"

The coffee shop manager arrived in time to cut off Darcy's reply. Looking down at Tres the man said, "I'm very sorry, sir, but—"

Tres looked up at the manager. "I'm a bit hungry this morning. I'll have everything on page two."

"You don't understand, sir. You cannot dine here dressed like that."

"What? You want me to take off my pants?"

"No. No. I want you to leave."

Tossing the menu onto the table top, Tres rose and looked down on the top of the manager's bald head. In a booming voice that likely could be heard across the street, he addressed the quivering man. "A Hollywood motion picture company is about to start filming on the lawn outside. I am the star of that movie and am dressed for the scene. I intend to have breakfast here while I wait for my cue call, and I expect to be treated as an important guest. Now leave us alone."

Turning to the other diners, Tres announced, "Some of you

may get to be extras in the scene." Then he sat down, winking at us in the process.

After blinking a few times, the manager retreated. He waved at the honey-blonde and pointed at our table before hiding behind the cash register.

She arrived, eyes wide. "Sir?"

"I'll have the country-fried steak with eggs over easy and a side of buttermilk pancakes. Better make that two sides of pancakes."

"And to drink?"

"A Bloody Mary followed by a pot of coffee."

"Sorry, sir, the bar isn't open yet."

"Then make it a tall glass of tomato juice with a celery stalk stuck in it. I'll pretend."

"Yes, sir." She scribbled in her order book as she walked away.

"You do know how to make an entrance," I said. "Where in hell have you been?"

"I spent a day and a half locked in that feed room you know so well. Then last night two guys dressed for a Martian Halloween came along, blew the lock, and drove me back to the good old U S A on some kind of car made of nothing but steel bars and big tires."

Leaning across the table, I asked, "Tres, are you lying to me again?"

"No, sir. Honest Injun."

"Yeah, right. Were they Americans?"

"Probably, but they really could have been Martians. What's new with you guys?"

Darcy sighed. "You tell him, Daniel."

"Well, for starters, Darcy over there is not a famous writer, he's a forensic accountant sent here by the Pinkerton Detective Agency to check out various frauds committed by our producer friend, Grant Griffin."

"No shit? Griffin's in jail?"

"He's dead. Shot by a hit man out of Vegas."

Our coffee arrived just then, and the blonde waitress was careful not to get too close to Tres as she poured.

Tres ignored her. "What happened to the hit man?"

"I killed him."

The waitress gasped and spilled hot coffee on Tres's leg. "Oh God," she whispered, "I am so sorry."

"Miss," I said, handing her a dime, "leave the coffee pot here and go read one of those morning newspapers for sale at the cashier stand."

She looked confused as well as contrite.

"When you're done with the Old Tucson shootout story, bring us the paper. My semi-naked friend here also has some catching up to do."

"Yes, sir. And I am really sorry about the leg."

By the time she returned with our food and the paper, I'd told Tres about Jubal and Sienna. It put a real damper on our

Indian's homecoming.

After breakfast, Tres left to find Sugar Holliday and—maybe—get some rest. He left a roomful of disappointed tourists behind, although a couple of persistent women followed him out the door. The honey- blonde waitress waved goodbye to him from behind the cash register.

Darcy paid the bill, then went to his hotel to pack. His job done, he was flying back to Los Angeles and the possibility of a writing career.

But I, on the other hand, had real work to do, and I started at HQ. The sheriff was at a Chamber of Commerce meeting, but the forensics crew had compiled a thorough report that pretty much backed up what I'd told the sheriff. Griffin's confiscated Cadillac contained the man's clothes and a lot of cash, but not much else. Whatever further evidence of malfeasance might exist, it was yet to be discovered.

Chapter 15

November 1957 – Old Tucson

After checking out a patrol car, I took the long, easy route to the movie set. A steady stream of cars was leaving the parking lot when I arrived, which was unusual since it was only eleven o'clock. Like a salmon fighting its way upstream, I made my way toward the movie set through the departing crowd. A clutch of crew members parted to let me pass, and I bumped into Pilar.

Tugging at my sleeve, she pulled me to one side. "I hear you had a tough day, yesterday," Pilar said, moving close to my chest. Real close.

"Bad enough," I said. God, she looked nice. "What are you up to?"

"Wrapping up some loose ends. Darcy's leaving you know."

"Yeah. I know."

She stepped back. "I don't see a badge. You on official business?"

"Snooping around, trying to find if Griffin left any incriminating evidence stashed someplace. You know where I can find Cromwell?"

"Try the saloon," she said, turning away and rejoining the flow moving toward the parking lot. She looked nice going away too.

Good old Justin Cromwell was standing on the saloon's porch when I walked up. "Well," he sneered, looking down at me, "you here to kill somebody else?"

"Don't push your luck, Justin. Why is everyone leaving?"

"I sent them home. We weren't going to get any film in the can today, everyone's too upset. Besides, I'm not even sure we're still in business. The company's backers are meeting in Los Angeles to decide how to proceed."

"What about security for the set here?"

"One of your fellow deputies spent the night out here and left when my crew came in this morning. The company that provided the last guard is lining up a replacement."

Stepping up on the porch, I looked toward the corral. "What happened to the dead horses?"

A county front-end-loader showed up first thing this morning, and we buried the horses about an hour ago."

"Where?"

He pointed to an area beyond the church. "We got the owner's permission to dig in a remote part of the property. You can't see it from here."

"Does Jubal Pearce know?"

"Gosh, I have no idea. Sugar Holliday arranged for a Pima

Indian shaman to come out and hold some kind of religious ceremony for the horses at the burial. I attended. It was kind of touching."

"Justin, you seem to have it all under control. I'm proud of you."

"Well, I like to think of myself as being capable."

"That is evident," I said. "What surprises me is that you also seem to have a heart."

Turning away, I hopped down from the porch and headed for the faux mission.

Griffin's desk yielded only one thing of interest to me: the keys to his pickup truck. I could finally get my rifle back.

But the sheriff was right; there had to be more to the story. I gave up on the desk and began an organized search of the building's entire interior, looking for a hidey hole.

The desk had been placed about ten feet inside the entry door. Behind it, in the rest of the fake church's nave, six rough-hewn wood pews had been arranged in three rows with a center aisle, all facing a single raised altar in the back.

Since I saved the altar for last, that's where I found something suspicious: one of the boards making up the floor of the altar wasn't as dusty as its mates. Pushing on one end of the board made the other end rise, revealing a metal film canister stuck in the narrow space under the wood.

As I lifted the canister from its earthen crypt, I had the odd feeling of being watched. Perhaps God didn't like me messing around an altar, even a fake one. Shrugging it off, I popped open the canister. Inside was a hardbound notebook.

Taking the notebook back to Griffin's desk, I spent some time going over the details inside it. There were notations showing dollar amounts wired to a bank account in Las Vegas and a balance remaining. Thanks to Darcy's testimony, I knew the account belonged to a Las Vegas bookie named Bunny Malone. And those entries could easily be read as payments to reduce a rather large gambling debt.

But other items appeared occasionally. Large amounts of cash would come in by some means, and then several smaller amounts would be wired separately to an account on Grand Cayman Island. And for each amount sent to Grand Cayman, five percent of it was deducted from what looked to be the gambling debt.

This was meat for a forensic accountant. I closed what I'd come to think of as an accounts ledger and headed for the door. I stepped out into the bright sunlight—and everything went black.

I regained consciousness in time to see a blurry figure running toward the parking lot. By the time I was able to stand up and my vision had cleared, the runner had disappeared. My head hurt, but then it's hurt worse. A question lodged in my aching brain: why?

Then I knew why; the notebook was gone.

The sound of a car engine racing penetrated my brain as I

staggered toward the parking lot, but there was only a lingering dust trail by the time I got there. And my patrol car's nose was drooping; someone had slashed one of the front tires. Fortunately, I had an ace up my sleeve, or at least in my pocket. I pulled out the Ford pickup's keys as I ran to it. I had to waste the better part of a minute unhitching the trailer, but it gave me time to form a plan.

Judging by the dust trail, the thief had turned north on Kinney Road. If they were headed for Tucson, which seemed a good bet, they'd soon turn east on Gates Pass Road. I might cut the corner if the pickup could handle a cross-country dash through the local desert. It was worth a try.

Turning the truck northeast, I blasted my way through a thin line of brush, then found some firm footing that seemed to go in my direction. Sand and bits of cacti flew around behind me as I jolted across the rocky remnants of ancient volcano ash and slewed around in their sandier remains.

After half a mile of this, I swerved hard right into a fresh dust trail and found myself on the stern of a red Chevy Bel Air doing well over a sane speed for a winding gravel road like this one.

It suddenly occurred to me that I was a bit like the dog that finally caught a car: what do I do now?

Having no better idea, I honked my horn twice, then stuck my arm out the open window and motioned for the Chevy's driver to pull over.

CRACK.

I'm not sure what I expected, but what I got was a bullet hole in the middle of my windshield. That did it. I slammed on the brakes and slewed the truck so it came to a stop at an angle to the road. Yanking my rifle from under the seat, I stuck its muzzle out the window and fired three quick rounds at the Chevy's fast-disappearing rear end.

One of them must have hit a tire, because the Chevy began to fishtail. A second later it dug a front wheel into the soft shoulder and flipped. The car rolled three times before it came to a stop inverted, lodged against a large palo verde tree.

Leaving the pickup truck idling right where it was, I ran toward the wreck, rifle at the ready. It turned out there was no need to hurry.

The driver lay alongside the vehicle; a pistol rested in the sand nearby. The driver's legs were at angles that indicated broken bones, and blood trickling from her mouth. She had to have serious internal injuries. Yeah. A woman. Pilar.

Pilar looked up at me and whispered, "Sorry, Brannigan." She tried to say more, but blood in her mouth intervened.

"Don't try to talk," I said. "I'll go for help."

She shook her head. After swallowing, she whispered, "Stay with me. Please." Swallowing again, she pointed. "Water bag. In the car."

The driver's door had been ripped off, leaving an opening to the front seat. I got on my hands and knees and crawled into the car far enough that I could reach the canvas water bag hanging from the passenger window crank. The ledger was lying on the upside-down roof near it, so I brought it out along with the water bag.

Pilar was waiting for me, the pistol now in her hand. She was almost smiling.

Kneeling close to Pilar, I pulled the stopper on the water bag and held the round opening close to her mouth. She kept her eyes and the gun pointed at me while she took a long drink. Then, coughing, she pulled away from the bag.

"Not much time," she whispered. "I work for someone … Bunny Malone. He sent me …" She coughed up some blood. "… to keep an eye on Griffin."

"Why?"

"Money laundering … Darcy can figure it out." Another cough, some more blood. "I telephoned Bunny after your trial. Told him … Griffin had screwed up. Sorry Fredo killed the pretty horse."

"Look, Pilar, if I get help you might make it."

She shook her head. "Kiss me good bye, Brannigan?"

The look on her face said it was a serious request, so I leaned forward and kissed her bloody lips. They tasted salty.

As I moved back, Pilar put the pistol to her head and pulled the trigger.

November 1957 – Tucson

Sheriff Branson looked at me a long time. "Dammit, Brannigan, that's three dead yesterday and one more today. This many people usually die around you?"

"Not lately."

"I'm glad. The department can't afford all this overtime for the forensics crew. By the way, I've gone over their report on the shoot out at the Old Tucson corral. It clears you of any misconduct."

"But now—"

"Yeah. Now there's another shooting, and I need another damn forensic report."

"Sorry." I glanced at Griffin's ledger lying on the sheriff's desk. "Is Darcy O'Rourke going to go over those accounts?"

"Yeah. I had Castillo yank him off the plane to Los Angeles. They should be here any time now. I hope O'Rourke can find something in the ledger that tracks back to that Bunny Malone character in Las Vegas; I couldn't do it. Four people dead, Jubal Pearce in the hospital, and it looks as if the bastard who started this whole mess will walk free."

"Maybe so, Sheriff. But I don't think the last card's been played yet."

"I hope not. As for you, check with the sergeant at the desk. You'll be helping him with paperwork for a while."

"Ah, Sheriff, I'm not much good at that sort of thing. Can I have a couple days leave without pay instead?"

"If that's what you want. It'll save the county some money."

He opened a desk drawer and pulled out a form. After a few strokes with a pen, he handed me a leave slip good for forty-eight hours leave without pay. "Give this to the desk sergeant, and report back on time. You have any money?"

"Yes, sir."

"Then be wearing a uniform when you come back."

Deputies get a special deal at one of the better tailor shops in town, so I stopped off there and got fitted for a uniform. After some pleading, the owner agreed to have one ready in twenty-four hours, with two more sets to come later. Then, feeling the need to unwind, I went home to Rosie's place, had a nice dinner and a fitful night's sleep. I suppose I should have had nightmares, but it was the future that bothered me, not the past.

Next morning I saddled up one of Rosie's horses and went for a long ride while I made up my mind about things. As noon approached, I drove into town and went to the hospital.

After frowning at me, the floor nurse said I could have one minute with Jubal.

To be honest, he looked terrible, but Becky was seated next to his bed, holding one of his hands, and he could have been worse.

"You look great," I said.

He grinned. "You ... bad ... as... Tres."

"Sssh," Becky whispered. "Don't talk." She scowled at me.

"He's getting better, but still very weak."

Jubal blinked several times, "Sienna?"

"He knows," Becky mouthed.

"Sienna was buried behind the Spanish mission there at Old Tucson. Sugar Holliday had an Indian shaman come out and conduct a service for the three horses. I'm told it was quite touching."

Smiling, Jubal closed his eyes.

The floor nurse stuck her head in the doorway and said, "It's time, Mr. Brannigan."

After I waved at Becky, I allowed the nurse to chase me out of the room.

Next stop was the sheriff's office, where Darcy was working at a desk in the back.

Pulling up a chair, I asked, "What have you figured out?"

Darcy leaned forward, as if to share a great conspiracy. "Griffin was a schmuck being jerked around by a big-time crook."

"I know that. But just who the hell is Bunny Malone?"

"Like I said in court, he's a Vegas bookie. He also dabbles in loan sharking and other criminal endeavors. Griffin apparently lost a bundle to Bunny gambling on college sports. Being a sweetheart, Bunny let him pay it off, with interest, in installments: a grand a week."

"Which Griffin got by skimming the payroll and submitting

false receipts. I understand that part. But Pilar made a point to say *money laundering*."

"Well, the ledger you found shows that, starting shortly after Paradise Pictures began shooting at Old Tucson, Bunny sent shipments of cash to Griffin a couple times a month."

"How?"

"Probably by courier. Based on the ledger notes, I got a warrant from Judge Hanrahan to go exploring this morning. Bank records show Griffin deposited these incoming amounts in various company bank accounts he opened up here in Tucson."

"Wait a minute, wouldn't a bank here be suspicious about large cash deposits?"

"Griffin split the incoming cash into smaller amounts and deposited them in three different Tucson banks. To the casual observer, they looked like normal operating funds."

"What did he do with the money?"

"In each case, Griffin withdrew small amounts over the next few days. Some of the cash would be used to pay bills, and be part of his skimming operation, but some would be wired to a bank account on Grand Cayman Island. The total going to Grand Cayman was eventually the same as the shipment recently received."

"So Griffin wasn't trying to skim any of that."

"No way, but Bunny apparently let Griffin deduct five percent of the amount sent to Cayman from his gambling debt."

"What about those wire transfers to the Cayman Islands?

Didn't they look suspicions?"

"The money went from Paradise Pictures to an account on the island owned by an entity called the Motion Picture Clearing House. If anyone looked, money being sent there would appear to be a legitimate expense."

"Oh yeah? What for?"

"Licenses to use patented equipment. Royalties for using someone else's script or canned film footage. Lots of possibly legitimate reasons."

"And Griffin took all the risk in order to help pay off his gambling debt. If the law caught on, there was no way to trace the laundered money back to Bunny Malone. Except possibly that ledger I found."

"Bunny must have known Griffin would keep such a record, and he didn't know how detailed it might be, how much it might incriminate him. That's why he ordered Pilar to get it."

"Yeah. I think we'll both miss Pilar. Were you able to find out anything about her?"

"Unfortunately, I was. She's wanted in Nevada, under another name, for accessory to murder. She apparently lured one of Bunny's enemies to a rendezvous where Fredo killed him."

"Jesus. That kind of changes her image, doesn't it."

"Yeah. I really liked her."

I sighed. "Me too."

* * *

The Mexican police had my .38, and the sheriff had his personal .45 back, so I felt pretty naked. Since I had a job to do that required some armament, I went looking for suitable hardware.

One of the advantages of being a law enforcement officer is you get to know the local criminals. I went to see Carlos, who was suspected of running guns into Mexico. He was clever about it, which is why he was only a *suspected* gun runner. I found him in his place of business, a small room attached to the back of a south-side grocery store.

One eye looked out through a peephole when I knocked, then Carlos opened the door. The butt of a revolver poked out of his trousers above the belt. It looked well-used.

"Carlos," I said, "good to see you again."

"Quit the bullshit, Brannigan, what do you want?"

"I want to buy a couple of guns, cheap."

"Oh yeah? Ain't you a deputy sheriff now?"

"Truth is, I'm on unpaid leave, a little short of cash, and I lost my thirty-eight in Mexico."

"Too bad. Why do you come to me?"

"Heard a rumor you might have some used guns for sale. All legit, of course."

"Maybe. What are you looking for?"

"A snub-nose thirty-eight and a two-shot Derringer."

"Jesus. You taking up a life of crime?"

"You always get nosy with your customers?"

He laughed. "Come on in."

Carlos stepped aside, then followed me into his dimly lit office. Several wood crates were stacked up against one wall, and empty crates appeared to serve as his only furniture. Pointing at one of the empty ones, he said, "Have a seat."

"Thanks." I had to grin. Carlos was undoubtedly more interested in keeping me from peeking into his crates than any concern about my comfort.

Walking over to one of the crates, he raised the lid. After peering inside for a few seconds, he lifted out a small gun. "Here," he said, "is a good little pocket gun, a Remington Model Ninety-Five. Uses forty-one caliber, rimfire ammo." He handed it to me, butt first, then closed the lid on his case.

The thing nestled into the palm of my hand like a newborn kitten. I rotated the barrels and made sure the hammer switched to the active barrel. "How old is this thing?"

"Don't know, it was made somewhere between eighteen sixty-six and nineteen thirty-five." He grinned. "No serial numbers on that block of Remington Derringers."

Setting the tiny gun on the case next to me, I asked, "What about the thirty-eight?"

Strolling over to a different case, he lifted the lid and extracted a revolver with what looked to be a two-inch barrel. "This is the one for you," he said, handing it to me. "The serial number's been ground off somewhere along the line."

"But not by you."

"Of course not."

"How much for the two of them?"

"Forty dollars and the story of how you lost your thirty-eight in Mexico."

"Throw in two rounds for the Derringer and you got a deal."

"Don't you want ammo for the thirty-eight?"

"Already have enough."

Now I needed transportation. Again, I knew someone.

Boomer Bradley was seated cross-legged on the cement floor of a small hangar out at the Tucson airport. His brand new Cessna 182 was parked nearby, one wing close enough that Boomer could reach up from his present position and touch it. He liked to be close to his new toy.

Even from fifty feet away, I could tell he was into a flying story; he needed both hands to demonstrate his aerial combat moves to an enthralled pair of ten-year-old kids—one boy, one girl—who squatted on the cement in front of him. Built like a fireplug, with a ruddy complexion and thinning hair, Boomer defied the image of a fighter pilot. But he'd been one.

He looked up as I approached. "Brannigan. What have I done to deserve you?"

"I need to rent you and your plane for a quick round-trip flight to McCarran Field. You up for it?"

"Fifty bucks each way ... cash up front. Can you handle that?"

Handing him a hundred-dollar bill, I asked, "You ready?"

Boomer turned to his audience. "Back to your books, kids, grandpa has to fly."

"Oh crap," the boy said.

"Watch your mouth," Boomer snapped. "If you aren't careful you'll grow up like your father. Now git."

As my pilot prepped his plane, I asked him, "Why do folks call you *Boomer*."

"Aw, I got to break the sound barrier a few times before I left the Air Force. The last time, I was a little too low over Las Vegas. Broke thirty-seven windows and the crystal chandelier in the Frontier."

November 1957 – Las Vegas

Five miles from downtown and only a mile from *The Strip*, McCarran Field is the main airport serving Las Vegas, Nevada.

Boomer lowered the landing gear and greased us onto one of its runways about an hour after local sundown. He taxied over to the transient aircraft ramp and allowed a pretty young female attendant waiting there to show him where to park.

"Haven't been back to Vegas since my low-level pass," Boomer said. "Don't tell anyone I'm here, okay?"

"You got it. I'm not here either. And if I'm not back by midnight, go home without me."

"Sounds mysterious."

"Bet your ass."

Being devious, I walked over to the main terminal and caught a cab from there. I had Fredo's name and address from his Nevada driver license, so I had a starting point, but I had the cabbie drop me off a couple blocks away. I didn't want him to associate me with that address.

It was a pleasant walk, but Fredo's address turned out to be a vacant lot. *Surprise.*

Fortunately, Fredo's vacant lot was close to the strip—which still had a few vacant lots of its own—so it was another easy stroll to the bright lights and a phone booth. It was probably too much to hope that Bunny Malone would be listed. He wasn't.

So, to plan B. I dialed the local newspaper.

"Las Vegas Sun."

"Is there a crime reporter there?"

"You must be from out of town. There isn't any crime here."

"Right. Give me the night editor."

After a pause, "Johnson here."

"My name's Adams," I lied. "I'm a reporter for the LA Times on a hot lead about one of your more colorful characters, Bunny Malone. You know where I can find him?"

"You think this is a directory service?"

"I need a quick answer. You give it to me and I'll cut you in right after I call LA with my story."

"Oh what the hell. This time of night he'll be in his office above the Shamrock Casino."

"Thanks."

"But watch your ass. He's got a body guard that breaks heads first and asks questions later."

"Only one guard?"

"That's been enough so far."

"Again, thanks."

I hung up and strolled toward the bright lights. The Shamrock was on the near edge of the action. Two stories, ground floor lit up, no windows on the second deck, clearly not in the same class as the Tropicana. I guessed no shows, no meals, no high rollers in from L.A. This would be where the locals and the cheaper tourists went to try their luck. And where Bunny Malone did his business. I pulled my beat-up cowboy hat low over my face and went in.

My luck was running hot; I played the slots for half an hour and made ten bucks. I also managed to case the joint. It was small as those places go, but still a standard, brightly lit, noisy as hell casino. And its oblong shape was packed to the gills with cowboys, locals, and tourist types.

One end of the casino was devoted to cashier counters and a locked door that just had to lead to offices and a vault behind. A long, one-way mirror overlooking the casino floor was mounted on the second-floor room above, no doubt home to the security types watching the action below. *Note to brain: Keep your face averted from the guys up there.*

At the other end of the casino was a long bar equipped with about twenty bar stools and a dozen outlying tables. Bunny Malone's office had to be in the enclosed room perched above it. A small window up there overlooked the casino action, but it was plain glass, so I could see that the light was on. Bunny was there. Alone? Just one guard? I figured I could handle Bunny and one guard. If there were more, I'd have to pretend I was lost and beat a hasty retreat.

A door labeled *Private* at one end of the bar attracted my attention. Whenever someone opened it, which was seldom, I could see stairs that appeared to lead up to Bunny's loft.

The gambling operation had the usual amount of both uniformed and plain-clothes security cruising around, but they didn't seem to mind if someone went upstairs to see Malone every now and then.

Those who did never stayed very long. Maybe they were placing a bet with Bunny, or collecting their winnings. At any rate, Bunny did not seem to be a talkative host. Get 'em in, get 'em out.

When I was pretty sure none of those transients was upstairs, I strolled over to the door marked *Private* and opened it. No one seemed to care.

There was another door at the top of the stairs; it was locked. I knocked and stood in front of the door's peep hole.

After a moment, a gruff voice asked, "Whadda yah want,

cowboy?"

"I have a message for Bunny Malone."

"Go away."

"It's from Fredo."

Several seconds went by. Then the door swung open to reveal a beefy man with limited sartorial taste. No jacket, no tie, just a .44 pistol slung from a shoulder harness. His sleeves were rolled up around large muscles. He glared at me and said, "Come in."

I found myself in a small tiled foyer that opened onto a dimly lit room with thick carpeting. The word *opulent* struck me. A very rich man worked here. The paneled walls were covered with what was probably expensive art. If this was a Bunny hole, it was a first-class one. And I could see only one guard.

A large desk was parked about thirty feet away. A slender, elegantly dressed man was seated behind it, looking at me.

Walking toward him, I asked, "You Bunny Malone?"

"Yeah. Stop right there. Frisk him, Al."

It was a pretty professional pat down, and Al found the snub-nose .38 in my right boot. Holding the gun up in the air, he said, "Look what I found, boss."

"Good work." Then, glaring at me with dead eyes, Bunny asked, "What's the message?"

"Fredo's dead."

"So I heard. Who shot him?"

"I did."

"Kill him," Bunny snarled.

Al pointed the .38 he'd taken from me and pulled the trigger. The gun blew up and did serious damage to Al's hand. This was probably the result of all the mud I'd tamped down in the gun's barrel back in Tucson.

Doffing my Stetson, I ripped the little Derringer loose from the threads that held it in the hat's crown.

Before Al could scream, I let him have the Derringer's first .41-caliber round right in his open mouth. He dropped like a pole-axed steer.

As I spun back toward Bunny, his right hand came up from behind the desk holding what looked like a .32 revolver. The Derringer's second round smacked him in the right temple. Bunny's head snapped back, and his .32 fired one round into the carpet at my feet. Then the springs in his tall executive chair pitched him forward, face down on the desk.

All those downstairs casino noises continued as before; apparently nobody down there had heard our little confrontation through the thick carpeting.

Now I had the opportunity to embellish. Paraffin tests would show that both Bunny and Al had fired weapons. I wiped my prints off the derringer, and wrapped Bunny's fingers around its butt. Then I laid hand and gun on the desk top. There wouldn't be any powder burns on Bunny's temple, but maybe that would be ignored.

Before I left, I picked up Bunny's revolver and stuck it in my boot. Then I tugged my hat low over my face, wiped the door handle clean, and went down to the casino.

Strolling over to the roulette table, I put the ten bucks I'd won playing the slots on double ought. The ball landed on thirteen. Just as well, if I'd won it would have brought way too much attention my way.

Just another losing gambler, I slunk out the door. A phone booth was parked down the street, so I donated a dime and dialed a number.

"Las Vegas Sun."

"Give me the night editor."

After a short wait, a voice said, "Johnson here."

"This is Adams from the LA Times. Here's your story: Bunny Malone just killed his body guard in a lover's quarrel. Then he committed suicide."

I hung up, went to a different phone booth, and called a cab.

Boomer was telling flying stories to the young woman at the transient parking line when I arrived a few minutes before midnight. Not wanting the woman to be able to identify me, I went straight to Boomer's plane and waved for him to come over. Fifteen minutes later we were in the air, bound for Tucson. I felt better about things.

Chapter 16

November 1957 – Tucson

I didn't get to bed until the wee hours, so I slept in. After all, my forty-eight hours of leave without pay wasn't up until late afternoon. Since Rosie was out riding around her mesquite patch, I raided the fridge for some orange juice, then drove into town for brunch.

As usual, I headed straight for the Santa Rita coffee shop. The manager seemed relieved that I was alone, and he pointed the honey-blonde waitress in my direction.

"Good morning," she said, hiding behind her little order book.

"Yes it is, Miss ...." I peered at a small nametag parked just above her left breast.

She leaned in so I could see it better, but she covered the bet by saying, "It's Melinda."

"A pretty name for a pretty woman."

"Please don't try that Irish blarney on me, Mr. Brannigan, I'm old enough to be immune."

"Oh really? At what age does immunity kick in?"

"In my case, twenty-six. What would you like for breakfast?"

"Since I've been chastised and now feel depressed, I'll just have a muffin with orange marmalade and a cup of black coffee."

"Yes, sir."

Brrrr.

The manager came over as soon as Melinda left. "Good Morning," he said. "Will that big Indian be joining you today?"

"I'm not sure. He's probably busy elsewhere with a movie."

"Oh I hope so."

"I understand your concern."

"But the other one who had breakfast with you that day, the older gentleman, he stopped by here this morning looking for you." The manager pulled a piece of paper from a pocket and handed it to me. "He asked me to give you this note."

"Thank you."

"My pleasure, sir." The manager beat a hasty retreat back to the safety of his cashier counter.

Darcy's note was short and to the point. *Have an early flight to Los Angeles. Will be in touch. Good luck in your new career. Darcy*

Melinda showed up with my muffin, marmalade, and coffee. "I'm sorry I gave you a hard time," she said as she set down the plate and poured my coffee. "The manager just reminded me that you've had a tough week."

"No apology required. And it wasn't all bad; I did get acquitted."

"So I heard. Tell me, is that big man I spilled coffee on still around?"

"He's taken."

"Too bad." She gave me a big smile and turned away.

After a short internal debate, I left Melinda a good tip

Surprise, the tailor had my uniform ready—and it fit. I wore it out the door and drove over to see the sheriff.

That man had a huge grin on his face when he waved me into his office. "Guess what happened in Las Vegas last night?"

"Frank Sinatra got laid."

"Probably, but that's not what I meant. Bunny Malone committed suicide after killing his bodyguard. It looks like a homosexual lover's quarrel."

"You kidding?"

"*Es verdad.*"

"How'd he do it?"

"A little two-shot derringer. He put one shot into the bodyguard's mouth and the second one into his own temple. Funny though, the bodyguard's hand was all mangled because his own gun blew up. The damn fool had gotten mud in the barrel."

"Huh."

"So," the sheriff said, "that kind of puts a wrap to the case and some kind of justice was done after all."

"Looks like it. How'd you get the word?"

"The Pinkerton guy in Las Vegas called Darcy O'Rourke here at the office first thing this morning. It's all over the media up there. I see you're in uniform. You back from leave?"

"Yes, sir."

"Good. You've been cleared of any malfeasance in the death of Pilar Espinoza, so you can go back on full duty." The sheriff pulled a badge out of his desk drawer, then stood up and came around the desk. As he pinned it on, he said, "The desk sergeant will issue you all the standard equipment."

"Guess I don't get to use your personal .45 any more."

"No, son. You might wear it out."

The desk sergeant not only issued me all the standard gear, he assigned a patrol car and, after some consultation with the sheriff, a beat: the valley west of Tucson from Marana Air Base down to Highway 80. Old Tucson was right in the middle of that stretch of real estate. I guess the sheriff figured I knew the territory.

And the territory was calm. There were speeders to ticket and an occasional drunk to pull out of his car and jail, but on the whole it was peaceful. Real quiet. Dull. It was very different from being a city cop.

I spent time getting to know the sparsely populated area and the people who lived there, mostly folks who liked their neighbors to be a long way away. Of course I swung by Old Tucson every so often, but there weren't many good memories for me there, so I never stayed very long.

December 1957 – Tucson

An invitation arrived by courier. Tres and Sugar showed up at Rosie's place one Sunday afternoon, bouncing their way up the ragged dirt road in Sugar's jeep.

Off duty for a change, I was busy chopping mesquite for Rosie's fireplace and welcomed the chance to put down the axe. Mesquite ain't ironwood, but its tough enough.

As the jeep rolled to a stop next to my wood pile, Tres grinned and called out, "*Ya-te-he.*"

Sugar just waved.

I wiped an hour's worth of sweat from my forehead and walked over. "What brings you two out here? Scouting for more scenery?"

"We bring tidings of great joy this Christmas season," Tres said. "Here." He handed me a crisp, white envelope with my name on it in fancy lettering. "Nobody knew your mailing address, so we figure we'd hand deliver this."

"What is it?"

Laughing, Sugar said, "Open it up and you'll find out."

"Looks like a wedding invitation," I said. "Yours?" They

both looked away. *Oops.*

The envelope was only sealed at the flap's tip, so it was easy to tear open. It was a wedding invitation, all right: for Becky and Jubal. To be on Sunday, December 22nd, at the Pearce ranch up on the Mogollon Rim.

Sugar did the little bouncy thing she always does when she gets excited. "You'll go, won't you?"

"Reckon so."

"That's good," she said. "Cause Jubal wants you to be best man."

"You have to be kidding. Why me?"

Tres chimed in. "He said he's only got two male friends in the state, and I'm too undependable."

"Jubal has a point, you know."

"It is my nature. What can I say?"

I glanced at the card again. "It's a morning wedding, which means we'll have to go up a day early. Where are you two staying?"

Grinning, Tres said, "I booked a room at the Old Apache Inn in Eagar for Sugar and me."

"Ah yes," I said. "For old times sake?"

Sugar blushed.

Winking at me, Tres said, "As I recall, they put on a good breakfast there."

"Yeah, right." I turned back to Sugar. "How goes the filming?"

"It's moving along," Sugar said. "Mr. Cromwell found a mare that looks something like Sienna, and they dyed her to match. It's kind of funny; she has a make-up call before every scene."

"You mean good old Justin Cromwell, Mr. Authenticity himself, is using a dyed horse?"

"Ironic, isn't it?"

The jeep groaned to life again. "We'll see you at the wedding," Sugar called out." Then she popped the clutch, and the jeep roared away, leaving a thin trail of dust trying to catch up.

A week later I checked into the sheriff's office at the end of my shift and found a note to call a Los Angeles number. When I did, a familiar voice answered: "Darcy O'Rourke."

"Hello, Darcy. This is Brannigan. What's up?"

"Good news, Daniel. They bought my story. The magazine will run it sometime in January."

"That's great, Darcy. So you're off on a new career."

"I'm keeping my day job, but I'm doing a lot of writing in the evenings."

"Well, at least that will keep you out of the pubs."

"Not quite. Where do you think I do my best writing?"

By swapping a couple of shifts, I was able to free up the two days needed to attend Jubal's wedding. But, not wanting to put a damper on Tres and Sugar's romp in the Old Apache Inn, I opted to spend the night before the wedding in Show Low.

A quiet place, Show Low has an interesting history. Corydon Cooley and Marion Clark settled there alongside a creek in 1875. They soon took to bickering and played a game of Seven-Up to see which of them would move. When the last hand was dealt, Cooley needed only one point to win. At that point, Clark turned his cards over and said, "If you can show low, you win." Cooley lay down the deuce of clubs, and thus won a hundred thousand acres of ranchland. The town's name was thereby set, and it's main thoroughfare is Deuce of Clubs Street.

Low clouds and a light dusting of snow followed me as I made the trek to the Pearce ranch the next morning. Having been warned about Boar Creek, I'd left the Edsel at home and borrowed Rosie's pickup truck. I was soon glad I'd made the swap; the creek was running strong from a previous snow melt and cold water came up to the truck's axels.

I figured to be a bit early, but there were a couple of pickup trucks and Sugar's jeep already parked in front of the Pearce ranch house when I rumbled into the yard.

An elderly woman I recognized as Mrs. Pearce came out on the porch to welcome me. The others might be getting ready to party, but this woman was obviously hard at work preparing one. Her apron and arms were spotted with flour, and a bit of what looked like a lost cranberry was stuck in her white hair.

"Hello, Mr. Brannigan," she said. "We're glad you could come."

"Thank you, ma'am. But please drop the mister."

"Everybody is down at the barn," she said. "They're taking a look at one of the wedding presents. Why don't you go join them."

"Yes, ma'am."

Five people were gathered in a semi-circle, their backs to me, when I walked into the warm barn. Becky and Sugar had Tres between them, and the peg leg gave away Jubal's father. The other man was clearly not Jubal, so I figured the about-to-be groom must be the center of their attention. I was almost right.

"Hello," I said to the assembled backsides.

They all spun around, and I finally recognized Becky's dad; I'd seen him at Jubal's trial.

Mr. Pearce stepped forward on his peg leg. Grabbing my hand, he shook it vigorously and said, "Thank you for coming, Brannigan. Jubal says you saved his life, and we're grateful as hell."

"I don't want to step on your son's story, Mr. Pearce, but as I remember it, he saved me from both a bounty hunter and a Mexican prison."

A voice from beyond the crowd said, "Let's call it a draw. Come here, Brannigan, and look at what Becky's dad got us for a wedding present."

Everyone shuffled to the sides and let me see into the straw-filled stall. Jubal was seated on a hay bale, his back to one of the stall's wooden sides. Standing beside him on skinny legs was a very young colt, red with flaxen mane and tail. Its head was nuzzling Jubal's lap, obviously looking for food and grateful for the attention.

"He's just been weaned," Jubal said.

Becky's father grinned. "I saw this mare and colt at an auction. A fella there wanted to buy the mare, but not the colt. Didn't take a genius to see that opportunity."

"Looks an awful lot like Sienna," I said.

"Yeah," Jubal said, a catch in his throat. "But this little fella is a colt, not a filly."

"I can always take him back," Becky's dad said, eyes sparkling.

Jubal laughed. "Not a chance. He's mine—I mean ours—now. We aren't ever letting this little guy go anywhere. He's going to be the stud around here."

Turning to Sugar, Becky whispered, "I hope he's not the only one."

The local Mormon Bishop and a few of the closer neighbors arrived over the next hour, and we all gathered in the ranch house for the ceremony. Since Becky was not an LDS member, at least not yet, this ceremony would marry them *for life*. Later, if they wished and were approved, they could go through another, more ritualistic, ceremony in a Mormon temple and be married *for eternity*.

As it turned out, the ceremony looked pretty much like the other wedding services I'd seen. Becky wore a modest white dress, Jubal had on a suit and tie, and the guests were reasonably attired. Tres even wore a shirt for the occasion.

After the deed was done, Mrs. Pearce brought out hot apple cider and showed us the way to a dining table laden with food. No one was going to leave hungry.

While the assembled folk moved toward the feast, I went over to offer congratulations to the bride and groom.

"Thanks," Becky said, giving me a quick peck on the cheek. "I've got to go change; this is the only dress I own, and I don't want to spill anything on it."

"I'll wait here for you," Jubal said, already falling into husband mode.

After Becky disappeared into a bedroom, I asked Jubal, "What are your plans?"

"We're going to stay here and build up the ranch again. Becky fell in love with a little meadow about a mile from here, and we'll make our home there."

"Sugar said you had a job offer from her dad but turned it down."

"Yeah. Mr. Holliday called me. Said he could use a man who knew how to shoot. Asked me if I'd be willing to go to Iran."

"Really? What kind of job was it?"

"He didn't say, and was kind of mysterious about it. Said they did contract work for our government. When I asked him which part of the government, all he said was it had to do with something called central intelligence."

"So you turned him down,"

"Yeah. Who the hell wants to go to Iran?"

Just then Becky came back wearing her usual attire: Levis and a shirt. She grabbed each of us by the arm and led us to the table.

Later, as I was getting into Rosie's pickup truck to leave, Tres wandered over wearing a hangdog look. "It's kind of sad," he said.

"What's sad?"

"Sugar and I have split. We came here together today just for appearances sake. We didn't want to put a damper on Jubal's wedding."

"What happened?"

"We had a long talk a few days ago. Sugar wants marriage and kids. I balked."

"Why?"

He shrugged. "It is my nature. What can I say?"

"So is Sugar moving back into Tucson?"

"No. She's going home. Back to LA."

"Then you're out of a job."

"Oh no. I've been hired to replace Sugar. I even get the jeep." He stepped back and waved. *"Ya-te-he."*

Rosie invited me in for coffee when I got back. "I've got to talk to you about something," she said as soon as I sat down at the kitchen table.

"Oh oh. I have a paying job again, Rosie. I'll catch up on my rent by the end of the year."

She smiled. "That's not it. You know I never worry about the rent." Taking a deep breath, she went on. "Your father and I are getting married."

"Wow ... I mean—"

"We know this is a surprise, Dan. We thought, I mean we hope that you'll ..."

"Relax, Rosie. Don't get all flustered. I approve. You'll be good for dad, and that's important to me. But there is one thing ..."

"What's that?"

"I won't call you *mom*. I'll never have another mother."

"That's fair. I don't mind being just plain Rosie."

"You will never be plain. When is the wedding?"

"Sometime in January. We're going to have a big Christmas Eve party here and make the announcement then. You dad is going to shut down the restaurant early and bring the booze, and I've invited most of the neighbors."

"Most?"

She laughed. "There's a couple I don't cotton to. Hell, they wouldn't come anyway. But you'll be here, right?"

I had to think for a moment. There was one loose end I had to wrap up, and Christmas Eve would be a good time to do it. "I'll be here, Rosie, but I'll be real late. Save me some of your cookin' and a lot of Dad's Scotch."

Nogales was lit up on both sides of the border when I steered the Edsel into a parking lot on the U.S. side. Mexicans love Christmas even more than us *gringos*, and Christmas Eve parties were in full swing everywhere.

Dressed in a dark shirt, Levi's and cowboy boots, I figured to blend in with the natives. I was off duty, and had left everything associated with Pima County at Rosie's, just in case. If I ran into trouble across the border, I didn't want to involve the sheriff.

My watch said nine o'clock when I got out, pulled on a light windbreaker, and made sure the roll of dimes I'd picked up at the bank was still in one pocket. Then, whistling a Christmas song, I locked up the Edsel and headed for the border check station.

The Mexican customs agent waved me through with a cheery, "*¡Feliz Navidad!*"

"Merry Christmas," I answered.

Throngs of people from both countries, and probably several more, wandered the littered sidewalks and much of the broken pavement that pretended to be a street.

It took me a while to find a uniformed policeman. I stopped next to him and asked, "Where can I find the police sergeant?"

"*¿Qué?*"

"*¿Dónde está el sargento de la policia?*"

"Ah." He pointed toward a brightly lit cantina down the street.

"*Gracias, señor.*"

So, as expected, the sergeant was out on the town this Christmas Eve. Probably collecting little bribes disguised as *presentos*. Keeping my well-used brown hat pulled down over my forehead, I went into the *cantina* and found an empty chair in a far corner.

Within moments an underage waitress with saucy eyes and riveting cleavage found me. "*¡Feliz Navidad!*" she said with a coy smile. "*¿Qué quieres?*"

"*Dos Equis, por favor. Verde.*"

"*Un momento.*"

While waiting for my beer, I admired the poinsettias, *las flores de Noche Buena*, arrayed along the bar. The police sergeant was also at the bar, in uniform, nursing a beer. I did not admire him.

My waitress dropped a cardboard coaster on the table and set a tall glass of beer on it. The foam overflowed and slid down the glass. She looked at me expectantly.

I gave her a quarter and a smile. "*Gracias.*"

She whirled away to another table without a backward glance.

Now I had to wait for the sergeant to leave. I knew that Mexicans celebrate Christmas Eve by going to a late mass, then home for dinner followed by the opening of presents in the wee hours. Worst case, the sergeant would stay here until it was time to go to mass, probably close to midnight. If so, he'd be in the middle of a crowd, untouchable, and I'd have made the trip in vain.

Luckily, I didn't have to wait that long. I'd just about finished my beer when the sergeant slapped the backs of several men drinking near him, then swaggered out the door.

Pushing back my chair, I followed. My plan was simple … well, I didn't really have a plan. I just needed to get the sergeant alone somewhere.

My target strolled south, away from the bright lights. Toward police headquarters? With beer on his breath? Hopefully not.

Crossing the street, I walked fast and gained a good lead on the sergeant. When I saw the opening to a dark alley on the same side as the sergeant's stroll, I crossed again. Now all I had to do was wait some more. There was infrequent foot traffic in this area, so I had to estimate the sergeant's arrival time.

Finally it was time, and I heard footsteps on the sidewalk. I ran a dozen yards into the alley and yelled, "*¡Ayúdame! ¡Ayúdame!*" Then I made a fist around that roll of dimes, fell face down on the ground, and began to groan.

Any respectable police sergeant hearing my cries for help would surely come to my aid. He did.

Footsteps approached, I felt a hand on my shoulder, and a voice asked, "*¿Estás herido?*"

Rolling over, I devoted a split second to making sure it was the sergeant bending over me, then I hit him in the gut just as hard as I could.

The sergeant grunted and doubled over even more.

As recognition bloomed in the sergeants eyes, I gave him a right cross that brought him crashing to the ground, unconscious.

My right hand hurt like hell, but the sergeant's jaw must have been worse. I pocketed the roll of dimes and searched the sergeant. My .38 was in his holster. I relieved him of it and stuffed it into my boot. Then, with the sergeant still passed out, I quickly stripped him. I took everything, including his underwear. The watch on his wrist was also mine, so I took it too.

The man drifted back to consciousness as I was wrapping his clothes into a tight bundle. He blinked several times, then leapt to his feet and opened his mouth as if to yell.

"*¡Silencio!*" I ordered, drawing my .38 and pointing it at the sergeant's gut.

His mouth closed.

"You are naked, Sergeant. I suggest you stay hidden in this

alley until everyone has gone to mass. Maybe then you can sneak out and find something to cover your body. It would be a shame if the people of this town saw your *pene pequeño*. They would all laugh at you. Forever."

"¿Por qué? Why you do this to me?"

"To get my property back. And to get even. *Adiós, Sargento*."

I figured I better get back across the border quickly. The sergeant might get lucky, or brave, and leave the alley in time to have me arrested at the border. Hailing a cab, I told him, "*Andale*."

When we pulled up at the crossing point, I handed the cabbie some extra money and the sergeant's clothes. "*¿Habla Englés?*"

"*Sí.*"

"There is a naked man in the alley where you picked me up. Take these clothes back to him and say, "*¡Feliz Navidad!*"

The man laughed. "It will be a fine present for a naked man." He was still laughing as he drove away.

The American customs agent waved me through with a cheery, "*¡Feliz Navidad!*"

"Merry Christmas," I answered.

My dad and Rosie were obviously having a good time at their party when I arrived a few minutes before midnight. About a dozen or so well-oiled guests were still around, and I didn't feel like drinking fast enough to catch up, so I did the courtesies and then headed for my bed above the garage.

Rosie caught up with me on the porch. "Your dad and I are having a real family Christmas dinner here tomorrow. You got a girl you can ask?"

"I've been too busy to acquire one."

"What about that girl in the jeep?"

"She went for a big Indian, then left him for the bright lights of Los Angeles."

"Huh. Well, after we open presents tomorrow morning, you go out and find a date. That's an order. I don't want you moping around the house and spoiling our Christmas dinner."

"Yes, ma'am."

The Santa Rita coffee shop was almost deserted, which wasn't too surprising for a Christmas morning. Sheila was the only waitress on duty and couldn't avoid me, so she carried a mug of black coffee over to my table and said, "Merry Christmas."

"*¡Feliz Navidad!*"

"You having breakfast, or just coffee?"

"Just coffee. I'm on a mission."

Sheila stepped back. "This isn't going to get violent or anything, is it?"

I took a sip of coffee. "It's a peaceful mission. I need a date for Christmas dinner."

"You're kidding."

"Nope. I'm invited to a family Christmas dinner and have orders to bring a date."

"Surely you're not thinking of me. I mean …"

"Well, actually I figured you'd rather skip Christmas than go out with me. But what about Melinda?"

Pulling out a chair, Sheila sat down across from me and looked thoughtful. "Why her? You know anything about her?"

"She's about the right age and was nice to me the last time I saw her. And she's pretty. That's about it. She's not married is she?"

"No. She divorced the bum. But what you're talking about is almost a blind date."

"Sort of. I guess. What do you think?"

"Hmmm." Sheila got a strange look in her eyes, then tore a sheet off her order pad and wrote on the back. "Here's Melinda's address, she said, handing it to me. "You might as well go for it."

"Thanks," I reached for my wallet.

Sheila put a hand on my arm. "The coffee's on the house. Merry Christmas."

The address took me to a small house in a working-class neighborhood about a mile north of downtown. One story, square, with a small porch in front, the place looked sturdy but tired. Lava rocks framed a small flowerbed that separated the porch from a dormant lawn, and cracked cement slabs made up a short sidewalk from porch to street.

A woman who looked a lot like Melinda was sitting on the porch steps. She was watching a little girl about three years old ride a stick horse up and down the sidewalk. Both were bundled up against the brisk morning air. The woman turned her face a little; she was Melinda all right.

I pulled up across the street, turned off the ignition, and sat there for a moment. *So, she has a kid.*

Melinda suddenly stood up and called out, "Katy, come here. Right now."

Pushing the car door open, I got out and yelled, "It's all right, Melinda. It's me, Brannigan."

From across the street, holding Katy in her arms, Melinda stared at me.

"I'm here to see you," I called out. "Is it okay to come over?"

She nodded, but kept a firm hold on the little girl.

I took off my hat as I approached them and said, "Merry Christmas."

The little girl's eyes lit up. "I got a pony." She held up the stick horse to show me.

"Looks like a good one," I said. "I had a pony almost like it when I was a little boy."

"Excuse me for interrupting," Melinda said. "But why are you here?"

Twisting my hat in my hands like some adolescent, I said, "I need a date."

"You what?"

"My dad and his fiancée are planning a family-style Christmas dinner this afternoon, and I have orders to bring a date."

"Are you thinking … me?"

"Well, yeah."

Melinda smiled, then laughed. "I couldn't. Thanks, but there's no way I could get a baby sitter."

"Bring her," I said. "It's at a ranch north of town." I looked at the little girl. "Lots of pretty horses there."

The child's eyes became big. "Real ones?"

"Yep. Real ones."

"This is nuts," Melinda said. "Are you sure?"

"Absolutely. Having a little girl there will make it a real Christmas. And we may be able to find some of my old t-o-y-s to wrap up too."

"When?"

"How about if I pick you both up at two o'clock?"

"Okay. We'll be ready. Can I bring anything for the dinner?"

"Can you sing?"

"Sure."

"Then bring your voice. After dinner we like to sing Christmas carols. I'll see you at two o'clock."

Back in the Edsel I finally remembered to put my hat on.

Katy waved to me as I drove away. I smiled. Rosie was going to be delighted. Me too.

The End

I hope you enjoyed this story. If so, and if you bought the book from Amazon.com, please go back to the book's Amazon.com page and post a favorable review. It sure helps sales. *B.K. Bryans*

Other books by B.K. Bryans

The Dog Robbers
Flight to Redemption
Those '67 Blues
Sand
Trouble in Tucson
Flying Low
Management Math

Most of them are available on Amazon.com at:
https://www.amazon.com/author/b.k.bryans

You are also invited to visit the author's personal website at:
www.brianbryans.com

Those '67 Blues

Those '67 Blues by B.K. Bryans is an almost-true story of naval aviators fighting a vicious air war over North Vietnam in the fiery autumn of 1967 ... and of the families waiting for them back home "in the world." The novel covers a two-week period in a day-by-day account of flight operations and the heroic acts of men flying the hostile skies of North Vietnam. Many of the exploits in the book are based on the author's Vietnam War experiences as an A-6 Intruder pilot.

Those '67 Blues is a 6" x 9" glossy paperback novel published by Patriot Media, Inc. The cover art, *Moonlight Intruders*, is courtesy of Craig Kodera, a famed aviation artist whose work is on display in the Smithsonian National Air and Space Museum.

REVIEWS: *The Association of Naval Aviation* reviewed *Those '67 Blues* in the fall 2011 edition of their magazine, *Wings of Gold*, as follows: *Those '67 Blues* by B.K. Bryans. As one reviewer wrote, "This is my kind of book. It has the accurate detail that satisfies the guy who's 'been there and done that' and intrigues the guy who wishes he could have. *Blues* takes you through virtually every aspect of the carrier war in 1967 and does it so precisely you feel as if you are right there getting shot at." This is a story about the aviators who went in harms way big time. "At night," writes Bryans, "Navy all-weather A-6 Intruders went in low and alone." A brief excerpt: "The SAM that hit their A-6 right after weapons release knocked out everything electrical, set the port engine on fire, and caused the plane to shake like a dice cup." Bryans knows his subject. He flew A-6s during the Vietnam war earning a Silver Star and DFC, and commanded VA-35 aboard USS *Nimitz*.

There are numerous four- and five-star reviews for *Those '67 Blues* posted on its Amazon.com web page.

The Dog Robbers

The Dog Robbers by B.K. Bryans. After the 1945 Battle of Okinawa, US forces built Marine Corps Air Station (MCAS) Futenma atop the rubble of several small towns. Surviving villagers returning home found that an air base now lay across their land. They could only settle nearby, where they remain to this day, waiting. This real-world conflict serves as background for *The Dog Robbers*.

Lieutenant Deuce Riley, a US Navy pilot, is content to be a flight instructor at Naval Air Station (NAS) Pensacola, FL. Then he's suddenly ordered to Japan to be an aide to Rear Admiral Brewster Brody, who has become enmeshed in the diplomatic argument over MCAS Futenma. Neither officer is real happy about their assignment, but the result is humor, action, and romance.

Flight to Redemption

Flight to Redemption by B.K. Bryans is a flying story about an ageing pilot and several classic old airplanes from yesteryear. It is also an adventure story where action is not the sole property of those who are young and strong. Here, two well-seasoned citizens wisecrack their way from crash to crisis and back in a story for the "baby boomer" generation. As this pre-publication reviewer said:

REVIEW: "In *Flight to Redemption*, the author gives us a novel that realistically depicts the drug and alien smuggling problems that challenge our southwestern border country, but he also gives us lingering romance, bantering friendship, and an exciting conclusion. An ageing pilot, reluctantly accompanied by a small-town doc, fly a stolen airplane into Mexico on an ill-conceived rescue mission. This is a page-turner that is difficult to put down."

Robert Jorgensen, Brigadier General, US Army-Retired

Made in the USA
San Bernardino, CA
11 September 2013